RAINY LAKE RENDEZVOUS

The long-awaited sequel to "Waters of the Dancing Sky"

JANET KAY

ISBN: 9798630656995 (paperback)

Independently Published

Cover design by Hannah Linder

"Life is a balance between holding on and letting go."

– Rumi

Other Books By Janet Kay

Waters of the Dancing Sky

Amelia 1868

The Sisters

www.novelsbyjanetkay.com

For my beloved children

Shannon & Will Graber
Shane & Sandi Jenson
Sherry Jenson

With love and appreciation
Always

Acknowledgments

I would like to express my appreciation to all who played significant roles in making this book possible. This includes:

My amazing first readers and reviewers, all of whom provided unique and valuable feedback:

Agnes Kennard, Marty Ruzzo, Peggy Roeder, Mike Williams, Shane Jenson, and Sherry Jenson.

To Hannah Linder for her beautiful cover design and internal formatting

To Maxine Bringenberg, my talented editor

I would also like to thank The St Croix Writers of Solon Springs for their feedback and support throughout my writer's journey. This is a truly special writers group that I feel blessed to be a part of.

To all my friends around Rainy Lake where this novel is set, thank you so much for welcoming me into your community, a special place that I've fallen in love with. You have been asking for a sequel to "Waters of The Dancing Sky." Here it is – finally!

Last but never least, a heartfelt note of appreciation to my readers, near and far. Please drop me a note anytime at janetkay@novelsbyjanetkay.com. I'd love to hear from you.

RAINY LAKE RENDEZVOUS

Chapter One

I *have a rendezvous with death…with death…with death….*

These familiar words echoed through his mind once again as he thrashed about in his sleep. Sweating, heart pounding, he flipped on the bedside lamp, trying to escape from the nightmare that had haunted him for the past ten years. He was still trying to figure out what the words meant.

Was this a premonition that he was going to die? Or was someone else going to die? Perhaps someone like Seth, the bastard who had stolen his wife. Yes, death seemed to be a just sentence for Seth, he smiled to himself. Perhaps the voice was telling him to get rid of Seth. Then Beth would surely return to him.

Rob stumbled into the kitchen of the little cabin he had just purchased at the remote Black Bear Camp near Nestor Falls, Ontario, Canada. Just a few secluded cabins were hidden in the woods down the hill from the lodge. The kind of place where he should be able to hide out without arousing anyone's suspicions.

He poured himself a tall glass of Jack Daniels, his hand shaking. Glancing at his image in the mirror over the stained sink, he barely recognized himself. Hopefully, nobody else would recognize him either. He'd made a major transformation recently, from a perfectly groomed, well-dressed lawyer, to a scroungy looking, unshaven man sporting a scraggly gray beard. He now wore old clothes from Goodwill, like the well-worn plaid flannel shirt he'd slept in last night. Hopefully, he would pass as a local fisherman up here in the woods.

After belting down the whiskey, he made a pot of coffee and settled his large frame in a chair on the screened-in porch, where he watched the sun rise through the bank of fog hovering over Lake Kakagi. Someday, after ice-out, he'd have to get out there on the pristine wilderness lake, also known as Crow Lake. It encompassed forty-three square miles and was fifteen miles long. With hundreds of remote islands, there had to be some good places to hide out. As it was, he was feeling relatively safe up here in the Canadian wilderness, about seventy-five miles north of the Fort Frances international border on Rainy Lake. Beth's island was another fifteen miles out across Rainy Lake.

A breeze off the lake suddenly rattled his old screen door, startling him. Cautiously glancing around, he saw nothing. Nobody. Focusing again on the view outside his window, he noticed that most of the snow had melted. Little streams of water trickled down the hillside towards the big lake where massive chunks of ice were breaking up, crashing against the shoreline. Spring daffodils were beginning to poke up through the gardens surrounding the nearby lodge. Summer was just around the corner. It was almost time for him to proceed with his mission.

As always, his thoughts drifted to Beth, his ex-wife, who he had foolishly divorced ten years ago. Ten long and lonely years.... He shook his head sadly. Yes, he had been a fool to leave her for his young, pregnant girlfriend. Who would have known that she would turn out to be such a disaster? She'd had the baby, a boy, and disappeared with him. The kid would be about ten years old by now. Rob had not seen or heard anything from or about him or his mother since they disappeared. He had been too busy defending wealthy clients through his law firm to worry about it. He had buried himself in his work to escape from his loneliness. To try to forget Beth, the love of his life. Why the hell had he ever let her go?

Beth had continued to haunt his thoughts and dreams over the years. She was his wife, after all, and damn it, she belonged to him. She still did. He would get her back one way or another, he had decided several years ago. Today, he was a man on a mission, a man who had left his previous life and identity behind, forging a new one for himself. It had taken some time, his lawyerly skills, and a considerable amount of money to create a new identity.

"Morning, Bob. Beautiful day, eh?" someone interrupted his thoughts. *Bob? Of course, my new name,* he remembered as he greeted the owner of Black Bear Camp, who was walking by on his way down to the lake.

"Yup, fine day," Rob replied. And it was. He was enjoying his little Canadian cabin almost as much as the fact that he had escaped from the United States, leaving no trace behind. There was the matter of having embezzled ten million dollars from the law firm before disappearing. He deserved it, didn't he, after all he'd done for the firm over the years? He'd earned most of that money. Besides, he needed a cushion of cash to complete his mission. He chuckled to think of law enforcement agents trying to find the old Rob, a man who no longer existed.

He should be safe up here in the wilderness, although his mission would require him to venture back across the border to the United States side of Rainy Lake, where Beth and Seth lived together on a wilderness island. Probably married, he grimaced. At least that was what Emily had told him. Emily, his daughter from his former marriage to Beth, lived in Paris, so he didn't see or hear from her often. Not that he ever had.

He'd never forget his first attempt to reclaim Beth ten years ago. He'd driven up from Chicago, rented a snowmobile, and hired a guide to take him out to Beth's island in the middle of the night. He'd talked his way into the cabin by telling her he had a real estate offer on their fancy penthouse suite in Chicago, which had to be signed by the next day or they would lose the deal.

Beth had reluctantly opened the door. He'd tried to ask for her forgiveness, told her he needed her and had come to take her back home where she belonged. Women always fell for his lines. Beth had done so many times during their twenty-year marriage. She'd even forgiven his many affairs. But this time, she would not budge.

"Leave now!" she had hissed at him as he tried to pull her into his arms.

"You're coming with me," he'd ordered her, backing her up against the wall. He was done being nice. He would force her if he had to. Someday she'd be happy to be back home with him.

The bedroom door suddenly burst open, and a big half-breed guy named Seth jumped out with a gun, ordering him to leave immediately and never come back. Seth's eyes were on fire. No doubt he would have used that gun.

Rob had stumbled out into the snow to his snowmobile, totally defeated, unable to believe what had just happened. He gunned the motor, shot past his confused guide, and roared off the island. That was one of a very few times in his life that he hadn't gotten exactly what he wanted. He wanted Beth back, and was determined to find a way. In the meantime, he'd turned to Jack Daniels, his best friend these days. In recent years, his highly successful career had begun spiraling down into the pits.

Rob had replayed this sickening scene in his head over and over again, furious that Beth had a man in her life. How could she? Then it dawned on him one day. Beth was actually being held hostage by this Indian with a gun! Rob had to find a way to rescue her. No, it couldn't be true that she had actually married this guy—unless he had forced her to do so.

Rob began planning her rescue. It would have to be a flawless operation, perfectly planned and executed. After all, she may be terrified and also brainwashed by Seth, afraid to leave on her own. She could even be a victim of Stockholm Syndrome, just like one of his former clients had been. A kidnapping victim, his client had developed an unconscious emotional response to the traumatic experience of being held hostage. She had actually bonded emotionally and positively with the bastard. Was that what had happened to Beth?

Maybe he was obsessed with Beth and bringing her back home where she belonged. That's what his few remaining friends told him.

They said he was drinking too much and not thinking rationally. His mother had even asked him to see a therapist. What the hell did she know? She was the crazy one in the family, too busy with her affairs and foolishness to be there for him over the years. And his father? What father? He'd never had time for him before, and was quick to let him know what a disappointment he was to him. It was their fault if he maybe had a few minor quirks. No, they had no clue. There was nothing wrong with him that having Beth back wouldn't cure.

He glanced around his cozy two-bedroom cabin. It was nestled in the woods overlooking a huge lake filled with wilderness islands, big walleye, lake trout, and record-setting muskie. A fisherman's paradise. It would be the perfect place for him to hide out and start a fresh new life with Beth. But...what about Beth? He'd imagined so many possible scenarios over the years. She should be thrilled that her loving husband had finally come to rescue her from that crazy Indian holding her hostage. Or she may not be thrilled. She would need to be dealt with. He would make her pay for the pain she had caused him for so many years. It was her fault that they would spend the rest of their lives together hiding out in the Northwoods instead of living a life of luxury in the big city of Chicago where they had once lived. Yes, she would have to pay somehow before he'd be able to really forgive her for all of this.

But first, he would have to deal with Seth....

I have a rendezvous with death. He repeated the words to himself as he spread his maps out on the antique wood table to continue plotting his journey to Rainy Lake and back again.

Chapter Two

M*y name is Bob, Bob Johnson. My birthdate is February 11, 1964. I live in Nestor Falls, Canada. I'm retired, a fisherman, that's what I do.*

He repeated the words to himself as he neared the international border in Fort Frances, Canada before crossing over to the United States. He had secured a fake passport, driver's license, and car title in his new name. Everything should be fine. Still, his palms were sweating as he rolled his window down to speak to the border agent. He knew enough to look him in the eye, to smile and be polite.

"Where are you headed?" the grim-faced border agent asked.

"Lake Kabetogama."

"And the purpose of your visit?"

"Gonna do some fishin'."

"How long will you be in the United States?"

"Probably close to a month, depending on how the fishing goes," he smiled, noticing the agent's eyes searching the back seat of his car. Of course, Bob had several rods and reels, a tackle box, fishing net, and life jackets visible for inspection. No need to tell the agent that he wouldn't be crossing back through this official border station. Instead, he'd be sneaking back into Canada through Rainy Lake in the middle of the night, with Beth at his side.

"Where did you say you were staying?"

I didn't say, and it's none of your damn business, Bob wanted to reply. Instead he calmly answered, "Arrowhead Lodge." He wasn't sure he wanted to relay this much information. At least he'd had the brains to book a cabin on a lake other than Rainy Lake where Beth lived. It would take some navigating to find his way through the lakes connecting his cabin to hers, but it would be worth it. It would help him keep a low profile in her area of the woods.

"Okay, good luck." The agent waved him through.

Breathing a sigh of relief, Bob slowly crossed the bridge into International Falls, Minnesota. Watching through his rear view mirror to be sure nobody was following him, he zigzagged his way through town on the way to the storage locker he'd previously rented. Thankfully, nobody else was there. He unlocked his unit and retrieved the guns he'd hidden there. Trying to cross the international border with weapons could have been his undoing, if they had torn his car apart. But he, Bob Johnson, was one step ahead of the law. He intended to remain that way.

Soon he was headed south on Highway 53 towards the little log cabin, where he would hide out as he made final preparations and executed the most important mission of his lifetime. He carefully watched and obeyed speed limit signs to be sure he didn't cause any undue attention or get stopped for a traffic citation. He didn't need that. Nor did he need to hit one of the many deer that had a habit of bounding across the roads in front of one's vehicle.

Rob Calhoun no longer existed, he reminded himself. The past had been erased. All that remained was an aging fisherman by the name of Bob Johnson, who was hell bent on fulfilling the old dreams that Rob once had—before Rob had disappeared from the face of the earth.

Yes, Rob's disappearance had been carefully orchestrated. He'd left no trace behind. He had called his adult daughter, Emily, to tell her goodbye—to tell her that he had retired and was leaving the country, going on a long journey to carry out an important but secret mission.

He was unable to provide any details. It would be a rather dangerous assignment, he told her, and he hoped it would be a success.

"But Dad, this sounds crazy. Are you all right?"

"Of course," he tried to reassure her. "Just wanted you to know I love you. Guess I should have told you before...and I'm sorry if I've let you down in any way, Em. I hope to see you again when all of this is over."

"Hold on, you need to give me more information than that. Like, who are you working for, and why? Where will you be?"

"I'm sorry, but I cannot disclose any of that information."

"What if something happens and we need to get a hold of you?"

We? He perked up. Did she mean *she* and her mother, Beth? Or perhaps Emily's husband and baby? He'd never met the baby since Emily lived in Paris. She was an artist married to a Frenchman.

"Dad, are you there?"

"Yes, but I...ah...I can't leave a phone number. No reception where I'm going."

"That makes no sense. There has to be someplace near your location with access to a phone or Internet. There are few places left in this world without access."

"Well, if I find a connection I will let you know," he lied. The old Rob would not need a phone. He would never be heard from again. Still, a part of him hoped that the new Bob would someday see Emily again, after he'd freed Beth. He wasn't quite sure how he would accomplish that yet, but he would. There was no doubt in his mind.

As a tear dribbled down his cheek, he'd told her he had to go and hung up. He hadn't been all that close to his only daughter, too busy working, and then she was suddenly grown up and gone. Still, she was his daughter, and deserved better than having her father desert her and disappear with no explanation.

He'd spent the rest of that evening in the company of his old friend, Gentleman Jack, belting down more stiff drinks than he probably needed. Why, he wondered, did everyone, even his own daughter, question his sanity? If they only knew what he was really up to, would they understand?

Maybe. Maybe not. Sometimes a man had to do what a man had to do, even if some people did not get it. Of course, he assured himself, he was actually doing a good thing—saving the love of his life from that evil man. He'd be a hero after all. Someday Beth would thank him, her green eyes shimmering with her love for him as she slowly undressed and invited him into her bed. He could hardly wait. It had been so long.

SHAKING HIS HEAD IN DISBELIEF, Bob turned left onto a winding country road surrounded by dense forest land. His turn was marked by a massive statue of a walleye mounted on a portable trailer. This was the entrance to the Kabetogama Lake resorts, and Chief Woodenfrog State Campgrounds. It felt like the middle of nowhere. He was about to head deep into the heart of the Kabetogama State Forest. That was good—a perfect place to hide out. At least, he noticed, there was a Gateway General Store across from the big fish. And, he grinned to himself, there was even a liquor sign blinking in the window. It was mounted above smaller signs advertising groceries, gifts, hardware, and clothing. What more would he need?

At the far end of the road, about the time he thought he was surely lost, he found a sign directing him to Arrowhead Lodge. A rambling log structure, painted red, loomed before him at the very tip of a peninsula jutting out into Lake Kabetogama. Probably built in the early 1900s, he figured, it perched upon ancient slabs of granite. Screened-in porches overlooking a large floating dock wrapped around the structure. Several guests sat on benches watching the white pelicans floating on the lake, as fishing boats bobbed on the waters of this island-studded twenty-six-mile-long lake that had been carved by glaciers long ago.

A massive stone fireplace dominated the main room of the lodge, surrounded by overstuffed antique chairs, a game table, and an antique hutch filled with books and games. Several old wooden dining tables were positioned along the window wall overlooking the lake below. A crystal vase of fresh flowers was placed in the center of each table. The room was filled with a variety of plants overflowing from old-fashioned metal plant stands. A mounted trophy wolf stood guard in the corner of the great room.

He had no trouble checking into his cabin. The owners were friendly, accommodating, and didn't ask too many questions. He was welcome to have breakfast or dinner with them any day, they told him, or he could book an American Plan. He declined that offer since he would not always be staying in his cabin. He had work to do that would probably require him to be gone for days at a time. That's why he had a tent and sleeping bag stashed in his SUV, along with his single shot 20-gauge shot gun and pistol. You never knew when a gun may come in handy; for hunting and survival; for protection. Or...who knew what, he grinned to himself.

He'd already made arrangements to park his fishing boat here, and was pleased to see it sitting at the pier waiting for him and his first adventure on the lake. He purchased a fishing license, although he doubted he'd ever use it. He'd be sure to throw all his gear into the boat every time he headed out to pursue his real reason for being there.

So what if he rarely, if ever, came back with any fish? Maybe he preferred to clean his fish and make himself a shore lunch out on one of the islands instead of bringing them back to the cabin with him. Or maybe he was just a lousy fisherman. Besides, catch and release was more popular than ever, right? Shouldn't matter anyway, should it? It was nobody else's business.

"Come on up and spend time at the lodge anytime you like," the owner intruded upon his thoughts as he left him at the door of his rustic cabin. "Folks like to sit by the fire and read a book or the daily newspaper, play games, or just sit out on the porch and watch the lake."

"Thanks, I will," Bob replied, not sure he'd take him up on his offer. The less people knew or remembered about him the better. Still, he would need to check things out and get to know a little about the people here so he could determine if this really was a safe place for him. What if he had, somehow, left a trace behind and the IRS or FBI were already on his tail? *Stop it,* he reprimanded himself!

His little cabin was all he needed. A big table for him to work at and plot his next moves. An efficiency kitchen with a small stove, refrigerator, and microwave. One bed and a bathroom. Most importantly, it was secluded, tucked into the woods. It stood on a slab of ancient bedrock with a little deck hanging out over the lake. The lodge was on one side, pretty much hidden from sight. On the other side, a path wound through the woods to the Woodenfrog Campground.

Once he was settled in, he took a walk around the premises to size it up and find a few escape routes if needed. As he hiked through the Woodenfrog Campground, a feeling of serenity came over him. He felt peaceful, protected. Could it be the spirit of the big chief himself who they said sometimes haunted these grounds where he and his tribe of Ojibwe once wintered? Maybe the chief's spirit understood the mission he was about to embark upon…maybe he had someone in his corner after all. Maybe this was a good place to come to think, be alone, and try to draw some wisdom from the universe.

He'd done a lot of research before deciding to settle in here, and although he'd never believed in spirits and such, it had been interesting to read. The chief and his people had lived a simple but self-sufficient lifestyle revolving around the seasons, spearing sturgeon and making maple syrup in the spring, picking berries in the summer, hunting in the fall. Chief Woodenfrog had paddled his birch bark canoe back and forth between his islands just across the water and the land where Bob now stood. He'd sold blueberries to the whites for eight to ten cents a quart, and he'd speared lots of sturgeon below the rushing waters of Kettle Falls. Yes, Kettle Falls was one of the next places Bob would visit—on his way to Rainy Lake.

As he hiked through the wooded park, he couldn't help noticing the lake glittering in the sunlight, a slight breeze ruffling its surface. A deer scampered out from the brush as loons called out to each other across the big lake. He sat on a picnic bench for a while, thinking, planning, wondering how Beth would react when he rescued her from that monster. So many scenarios played through his mind—some good, some bad. It was hard to know how this whole thing would go down.

Heading back through the park towards his cabin for dinner, he passed an unusual looking old building made of hand split stone. It seemed to be abandoned, and was overgrown with moss, trees, and plants. A sign informed him that this was a "refactory," whatever that meant, that had been built in the 1930s as a Civilian Conservation Corps project. Peering in through the cobweb-framed windows, he found it to be pretty much empty aside from an old wooden table and a few chairs. The door was locked with a rusty padlock. Not a bad place to hide out, he decided. Not a bad place at all.

Back at his cabin, he made himself a peanut butter sandwich and washed it down with whiskey. He'd need to stock up on groceries soon, or maybe eat a few meals up at the lodge after all. The aroma of fish frying wafted through the air from the nearby lodge, making him hungry for real food. He'd never been much of a cook. Even after Beth left, he'd eaten out or hired a cook. Those days were pretty much over, he feared.

He spent the rest of the evening sitting out on his secluded deck, hidden from the rest of the world. Peering out through the overhanging trees, he watched a few fishing boats come in, a few guests strolling around the grounds of the lodge or sitting on the log benches enjoying the view. Normal stuff that normal people liked to do.

Not like me, he chuckled to himself as he downed another glass of whiskey. A glorious sunset, impressive enough to catch his attention, soon swirled through the sky overhead, intermingling with a few clouds moving in. Somehow the shifting shapes of the clouds reminded him of Beth. He could almost see her face floating above him. Was she smiling? Smiling the way she used to smile at him?

Once darkness descended, a sliver of a moon appeared and the sky was soon filled with brilliant stars. They seemed to be twinkling at each other as if they were trying to communicate. Maybe they were laughing at the world below. He had to admit he'd never seen a sky quite like this before. He felt compelled to sit out there in his rocking chair, staring up into the sky, listening to the waves lapping gently along the shore, mesmerized by the stillness of the night. The sound of a wolf howling in the distance startled him. He knew there were wolves and bears out there in the woods. He might even encounter one as he trekked through the wilderness and escaped back into Canada with Beth. That's why he'd brought his guns with him—one of the reasons, anyway.

Finally, he turned in for the night, passing out immediately. But before long, he was thrashing about in his sleep, trying to escape from another of his nightmares.

"Can't you do anything right? What the hell is wrong with you?" his father was yelling at him while his mother laughed hysterically in the background, a drink in hand. The three of them were gathered around a body bag that thrashed about on the shore of the lake like freshly caught fish. Several eerie faces, glowing in the dark, began to float up from the bag, shrieking into the black night, circling around Bob's head, laughing at him. Laughing at him because he had apparently failed in his mission to rescue Beth. Three faces—Beth, Seth, and a young boy. As the faces moved in closer and closer, hysterical laughter filled the sky. Even the wolves and loons were laughing—laughing at him. "But I have a rendezvous with death!" he began screaming. But nobody could hear him. Nobody cared.

As the faces grew fangs and began attacking him, Bob struggled to wake himself up. "It's only a dream, only a dream," his conscious mind finally broke through his dream state. Heart pounding, he stumbled from his bed and rushed out of his cabin onto the deck, breathing deeply of the night air. No more sleep for him tonight, so he made himself a pot of coffee and tried to escape from his latest nightmare.

Chapter Three

As the early morning sky began to swirl with shades of pink and yellow, Bob dressed in his fishing clothes and headed out to begin his first day on the job. It was quiet—nobody else seemed to be up this early. That was good, since he had some security work to take care of first. He quietly walked through the parking lot, making a note of license plate numbers on the cars parked by the lodge. Then he snuck around the cabins, noting their cars' license plate numbers as well. It was important for him to know who was hanging around this place, just in case.

After a hike through the campground, he could smell bacon frying in the lodge. He was hungry and decided to stop in for breakfast.

"Good morning, Bob," the owner greeting him. "You're our first customer this morning. Sit wherever you like."

Bob chose a table in the corner with a view of the lake. *Always good to have your back to the wall.* Outside, white pelicans were bobbing and dancing on the waves. Strange birds. Lost in his sleep-deprived thoughts, he startled when a petite waitress approached his table, probably a high school girl.

"Good morning, sir. I'm Kathy, and I'll be your waitress this morning," the brown-eyed, brown-haired girl announced. "What can I get ya?"

"What do you recommend?" he asked her with a smile. It was important to make a few friends here, after all, if he wanted to get the information he needed.

"If you like pancakes, our blueberry pancakes, made with fresh blueberries, and our homemade maple syrup is one of our best-sellers."

"You sold me. I'd also like bacon and a strong cup of coffee."

After devouring his breakfast, he lingered with his coffee, waiting for her to return with his check, planning to ask her a few questions.

"Great place you have here. Do you live around here, maybe grew up here?" he began.

"Not here exactly. Like, I'm from Ranier, a ways up the road," she smiled at him.

Ranier? Bingo! That's where Beth and her family used to hang out when they weren't out on her grandmother's island. Ranier. That's where they parked their vehicles. That's where he'd inquired about Beth, in a Ranier bar, about ten years ago, before his humiliating snowmobile trip out to her island.

He caught his breath before carefully continuing the conversation. "Yes, I think I remember Ranier—a quaint little town with a Voyageur's statue at the entrance and an old railroad depot?"

"That's it," she beamed proudly. "I live there, but I go to high school in International Falls. I'm working here this summer to save money for college."

"Good for you! I used to know some folks from around there. They lived on an island on Rainy Lake, I think, but used to come into Ranier often. Let me think...." He paused as if trying to remember their names. As if he could ever forget! "Hmmm...I think it was Peterson. An old lady by the name of Emma. She had a granddaughter named... Barb? No, maybe Beth?"

"Why yes! I know them. Emma passed away some years ago, but Beth is still around. She and her husband live on Emma's island on Rainy Lake. But they also have a house on Houska's Point in Ranier where they spend some time—used to be Jake O'Connell's place. He's gone, too."

"Sorry to hear that," Bob managed to respond. So Beth had married after all. How could she? "I think I do recall Beth having married...what was her husband's name again?"

"Seth. Seth Davis. They are a nice family. I used to babysit for them sometimes."

Babysit? What the hell? Beth and Seth had children? Oh my God! This certainly complicates the situation. How could she marry another man? And have children with him?

He managed to collect himself, to control his simmering rage. "How many children do they have?" he simply had to know.

"Just one. Jason must be like close to ten, I think. Nice kid."

Suddenly, more customers came in and Kathy had to excuse herself, thankfully. He left her a nice tip and thanked her. "Small world, isn't it, Kathy? Nice visiting with you. See you later."

Stunned, he walked out of the lodge in a daze, recalling the three floating heads in his nightmare—Beth, Seth...and a kid! He retreated back to his little cabin. Pounding his fist on the table, he knocked his maps and books onto the floor, then proceeded to kick them across the room. How could she? Why, she must have been pregnant—with Seth's baby—when he'd paid them a visit on the island ten years ago.

What now? This shocking revelation would require some re-thinking, and some changes in his plans. He had some sleuthing to do, a lot of spying on Beth and her little family, before he could make some decisions. What was he going to do with the kid when he captured Beth? Taking a mother away from a child was different than taking a wife away from a husband who was holding her hostage and didn't deserve her. Seth had probably raped her, resulting in the birth of this kid. He deserved to rot in hell for that. What to do with the kid? What to do with the kid? Bob had to admit it wasn't the kid's fault that he'd been born.

But he sure as hell didn't need a kid underfoot—certainly not the child of another man. His head was spinning, trying to make sense of this evolving situation. Maybe he needed a good stiff drink and a nap to make up for his sleepless night. After that, it probably wouldn't hurt to hang around the lodge and see if he could discover anything else that he should know. It wouldn't be a good day to get out and explore the lake anyway, he decided, as thunder boomed across the lake and the heavens unleashed a torrential downpour of rain.

How could she do this to me? To us? To what we once had together? he mumbled to himself as he crawled beneath the vintage quilt, trying to escape from memories of the past. Memories of making love to her on the beach on a moonlit night consumed his thoughts. Of the way she would twist a strand of her long auburn hair around her finger when she was deep in thought, a thousand miles away. What had she been thinking? Was she plotting against him? And why had she kept her thoughts a deep, dark secret? He had a right to know. She was *his* wife, after all.

The rain was letting up a bit by the time Bob headed up to the lodge early in the evening. He was surprised to discover how cool it was up here in the summer. He even needed a jacket.

After a good dinner of fresh walleye, he settled in a heavy leather rocking chair to warm himself by the fireplace. He pretended to be reading the newspaper while he was actually trying to eavesdrop on anyone within hearing distance as they passed through the great room, stopping to visit and swap stories. Mostly fish tales, some local gossip. One scary encounter with a friendly bear.

Before long, two rowdy guys came in, laughing at each other's stupid jokes. They settled at the game table after selecting a game from the shelf. They guzzled beer and traded insults as they shuffled and dealt the cards.

"You suck, Wee Willy." The heavy set guy wearing suspenders over his plaid shirt threw his cards on the table in frustration.

"Screw you, Big Billy, you asshole," the other guy replied, stealing a curious glance at Bob out of the corner of his eye. He was smaller than his friend, slim, in good shape, with sharp piercing eyes. He seemed to be continually scanning the room as if he was looking for something or someone.

As they continued joking and insulting each other, a third man stopped at their table. “I hope you two aren’t flying tonight. Leave your plane at the dock and pick it up in the morning when you sober up.”

“Hey, the Minnow Man here can fly any day, any time, drunk or not. It’s what I do.” The fat one, Big Billy, was beginning to slur his words.

The other one, Willy, seemed to be drinking less and holding his booze much better. “Well, Butch is right, you are not flying tonight. I’ve got the keys.” He dangled a set of keys before Billy’s eyes, taunting him as he quietly glanced at Bob once again. Then he escorted his friend out onto the deck and they disappeared into the rainy night.

The guy named Butch walked over to the fireplace, warming his hands. “Mind if I join you?” he asked before plopping down in another chair.

“Sure,” Bob replied. Why not? Did he really have a choice?

“Sorry about the commotion at the game table. Looks like you’re just trying to read and relax. I’m Butch Olson, a neighbor and regular here. Great food, friendly people.” He held out his hand.

Bob shook it carefully. “Bob Johnson here. Retired. Just up here doing some fishing.” Before Butch could ask him any questions about himself, he immediately changed the subject to Billy and Willy. “Who are those guys, Billy and Willy?”

Butch chuckled. “The Zolinsky boys may be a little off, but they are harmless. Real characters. Twin brothers, actually. Billy lives in a shack in the woods not far from here, the one their fur-trading great-grandfather built years ago. No electricity. No plumbing. Their mother was a squaw, their father a Pollock. They say that the father always wanted a son named William. Well, they had twins, so he named them William I and William II. That got too confusing, so they were nicknamed Willy and Billy.”

Bob shook his head in disbelief. Sounded like something out of a movie. “But they own an airplane?”

“Yes, Billy owns a little Cessna. It is called The Minnow Man since Billy seines minnows, then flies them around to the various resorts and bait shops that purchase them. Yeah, Big Billy is a character. They call him The Minnow Man, same as the name on his airplane."

"What about Willy?" He was the one to keep an eye on, Bob thought to himself.

"Not sure where he actually lives. He disappears for long stretches of time and nobody really knows where he goes or what he does. Then he shows up now and then to visit Billy. He's more educated, loves to read and philosophize. Quieter, more of a thinker, believe it or not—except when he and Billy get together and start drinking. Then look out! Anyway...." Butch yawned as he rose from his chair. "Just wanted to apologize if they interrupted your reading. I gotta get home to the wife and get ready for a long day of fishin' tomorrow—if the rain ever quits."

All was now quiet in the great room. Bob wasn't sure he liked the way Willy had kept glancing at him, his steely eyes constantly scanning the room. Maybe he was being paranoid, as he'd so often been accused of being. Still, he would keep an eye on these characters. Harmless, probably, like Butch told him, but it never hurt to be cautious in a case like this.

Not yet tired after his long nap, and needing to find some diversion to keep his thoughts away from his mission and the recent complications, he decided to search the library by the fireplace for a good book to read. He'd never been much of a reader in the past, except for legal briefs and research. Too busy. But tonight he was drawn to the bookshelves, which were full of dusty old volumes, popular new novels, and non-fiction.

He gravitated to the historical section, where his eyes were drawn to an interesting title. *The Mad Trapper of Rat River*. Hmmm...Rat River. Interesting. That was the route he planned to use to escape back into Canada with Beth. Would she come willingly, he asked himself for the millionth time, or would he need to tie her up and duct tape her mouth shut until she realized this was actually a good thing?

Enough of that, he scolded himself. He needed a break from himself, from worrying about the challenges that lie ahead. He needed to escape into another world tonight. The Mad Trapper just might be the answer. Paging through the tattered book, he discovered it was based on a real-life mystery from the 1930s.

Clutching the book beneath his rain jacket, he stepped out onto the deck overlooking the lake, breathing deeply of the night air. The rain was still falling and a dense bank of fog was creeping slowly across the lake, threatening to swallow him in its ghostly arms. It felt surreal. Shivering as a rush of cold air passed through him, he cautiously walked down the stairs to follow the trail back to his cabin. Peering through the mist, he could barely see the airplane anchored by one of the big docks. Looked like the Cessna 180 he used to own and had enjoyed flying in his past lifetime. Must be The Minnow Man, he figured, shaking his head. A light glowed from within the plane. That was odd. Were those strange dudes hiding out in there, watching him?

It felt good to get back to his little cabin, lock and bolt the door, and pull the curtains shut so nobody could see in. After shedding his rain gear and taking a shower, he climbed into bed with *The Mad Trapper of Rat River* and Jack Daniels.

It was an intriguing read. This guy, known as Albert Johnson by some, arrived on the banks of the Rat River in the early 1930s. He'd navigated his way from the Mackenzie River Delta on a native-built raft, and proceeded to build himself a small 8 x 10 foot cabin on the Rat River. A total recluse, he hid out in his cabin and spoke to nobody. Although he was allegedly a fur trapper, he never bothered to secure a trapping license. Instead, he was accused of springing the traps of the other fur trappers in the area.

The Royal Canadian Mounted Police eventually executed a search warrant of Johnson's place after a number of complaints. Johnson refused to talk or let them in. When one of the officers tried to force the door open, Johnson shot him through the wooden door and a firefight broke out. The officers retreated to plot their next attack.

A posse of nine men and all their dogs was formed with the goal of blasting this fugitive out of his cabin with dynamite. After successfully blowing the place up, the posse rushed in to find his body. But The Mad Trapper was still alive and hiding in a dugout below the ruins of his cabin. He opened fire upon the officers, injuring several of them.

With blizzard conditions setting in, the posse decided to wait before regrouping and coming back for this guy. He was gone, however, when they arrived. Setting out on a foot chase, they eventually caught up with him several weeks later and surrounded him in a thicket. A firefight broke out in which Johnson killed a constable, shooting him through the heart, before escaping into the wilderness. The Mad Trapper managed to climb a seven-thousand-foot mountainous peak in blizzard conditions to elude the officers.

Way to go, dude, Bob chucked to himself, intrigued with this guy who also happened to be named Johnson.

Now the hunt through the frozen Canadian wilderness was intensified to capture this fugitive who had murdered one of their own. They eventually hired a post-war aviator to help in the hunt by scouting from the air.

The Royal Canadian Mounted Police finally caught up with him on foot as they rounded a bend in the Eagle River and discovered his campsite. He was standing just a few hundred yards in front of them, with no snowshoes on. A gun battle broke out in which one of the officers was seriously wounded and Johnson was killed, after a 150 mile foot chase and a month in the wilderness that winter of 1932..

Although extensive research had been done, nobody was able to conclusively identify The Mad Trapper. He apparently used a number of aliases. Whoever he was, The Mad Trapper had been a mysterious fugitive, hiding from justice.

Brilliant! My hero! Bob was impressed with what this guy had been able to accomplish against all odds. Too bad he had to get himself killed, however. Still, he'd made a name for himself and would go down in history as The Mad Trapper. Interesting that one of his aliases was Johnson, just like Bob's new name. Perhaps there was a reason he'd pulled the name "Johnson" out of nowhere. Did he have some kind of connection with this guy, whoever he really was? Maybe that's a strange thought, he sighed to himself, but stranger things had happened.

Reading The Mad Trapper's tale taught Bob a few things about escaping through the wilderness while being pursued. Hopefully, his mission wouldn't end up quite like the other Johnson's had. Still, it didn't hurt to be prepared. It may not hurt to build a dugout beneath his new cabin in Nestor Falls, just in case. He'd need to do it after Black Bear Camp shut down for the winter, after the owners and other cabin people headed south but before freeze-up—or after the ground thawed out enough in the spring so he could dig. It would also be a good place to hide Beth if she tried to escape. But she wouldn't do that, would she? He knew that somewhere deep down within her soul, she still loved him. Always had. Always would...even if she didn't realize that yet.

Here's to you, The Mad Trapper of Rat River. Bob swung his glass of Jack Daniels high into the air, toasting his new hero as a bolt of lightning flashed through the sky and the rain continued to fall.

Chapter Four

The rain finally stopped early the next morning and the sun came creeping up over the horizon, flooding Bob's cabin with rays of sunlight. Outside, a flock of white pelicans bobbed on the gentle waves, chattering to each other as they welcomed a sunny new day.

Bob was ready, finally, to venture out onto the lake with his maps, GPS, and all the items he'd methodically checked off on his long list. Pistol, shot gun, ammunition, camping gear, rain suit, extra clothes, water, food supplies, frying pan, old-fashioned coffee pot, matches, his newly acquired high powered binoculars, camera, and smart phone... he was not sure it would work where he was headed, but it didn't hurt to have it with him. He'd carefully concealed the shotgun in the tent sack to be sure nobody saw it on his way down to the boat.

Grinning, he carefully packed his shiny new survival knife, rope, and several rolls of duct tape, just in case. One never knew about the fickle moods of a woman, including his own wife. *Yes,* my wife, *damn it,* he grumbled to himself. *Got that, Seth, you son-of-a-bitch?*

He tucked his private journal, the one with all his plans detailing every aspect of this important mission, into his duffle bag. Once upon a time, he'd thought he had every minute detail perfectly planned.

He'd have to make a few revisions, now that the kid was in the picture. He'd do that while camping out and keeping an eye on Beth's island. He needed that journal with him at all times—it was incriminating evidence. He sure couldn't leave it behind at the cabin. *Can't trust anyone these days,* he mumbled to himself as he locked up the cabin and headed down to his boat.

It was early, and he figured he'd be the only one up at this time of day. Perfect. But just as he tossed the duffle bag into his boat, rearranged his fishing gear, and turned on his navigational device, he was startled by heavy footsteps approaching from the dock behind him.

"Great day for fishin', eh?" a loud male voice boomed out.

Spinning around, he found the Zolinsky brothers standing there with their fishing gear. Willy and Billy were in matching red plaid flannel shirts, grinning as if they didn't have a care in the world. *What morons,* Bob thought to himself.

"Yup, got that right," Bob replied, busying himself untying the ropes so he could launch his boat. Sure didn't need any conversation with these guys. Why did they have to keep showing up?

"We're Billy and Willy," the fat one grinned, displaying a big mouth with a front tooth missing.

"Bob," he replied curtly. Reminding himself he had to be a little friendly or these assholes may think he was up to something, he continued. "Think I saw you guys up at the lodge playing cards the other night."

"That was us," Billy chuckled as Willy stood in the background scoping out Bob's boat and gear, as if it was any of his business. "Hope we didn't cause anyone any trouble. Sometimes we get a little loud, especially when my brother cheats."

Willy finally spoke. "That's enough, Billy. Bob doesn't need to hear anymore. Time to go fishin."

"Where ya headed?" Billy inquired as he began to follow Willy towards another boat tied up at the pier.

None of your damn business, Bob wanted to reply. Instead he forced a smile and replied, "Just exploring the lakes and doin' a little fishin'. Good luck, you guys."

With that, he fired up his engine and was off, maneuvering his boat around the wooded islands into Lake Namakan, and up towards Kettle Falls, where he would portage the boat into Rainy Lake. That's where Beth's island was located. He already had this destination plugged into his GPS unit.

It was a calm day on the lake, with just enough of a breeze to be comfortable in a light jacket. As he maneuvered his boat through Squaw Narrows and Squirrel Narrows, he realized that while he was still in American waters, the islands and land on his right were, in fact, a part of Canada. Strangely enough, when the international borders were created way back when, the countries had agreed to use the route that the French-Canadian voyageurs had used for hundreds of years. He'd read that once he arrived at Kettle Falls, a person could stand by the falls looking *south* into Canada.

Yes, he'd tediously researched every step of his journey, and thought that Kettle Falls would be a very interesting place to visit, maybe even spend a night in the remote historic lodge there if he needed to hide out someday. Now a part of Voyageur's National Park, this wilderness retreat was accessible only by water.

He would arrive on the Lake Namakan side, then have his boat trailered over the portage to the Rainy Lake side. The only problem with that, he decided, was that once he was ready to actually rescue his wife, he didn't want anyone at Kettle Falls to remember him portaging his boat into Rainy Lake. Maybe he'd have to stash another boat on the Rainy Lake side or find a way to portage his boat around Squirrel Falls himself. He may even have to wait until the tourist season was over and the Kettle Falls Hotel closed for the season. That could make it difficult, however, if winter weather arrived earlier than anticipated. After all, he and Beth had to make their way back to Nestor Falls before winter set in.

Stop your worrying, he scolded himself. *This is meant to be. It will work out just fine—one way or another*. One way, she came with him willingly. The other way.... He glanced down at the guns he'd hidden beneath the console, a wry smile curling his lips. The other way would give him a great deal of satisfaction. He had a rendezvous with death, after all. Seth's death.

Before long he arrived at Kettle Falls, where he tied his boat up at the dock. Several other boats bobbed in his wake. An old log cabin stood on the shore, abandoned most likely. Nestled back into the woods was a cozy white house with a red roof. A building that appeared to be a boathouse or bait shop stood at the shoreline.

Nobody else was around, so he hiked up the road until he found a wooded trail with a sign directing him to the lodge. Several deer crossed his path as he made his way along the trail and down the rustic log stairs, swatting away a swarm of hungry mosquitoes. This certainly was the middle of nowhere, he thought to himself. Had he taken a wrong turn and gotten himself lost—already?

Then he suddenly found himself in a clearing. Emerging before him, tucked into the forest, was an expansive white frame structure with a red roof and red and white striped awnings. As he approached the lodge, he noticed hanging baskets of flowers framing the stairs to the veranda. An assortment of vines wrapped themselves up the sides of the porch, spreading across the building and framing the old windows. Beth would love this place, he sighed to himself. Did she ever come here?

He felt like he'd just stepped back into another era, as he walked up the stairs into the screened veranda filled with old wicker furniture and antiques. Hearing voices coming from the end of the veranda, he followed the sounds, walking through the porch where several guests were leisurely sipping lemonade—or something stronger, perhaps—reading books, and visiting.

What is this? He found himself in a bar—a bar with a sloping floor. In the background, an antique player piano played scratchy music from long ago. An old wooden bar filled the length of the room, and the walls were covered with historic photos, along with a number of framed girlie prints from long ago.

"Wow!" he found himself exclaiming as he took it all in. Was this for real? Time seemed to have stopped out here in the middle of nowhere. He felt like he'd slipped back into the world of *The Mad Trapper of Rat River.*

The friendly bartender chuckled. "Welcome, sir. Guess you've never been here before, eh?"

"That's right. So what's the deal with the floor, and all of this? I feel like I'm in a time warp here." Settling himself on a stool by the massive antique bar, he decided that he needed a drink after all, even if it was only noon. "Jack Daniels on the rocks, please."

"Comin' right up," the bartender grinned. "Name's Mike."

"Bob here."

"So," Mike began after handing Bob his drink, "This old hotel was built in 1913 on a bed of clay with no foundation. Heavy rains would wash away the soil beneath the building, causing the walls to sink and the floors to slope. The sloping floor of this old bar soon became a beloved landmark. In 1918, Robert Williams bought this place for $1,000 and four barrels of whiskey. The floor continued to slope for years until the park service took over and renovated the hotel. They decided to preserve the sloping floor for the sake of history."

"Interesting." Bob sipped his drink, trying not to gulp it down. He had lots to do today; not a good idea to get drunk this early in the day. His eyes focused on the pictures hanging over the bar.

"Those girlie photos are from the good old days here," Mike chuckled. "You see, during prohibition, they made moonshine here. Lumberjacks and ladies of the night spent time here together. Even the famous Chicago gangster, Bugs Moran, used to show up now and then as he smuggled whiskey into the country from Canada. Then there was old Moonshine Joe...the stories go on and on." He walked away to serve another customer, a young woman about thirty years of age or so, probably about Emily's age.

Bob had always enjoyed history, and was anxious to hear more. For now, he listened to the conversations flowing around him, trying to learn anything he could. After another drink, he asked Mike how long the place stayed open for the season. That may determine when he made his move through Kettle Falls on his way to rescue his wife.

"Closing party is usually around the end of September, depending on the weather," Mike informed him.

"So is anyone here over the winter to take care of the place? I mean, with all this historic stuff here—"

"Not anymore. Used to have a caretaker all winter. These days, we just snowmobile in after freeze-up to check it out. We fly over now and then to make sure the place is secure."

Perfect, Bob thought to himself.

"Not to worry if we're not here all the time. Our resident ghosts are, and they would drive away anyone who dared to break into this place!"

"Ghosts?" The young woman sitting several stools down the bar from him perked up and moved closer. "I am totally into ghosts. Tell us more."

Bob shook his head, wondering if he was already getting drunk. *Ghosts? Really?* Shaking his head, he focused on his drink.

As more customers gathered around the bar, Mike was off and running with his stories about the Kettle Falls resident ghosts. Stories about waking in the middle of the night to hear footsteps roaming the halls past the bedrooms on the upper floor of the old lodge. About the old juke box playing in the middle of the night when nobody was anywhere near the bar.

"One time my mother woke during the night to the sound of music playing downstairs. She thought that was odd. Had somebody forgotten to turn the Victrola off? Or had someone forgotten to lock the door to the bar, so someone got in and turned it on during the night? So...." He paused for effect. "She bravely tiptoed down the stairs to the bar. The door was locked, so nobody could have gotten in. When she unlocked the door...." He paused again, gazing at the customers gathered around him. "Well...the music suddenly stopped, just like that. The smell of cigar smoke filled the room, although nobody she knew smoked cigars anymore. An open bottle of whiskey and several glasses stood, half-full, on the bar."

"Then what happened?" the young woman asked breathlessly.

"Well," Mike continued, "as my mother stood there, mouth

hanging open, a chilling invisible presence seemed to pass right through her. It felt like someone had been there, like a party had been going on and she had interrupted it. She fled the room, running up the stairs, screaming for my father."

"How could that be? I mean, who could have been there?" another customer asked.

"The only thing we can figure out is that the spirits of Bugs Moran —you know, the famous gangster—and his cronies stopped in for one of their famous parties in the Kettle Falls Hotel. They always smoked those smelly cigars, drank whiskey, and loved to play that old Victrola. That's our best guess, anyway."

"Wow!" The young woman frantically scribbled notes in a little notebook she had retrieved from her purse. "I can't wait to write to my friends about this!"

Bob shook his head. Old Mike was a good storyteller, he had to admit, but ghosts? That was crazy.

Suddenly starving, Bob realized that he hadn't eaten since early that morning. He was shocked to realize it was already three in the afternoon. Maybe it made sense to stay here tonight, portage his boat in the morning, and get a fresh start to Beth's island then. Maybe he'd have lunch in the restaurant, then take a little cruise around the area to get an idea how far he was from the Rat River that would eventually take him back to his new home in Canada.

Feeling a bit wobbly, he carefully made his way to the dining area at the other end of the veranda. Seating himself at a glass topped bamboo table-for-two on the porch, he gazed out at a dirt road leading down to the roaring falls near the Rainy Lake side of the peninsula. Golf carts transported guests from their boats to the lodge. A hungry fox lurked at the edge of the forest, as if waiting for any scraps from the fish cleaning house.

After consuming a delicious fresh walleye sandwich, he felt better, good enough to check himself into the lodge for the night. He climbed the old stairs to find his room, a cozy old-fashioned bedroom with an antique dresser, even an old-fashioned water basin and pitcher. It was only five, but he couldn't help flopping down on the bed, and was soon out like a light.

Several hours later, he woke to the sound of music and laughter flowing up the stairs from the bar below. Ghosts? He laughed at the very notion, but decided to get up and take a look. More customers had come in by boat and were simply enjoying time together in the old bar. Some were playing pool on the sloping floor. Bob couldn't help wondering how often a drunk slid his way down the sloping floor onto the wrap-around veranda.

He hiked down the road towards the sound of the roaring falls and climbed up the path to the top, where he found a deck overlooking churning pools of root beer colored water bubbling and boiling beneath the falls cascading over the dam. Mesmerized by the power of the falls and the glowing reflections of the setting sun, he stood there for quite a while, just thinking. What if someone were to slip and fall from the top of the dam into the falls? Would he survive? What would happen to a body that somehow got dumped here? Would it be sucked into the churning falls and disappear forever? Would it sink to the bottom and stay there, especially if it was weighted down with concrete blocks?

As he roamed around the grounds in the emerging moonlight, he vaguely remembered a story that Beth once told him about her grandparents—Emma and Pete? They had loved these falls, had picnicked beside them. They'd felt a spiritual connection to the falls and to the lake. Both of their ashes had been scattered here after they died. So they'd, in a sense, become a part of the lake, a lake that may someday claim another of Beth's relatives. Maybe. Maybe not. It all depended on how things went down with Beth.

Finally, he decided he was thirsty and headed back to the bar. It was too late to get out on the lake and do any exploring tonight anyway. Tomorrow he'd get an early start.

AFTER A HEARTY BREAKFAST of stuffed hash browns loaded with

mushrooms, green peppers, onions, ham, and cheese, and lots of black coffee to sober up, Bob had his boat hauled across the portage to the Rainy Lake side and headed out on the lake. Another calm day on the big lake, thankfully. He had some exploring to do on the way to Beth's island. It was important for him to stake out several places along the route where he could stop, perhaps pitch a tent, and hide out from anyone on his trail.

Most of the islands scattered throughout this part of Rainy Lake were located within Voyageur's National Park, and no longer had any cabins or buildings on them. They'd become a part of the wilderness, preserved for future generations. People fished, sometimes camped at various sites, but cabins could no longer be built in the park area.

Several miles or so from Kettle Falls, not far from the mouth of the Rat River which would eventually take him back into Canada, he spotted an island with what looked like an abandoned cabin and a tilting shed hidden amongst the trees and brush. Interesting. Skirting around the entire island, he noticed no signs of activity or human life, so he decided it was safe to park his boat in a secluded inlet on the far side of the island, get out, and explore.

A rocky path covered with brush and downed trees led to the old cabin, its door hanging open and falling off its hinges. Stepping inside, he was surprised to find a shabby table and several chairs in one room beside an old wood-burning stove. A coffee pot sat on the stove. The remnants of several broken plates and coffee cups were scattered over a dirty floor littered with mouse droppings. A corner of the ceiling was falling down, and it looked like rain or snow had been seeping in for some years. A hanging curtain separated the main room from a bedroom that still contained several lumpy mattresses. Looked like the mice had been nibbling away at them. Still, the place certainly had possibilities if he needed to hide out here for a few days on his way back to Canada.

Hiking around the property, he found a lop-sided outhouse and a shed that contained what was left of an old wooden row boat, a motor that had to have been half a century old, miscellaneous rusty tools, and pieces of hand-hewn lumber. An old sign hung from the wall of the shed. The words "Rabbit Island" had been carefully carved on the rotting wood.

Rabbit Island—a perfect place to hide out. He could fix the place up enough to spend a little time here if he had to. He could put a tarp over the leaky roof, and repair the sagging door with lumber from the shed. Sweep out the mouse turds. Cut some wood to heat the place and cook on the old stove.

He could almost see Beth standing there by the stove frying bacon for his breakfast, wearing that sexy black negligee he'd bought her in Paris. Smiling at him the way she used to so many years ago.

Bob walked down to the lake, where he found himself a slab of granite near what was left of a rotting dock with loose boards washing up along the shoreline. He sat for a moment. Pulling his pocket journal from his pocket, he began making notes about the location of this place and what he'd need to bring with him to fix it up. Then he impulsively burst out in laughter, his belly shaking, laughing louder and louder, unable to control his emotions. Once upon a time, he'd had it all...a prestigious law firm, millions in the bank, a penthouse suite in Chicago, and a doting wife.

Look at me now. He shook his head. He had been transformed into a scruffy recluse who was actually thankful to find a mouse-infested, deserted, leaky, pile of shit abandoned cabin with no plumbing or electricity in the middle of the wilderness! Whoever would have guessed? Nobody, perhaps, except his own father.

"You'll never be any good, son," his father had reminded him over and over again throughout his growing-up years, shaking his head in disgust as he poured himself another Scotch. "You just don't have it. Why can't you be on the football team instead of wimping out on the debate team? Be a man, not a pussy that nobody will ever respect!"

Later, his father's drunken rants had escalated to, "Not sure you can ever possibly become a partner in this law firm. You just don't have it...just don't have it." To this day, his words continued to echo in Bob's ears from beyond the grave where his father was buried.

"Go to hell, Dad." Bob flung a rock into the lake, watching it skip across the surface of the still waters. Despite his father's put-downs, he had, in fact, joined that law firm and taken it to new heights after his father finally retreated into the background.

Of course, those days were long gone. Bob had now absconded with ten million dollars and disappeared into the wilderness—to save his beloved Beth. Small change, he figured, for all he had gone through, and for the future that he and Beth would soon have together.

A man has to do what a man has to do, he reminded himself. No, this wasn't exactly paradise here, nothing like the penthouse suite he'd left behind in Chicago. At least nobody would ever dream of looking for him here.

Chapter Five

Bob's heart began to pound in his chest as he maneuvered his boat through the channels and around the many islands scattered throughout Rainy Lake. He was on his way to Beth's island. What if she was down there by the lake when he got there? What if she somehow recognized him or sensed that it was him? He pulled his fishing cap down over his eyes and donned an oversized pair of mirrored sunglasses to complete his disguise.

The island was quiet when he arrived, and he found a secluded fishing hole with a good view of her island. He set up his fishing rods and began casting into the rippling waters. He could barely see her cabin through the woods, the rustic home where she'd been raised by her grandmother after her mother had drowned in the big lake. The old log structure was perched high on a cliff, with stunning views of the lake below. He could see several boats tied at the dock, along with a birch bark canoe.

He waited patiently, binoculars within reach, reminding himself to keep on casting his lure into the water as if his purpose in being there was to catch some fish for dinner. Several other boats were anchored or trolling around the bay, he noticed. That was good. He wasn't the only one hanging around this area of the lake.

Glancing around, he noticed a number of small rocky islands scattered within sight of Beth's island. He would set up camp on one of them, he decided, so he could continue to keep an eye out. He needed to know their routine and habits. When did they come and go? When did they leave the island to head to the mainland, perhaps to the place they owned on Houska's Point in Ranier? Most importantly, when was Beth alone, all alone?

The hours dragged by as he continued to wait for some glimpse of activity. Suddenly, he heard the slam of a door and the shout of a young boy running down the path towards the lake.

"Come on, Dad, let's go," a boy's voice shouted as he ran out onto the dock, tossing some buckets and gear into one of the boats. He was probably about ten, just like the waitress had told him. He had dirty blond hair, nothing like Beth's auburn hair.

Breathlessly, Bob waited for the kid's father—and Beth—to come down the path. Finally Seth stepped onto the dock, grinning at the kid. Seth—the bastard who had stolen his wife from him. Fire began to surge through Bob's veins. *Stay cool, or you will screw this whole thing up,* he reprimanded himself. This was not the time to take Seth on, to get him out of the picture.

"What's your hurry, young man?" Seth ruffled the boy's hair affectionately.

"We need to get out to Blueberry Island and pick the blueberries before the bears get them, don't forget!" The kid smiled up at his father. It looked like they had a close relationship. That was good. Maybe the two of them would get along just fine after he took Beth away. Maybe. Maybe not. Who gave a shit? The damn kid was not going to screw up his plans. That was for sure.

Bob's eyes anxiously scanned the path leading down to the lake, waiting for Beth to appear. Where was she? Then her voice broke through the silence, coming from the cabin on the cliff. "Have fun, you two," she called out. "Jason, don't forget to put your life vest on."

"We will bring home enough blueberries for you to make a hundred pies! Love you, Mom!"

With that, Seth started the boat and they headed out onto the lake.

Hopefully, they'd go a long way and stay away long enough for Bob to...to do what? This wasn't the time for him to rescue his wife. Not yet. He still had too much planning and preparation to take care of. However, if father and son had a habit of taking off on excursions together, that was a good sign. Once he got a better feel of their routines, he'd be ready to make his move.

He watched Seth and his son heading out across the lake, and was disappointed to see they didn't go far. They crossed the channel and pulled up at another little island within view of Beth's place.

Bob waited patiently, hoping to catch a glimpse of Beth. She was so close, yet so far away. What would he do if he saw her? What if she saw him? Of course, he was just a stranger, a fisherman, that's all. She had no way of knowing someone was out there watching her. Their daughter, Emily, had probably already told Beth that he had left the country. Beth would have no clue that he, her true love, was right there watching her every move, just waiting for the perfect opportunity to rescue her and bring her home where she belonged.

He was sick of fishing—or pretending to be fishing. The afternoon sun was beating down on him. He was sweating, sleepy, and thirsty. Not much of a breeze to cool things off today. Where was she? He treated himself to a swig or two of whiskey from his thermos, reminding himself he needed to stay sober and alert or he could blow everything.

Hours later, Seth and the kid returned to the island, hauling big buckets of blueberries up the path to the cabin, where he could vaguely hear the three of them chatting about their day. Beth's laughter rang out from time to time. She almost sounded happy with her little family. Had she been totally brainwashed? Had she completely forgotten him? That couldn't possibly be, he assured himself.

Finally he decided to call it a day and set up camp on a nearby wooded island with a good view of Beth's place. He pulled his boat into a secluded cove and got out to search for a good place to set his tent up before dark. Cautiously, he hiked around the island to make sure he was the only one there. He certainly didn't need company.

He climbed up a rocky ledge above the cove where his boat was parked and found a flat slab of granite surrounded by trees. A perfect place to pitch his tent. Nobody would see him here. Just steps away from his campsite, he found a spot hidden in the brush with a perfect view of Beth's island.

After setting up his tent and sleeping bag, he made himself a peanut butter sandwich and headed out to his observation post. He belted down several Jack Daniels as he sat there on a rock watching the sun set over the lake. Spectacular, he thought to himself—or, it would be if Beth was there beside him to enjoy the swirling shades of pink and gold lighting up the sky. Across the lake, he could see the glow of a campfire on the cliff overlooking Beth's beach. Voices around the campfire floated across the still lake—laughing, teasing, happy voices. Beth. Seth. And the kid.

Days crawled slowly along. Bob plotted in his journal and spent many hours with his binoculars at his observation post. Sometimes he got out on the lake and fished or explored, but he never got far away from Beth's island.

Finally, he saw her one day. She came down to the beach in a yellow bikini, large floppy hat, and huge sunglasses. God, she was still beautiful—what he could see of her. His heart began to pound in his chest as he imagined running his hands over her slim tanned body as she leaned into him, touching him, wanting him. Someday, someday soon, he would have her again. He would have her all to himself. Seth would be history, one way or another.

Beth waded out into the lake, swam for a while, then laid down on a lounge chair and picked up a book to read. Bob just watched, unable to take his eyes off her. Suddenly, Seth and the kid appeared, ruining the whole experience for Bob. The three of them. Together. Laughing. Splashing each other. Playing in the lake.

Soon they disappeared up the path to the cabin, only to come back down dressed in jeans and light jackets. Seth entered the old boathouse by the lake. The rumble of a loud motor echoed across the lake as a classic mahogany Chris Craft launch carefully backed out and tied up at the dock. Bob could see, through his high-powered binoculars, the words "Misty of Rainy Lake" inscribed in bold gold letters on the side of the vintage boat. He remembered it from his previous visits to the island. It had belonged to Beth's grandfather half a century ago, and had been the old man's pride and joy.

As the family prepared to head out on the lake, another boat pulled in close to the dock. It looked like one of the boats Bob had noticed on a neighboring island.

"Hey there," a heavy-set guy called out to the three of them. "I bet you're headed in to pick up the mail in Ranier, right?"

"Just like clockwork. It is Monday, you know," Seth laughed. "Anything you need in town?"

"I do have a package there waiting for me. Would you mind picking it up? I'd do it myself, but the wife isn't feeling too good these days."

"I'm so sorry to hear that," Beth replied. "Please give her our best, and tell her I'll be sending a blueberry pie over for her soon."

"No problem, John," Seth added, "I'll get your package."

So Monday was the day to pick up mail in Ranier. Bob made a note of that in his journal. Then, as soon as they headed out in their boat, he started his up and cautiously made his way to their island.

Making sure the coast was clear, he pulled up in a hidden spot, jumped out, and pushed his way through the brush and up to the cabin. He had to scout it out quickly before they returned. He made mental notes of entrances and exits and the layout of the place. That was all critical information he needed to have before making his move.

He vaguely remembered the old log cabin from years ago when he'd come home with Beth once or twice to visit her grandmother. He'd never stayed long, never paid much attention, was always preoccupied with pending deadlines and his briefcase full of legal briefs. And, of course, he'd been here ten years ago when he made his clumsy attempt to retrieve Beth. He'd barged into the living area and been escorted out by Seth—at gunpoint. It had been a humiliating experience, one that Seth would pay for someday.

Bob brought himself back to the present. This was no time to regress into the past. He had to hurry and get the hell out of here soon. He carefully opened the sagging wood door that had been there for close to a century. Never locked. People up here didn't bother to lock their doors. They trusted their neighbors. Idiots, he thought to himself.

As he explored the house, he noted sleeping arrangements, figuring he would probably strike while they were asleep. Beth and that asshole apparently slept in the downstairs bedroom. Upstairs, a small room surrounded by windows was probably where the kid slept. It was Beth's old room. There were kid's books, toys, and boy's clothes scattered around the room. Downstairs, a screened-in porch with a rumpled bed in the corner appeared to be a summer sleeping room, a place where a cool lake breeze would provide welcome relief from sultry summer nights.

As he prepared to leave, his eye caught upon a large framed photo on the mantle over the rock fireplace—a photo of Beth and Seth, arms wrapped around each other, in a gazebo decorated with white flowers and twinkling lights. She wore a long white dress that clung to her curves. Delicate white daisies were woven though her auburn hair, sparkling in the receding light. The sun was setting over the lake in the background. The two of them, grinning at each other, on their wedding day. That was entirely too much for him. He grabbed the picture and threw it down onto the floor, relishing the sound of broken glass, before storming out of the cabin and back to his boat.

Damn, that was stupid! He cussed his way down to his boat and back across the lake to his campsite. He'd been so careful not to touch anything, not to leave a fingerprint. Next time he'd wear the gloves he'd carefully packed in his duffle bag, along with rope, duct tape, and his pistol. Next time, he'd have to remove that picture and destroy it.

Can't you do anything right? Anything right? Anything right? the slurred voice of his deceased father echoed through his mind. His message was punctuated with a slap across the face.

"Yes, sir. I mean, no sir." A whimpering young Rob had ducked to avoid another blow from this man, his father, who he had tried so hard to please over the years. In the background, his promiscuous mother, Nora, laughed loudly as she poured herself another drink.

Chapter Six

Pacing around his island that afternoon, Bob was restless. He needed some diversion. Maybe he'd head to Ranier. Maybe he'd catch a glimpse of Beth, follow her from a respectable distance, and figure out where she spent her time—and whether she was ever alone during what was apparently their Monday excursions to pick up the mail.

A fresh breeze ruffled the lake today as seagulls soared through a brilliant blue sky. He nosed his boat around the islands. As he rounded the point into the quaint village of Ranier, a Canadian train lumbered over the hundred-year old cantilevered bridge spanning Rainy Lake. It pulled to a stop at the old railroad depot where Homeland Security would be waiting to process the cargo and authorize the train to proceed through the international border.

Locating the town docks just ahead of him, he didn't see any signs of Seth's boat. He did, however, notice a little Cessna float plane tied up at the dock—bright yellow, with large red letters splashed across the side. The Minnow Man!

Shit! Is that moron following me around or what? Should I stay, or should I go?

Throwing caution to the winds, he pulled in anyway, hoping that

Big Billy was not around. Just as he tied his boat up and got out, a voice bellowed from the shoreline.

"Well, I'll be damned," Big Billy chuckled. "Look who we have here! Was wonderin' what happened to ya. Haven't seen ya at The Arrowhead lately."

Bob forced a casual smile in his direction. "Just doing some fishin' and exploring."

"Good, good. I'm deliverin' my minnows. Need any?"

"Not today. Thanks," he dismissed the big guy standing there in his red suspenders that bulged over his protruding belly.

Pulling his cap down over his large sunglasses, Bob hiked up the main street, watching for any sign of Beth. Just beyond Tara's Wharf where he'd landed, he noticed a little restaurant—Rainy Lake Grill. The little village was filled with charming historic buildings, and lots of friendly dogs running loose. He found the post office and anxiously peered inside. No sign of Beth and family. Maybe they had a car here and had picked it up to go someplace else. Or maybe they were still around somewhere.

He knew that Beth also had a place here... Houska's Point. Where could Houska's Point possibly be? In a small village like this, certainly somebody should know, right? Maybe he'd stop in at that historic looking bar he was just passing, Loony's Pub. It looked familiar... wasn't that the place where he'd stopped that cold winter day ten years ago looking for directions to Beth's island? They hadn't been too helpful, he recalled. He'd had to drive to International Falls to find a snowmobile and guide to escort him to the island.

Still, Looney's Pub sounded like a great idea. It was a brew pub, advertising a beer of the week. Hopefully they'd have some whiskey as well. His stash of Jack Daniels was running out.

Preoccupied as he hiked down the street, he almost missed three individuals leaving the Rainy Lake Grill and heading down towards the lake. Suddenly, Beth's voice drifted across the street, freezing him in place. It was Beth, Seth, and the kid. Where the hell was their boat?

"I need to stop at the house before we leave," she gazed up at Seth, "to pick up some things."

"No problem," Seth replied. He was carrying an armful of mail and magazines.

Bob forced himself to turn away, trying to prevent them from seeing his face—or hearing his pounding heart. Once they'd passed him, barely acknowledging his presence, he glanced back to see where they were headed. They hiked a block down towards the lake and stopped at a log home perched on a point jutting out into Rainy Lake. Must be Houska's Point.

Skirting cautiously around a neighboring house, hiding in the shadows of the dense trees framing the property, he could see their boat tied up beside their own dock. The kid ran around the yard exploring while Seth settled himself in a rocking chair on the porch, going through their mail. Beth disappeared into the house, coming out later with a shopping bag.

"Where's Jason?" an exasperated Beth sighed as she came out of the house. "Disappeared again?"

The kid had wandered down the shoreline, following one of the neighborhood dogs, throwing sticks out into the lake for the dog to retrieve.

"Probably out exploring as usual. Jason!" Seth called loudly. "Get over here. We're leaving."

The kid, shoulders drooped, head hanging, gave up his pursuit and returned. "Mom, Dad, we need a dog. I really want my own dog. Maybe a German shepherd. You know, they are really good watch dogs too."

"Not sure we need a watch dog on the island—or here, young man," Seth replied.

"Not anymore," Beth sighed. *What was that supposed to mean?*

"Well, maybe someday, son." Seth softened his tone as he watched the look of disappointment on his son's face.

"We will see." Beth gave her son a hug.

Bob made a mental note as they boarded their boat and headed out into the lake. It would be one hell of a lot easier to kidnap the boy while he was off exploring. But why would he want to do that? Unless...unless he could hold him hostage in exchange for Beth.

His mind reeling with new options, Bob decided he most definitely needed a drink. Now that the coast was clear and even The Minnow Man's plane had taken off, he made his way back to Loony's Pub, where he was greeted with a skeleton wearing a baseball cap hanging on the wall. *Loony's, all right,* he laughed to himself as he stepped back in time and into the old pub.

He slouched down onto a cracked vinyl stool that had probably been there a hundred years, noticing about half a dozen guys bellied up to the bar. Laughing. Telling fish tales. Cussing. Guzzling down glasses of Loony's homemade beer. If only life could be so simple, he thought to himself. He was willing to bet none of these dudes had the IRS on their tail. Bet they'd never had to change their names and go into hiding. Hell, they each probably had a little woman at home waiting for them to return with the day's catch of nice fish. *Nice fish... why were fish always "nice"?*

Someday, he'd have his own little woman back home with him, waiting for him in his new cabin in Nestor Falls, Canada. Someday. For now, he needed a good stiff drink.

"Jack Daniels," he nodded at the bartender.

As Bob quietly nursed several more drinks, trying to stay sober enough to make his way back to the island, he thought about seeing Beth today. The first time he had seen her up close in ten long years. The first time since she and Seth had run him off the island. She was more beautiful than ever. Her waves of long auburn hair spilled over her bare shoulders, gleaming in the sunlight. She wore tight shorts that revealed her shapely tan legs. God, he wanted her more than ever. This time he would not let her get away. He'd have to keep a close eye on her at all times, just in case she was foolish enough to try to leave —maybe to find her son again.

That was a close call today—too close for comfort. He couldn't risk her identifying him, or hearing his voice. Maybe it was time for him to pack up his campsite and head back to Rabbit Island, where he could busy himself fixing the place up to be almost livable. He also had to journey up the Rat River into Canada to find himself a good camping spot where they could stop on their way back to Nestor Falls. He needed options. Lots of options. Lots of places to hide out after he had accomplished his mission.

His ears suddenly perked up, bringing him out of his reverie, when a bearded guy at the bar commented, "Ran into Seth today. He and the wife and their boy were having lunch at the grill."

"So what's up with them these days?"

"Still living on their island, but said they might move back to Houska's Point before freeze-up so their son can go to school here. Guess they'd still spend weekends out there when they can. Beth loves it there. Seth too."

Nursing his drink, Bob filed this information away in his mind. It might be easier rescuing her at her place in Ranier instead of out on the island, sometime when Seth was out running errands or whatever he did.

"That was one hell of a good match, Beth and Seth," the bartender spoke up.

"You got that right," another guy jumped in. "I knew Beth as a little girl. Her mother and grandmother also. Poor kid went through hell with the first dipshit she married. Nice to see how happy she is now."

Dipshit? Me? She's happy with Seth? What the hell do they know? That was about all Bob could tolerate. Tossing a tip on the bar, nodding at the bartender, he stomped out of Loony's Pub.

Dipshit? If they only knew what he'd gone through. Maybe he hadn't always been the perfect husband, but look at the good life Beth had led with him back then in their penthouse suite. Fancy clothes. Expensive jewelry. Travel. Anything she desired. What more could any woman want? And someday, she'd have it all back again—everything but the money and fancy house and travel.

Chapter Seven

"Good morning, sun," Beth repeated her grandmother's words as the sun broke through the mist hovering over their island on Rainy Lake. She was settled in an antique wicker rocking chair in her Victorian gazebo on the point that jutted out above the big lake.

She was surrounded by flowering shrubs and perennial flowers she'd planted and tenderly nurtured over the years. Their fragrance filled the air this morning as she sipped her coffee. This was a special place for her, her quiet place, a place to think and remember.

Just beyond the gazebo, nestled in a grove of trees, laid the grave markers of her mother Sarah, grandmother Emma, grandfather Pete, and father Jake. Both Sarah and Pete had been claimed by this lake. Some of their ashes were buried here; the remainder had been scattered over Kettle Falls, one of their favorite places on Rainy Lake.

She'd never known her grandfather, and her mother had drowned when Beth was only six years of age. Nana, her grandmother, had raised her here on this island all by herself. And she had cheerfully greeted each morning with those words; "Good morning, sun." It hadn't mattered if she could see the sun or not, if it was raining, snowing, or sleeting.

"But I can't see the sun, Nana," a young Beth had protested as she ate her oatmeal, peering out the kitchen windows as rain splattered against them.

"It's still up there somewhere," Nana had smiled at her, "up above the clouds, watching you, just waiting to come back out and spread sunshine through your life." She had been the eternal optimist, despite the struggles she'd faced living alone on this island raising her granddaughter by herself.

"Just like Mommy watches over me?" Beth had inquired.

Her grandmother had turned her head to wipe a tear from her eye. "Yes, just like Mommy. She will always love you and watch over you, honey."

Inhaling deeply, so many years later, Beth watched the rising sun cast its glow over the still waters. She also wiped a tear from her eye. Sometimes she felt like the spirits of her dear mother and grandmother were here with her during these quiet moments on this island they'd all loved. Now it was Beth's turn to love and care for it, as she had for the past ten years.

It was hard to believe how her life had changed since she'd come back to the island ten years ago, running from an abusive marriage to her former cheating husband, Rob. Running home to her dear Nana, just in time to sit beside her death bed, telling her how much she loved her and how sorry she was for not being there for her. Rob had controlled her totally, and refused to allow her to go home often. But that was all in the past, thank God.

She'd met and fallen in love with her neighbor, Seth, who lived alone on his little island just across the channel from Beth's island. She remembered how their eyes had connected the first time they'd met at The Thunderbird. She'd been frightened at the time, afraid that the husband she'd just escaped from would find her. But she'd also been frightened at the mysterious connection she'd felt with this stranger. She wasn't ready for another relationship, not after all she'd been through. But Seth had proceeded very cautiously, helping her out with chores on her island, befriending her, being there for her unconditionally. It was their destiny to find each other and fall in love—again—in this lifetime.

Seth was a talented artist. To this day, he continued to paint in his cabin studio on his island, selling his work via the Internet and at several shops in Ranier and International Falls.

Seth, she sighed to herself. She could not have wished for a more wonderful husband. He was part Ojibwe, very spiritual, very much connected to nature and the world of his ancestors. She was learning so much from him. And now they were raising a son together. Seth was teaching him valuable lessons in life, lessons passed down from his ancestors.

Lost in thought, thanking the universe for her many blessings, she noticed the ring on her hand sparkling in the sunlight. The green turquoise stone was set in an intricately carved sterling silver setting. Seth had given it to her the day he asked her to marry him. She had worn it ever since. It had once belonged to Seth's dear grandmother, and allegedly had spiritual powers.

Sometimes she wondered if it could be true that this ring played a part in the happy life they shared together. Seth felt his grandmother's presence from time to time, sometimes relaying important messages from beyond and trying to guide him. She was his spirit guide, Seth told her. He believed that she had lived many lives upon this earth, learning and enhancing her own spirituality so she could guide others still on this earth.

"A penny for your thoughts," a familiar voice spoke softly as Seth crept up behind her and wrapped his arms around her.

"I was just thinking how lucky I am to have you in my life, if you really want to know," she teased him.

"Likewise, Ninmosche," he held her close. That was his pet name for her, meaning "my love" in Ojibwe. "You know, we have a special occasion coming up next month."

"Our tenth anniversary," she sighed, remembering the small candlelight wedding ceremony they had held right here in this gazebo. The gazebo had been decorated with white flowers, contrasting with the red geraniums Beth planted around the gazebo each year, Nana's favorite flowers. Today, she could still almost smell their fragrance and hear the violin music floating through the air as she'd gazed up into the eyes of the man she would always love.

It was a shame that their wedding portrait had somehow fallen off the fireplace mantle and shattered. They were trying to get another print from the local photographer who had filmed their ceremony.

"So, what would you like to do for our anniversary?" Seth nuzzled her ear.

"Maybe dinner at The Thunderbird?"

"That's a start, but we could also take a trip someplace—you know, just the two of us. I'm sure Evelyn would be delighted to watch Jason for a few days."

Evelyn. It was quite interesting how this eighty-year old woman, a former adversary, had become an important part of their lives. Once upon a time Evelyn had been the wife of Jake O'Connell, a local real estate broker. Jake, however, had fallen in love with Sarah, Beth's mother, who was his office assistant.

Beth was the result of this affair between soulmates who finally found each other in this lifetime—too late. Evelyn had refused to give Jake a divorce, holding him hostage in a loveless marriage. She had done everything imaginable to humiliate both Beth and her mother over the years.

Jake had finally found a way to leave Evelyn and marry Sarah. He'd given Sarah a ring and officially proposed to her on a camping trip that had turned deadly. Just as the newly engaged lovers were canoeing back home, a freak storm blew in out of nowhere. Despite Jake's relentless efforts to save his beloved, she had drowned in the big lake. A devastated Jake had pretty much given up on life, burying himself in his real estate business. He never bothered to divorce Evelyn. Sarah was gone.

Beth had not known who her father was, not until she came home to the island ten years ago and discovered her mother's old diaries hidden in a trunk in the attic. She had been shocked, infuriated, to discover that her dear Uncle Jake was actually her father! She'd eventually forgiven him, realizing how much he had done for her and her mother over the years. He had continued to care for her, and finally announced to the world that she was his beloved daughter.

Jake had passed on shortly after he learned that Beth and Seth would be married, something he had hoped and prayed for. His mission on this earth had been accomplished. Seth would now care for his beloved daughter. He knew that Sarah was waiting for him on the other side. It was finally time for him to go "home" to her. He'd left his house on Houska's Point and a healthy inheritance for Beth.

It had been a complicated, emotional time after Jake died. Shortly before he died, he had asked Beth to watch over Evelyn since she had nobody else. Love was complicated, that was for sure. There were so many kinds of love and caring for others. So many times that shared history, good or bad, entered into the equation. So many trespasses, people and things to forgive. And so easy to wallow in bitterness and hatred instead of freeing oneself by forgiving others.

Sure, Evelyn had known about Sarah and Jake, and that Beth was their daughter—even if nobody else was aware of it. Evelyn felt compelled to hide that truth from the world to save face. She'd suffered in silence, drinking a lot, and taking her frustrations out on her estranged husband. She'd spread gossip around town to discredit Sarah and Beth.

Evelyn and Jake had never had children of their own. In the early days of their marriage, she had aborted his unborn child, knowing how much he wanted children. Why? It remained a mystery to this day. She'd stiffened, eyes hard as ice, lost in the past, as she explained that she simply did not want children. Not ever. After that, she retreated to her own bedroom for the rest of their married life. It was only after Jake's death that she began to deeply regret having no family of her own. She wanted very much to become a part of Beth and Seth's family. After all, Beth was Jake's daughter. Emily and Jason were his grandchildren. Weren't they a part of her family also, despite the circumstances?

While Beth had initially struggled to get over the fact that Evelyn had been responsible for keeping her parents apart and the fact that she had grown up fatherless, Seth finally convinced her to give this lonely old woman a second chance. He lived by the Ojibwe values he'd grown up with, one of which was compassion for others. His family had adopted relatives, even taken in strangers in need of a home. He felt they should try to be there for Evelyn also.

Little by little, they began to invite Evelyn to family gatherings. They checked in with her on a regular basis to be sure she was all right. She still lived in her own home in International Falls, but loved to visit and spend time with them on the island.

These days, Evelyn was almost like a grandmother to Jason. She thrived on babysitting for him and helping out any way she could. And she was always anxious to see and hear from Emily, although Emily's visits from France were obviously few and far between.

Emily was now thirty-three years old, married to a Frenchman, and living in Paris. Beth missed her free-spirited daughter, and tried to stay in touch with her as often as possible. Emily and her husband, Jacques, had just had their first baby two weeks ago, Beth's first grandchild. Beth couldn't wait to visit as soon as possible. She'd been on line checking airfares the moment Emily had called to announce the wonderful news.

"What did you say?" Beth came back to the present, noticing Seth grinning at her as if waiting for an answer. "Sorry, guess I was preoccupied, thinking about Evelyn and about visiting Emily and our new grandbaby."

"Do you want to go to Paris to celebrate our anniversary?" He held his breath.

"Oh no, I know you can't get away right now with all your painting deadlines," she sighed. "And we can't leave Jason for that long, not even with Evelyn. He can be a bit of a handful, you know, always exploring and disappearing. She loves babysitting for him, but he wears her out. She's not a spring chicken anymore."

"You're right. You can go to Paris yourself, you know, like we planned. Then we will all go together later when the baby is a little older."

"Sounds like a plan to me." She smiled up into his deep chocolate eyes, connecting on an intimate soul level.

"We can still take a little trip, maybe for a weekend, Beth—just the two of us."

"I'm up for that, if Evelyn is. I know—what about Kettle Falls? We haven't been there in ages. There is something magical about that place. I've loved it since I was a little girl when my mother and 'Uncle' Jake would take me there. It's past time for us to pay a visit to the falls," she continued with a wistful look in her eyes.

The roaring Kettle Falls that separated the United States from Canada was the place where the ashes of her grandfather, grandmother, and mother had all been scattered. It was a sacred place for Beth. While some of their ashes were also interred beneath gravestones just beyond the gazebo, there was something so liberating about the thought of their ashes also drifting back into the big lake they'd loved, becoming a part of Rainy Lake, floating freely into eternity.

Seth got it, of course. He understood, hugging her close once again. "Kettle Falls it is. Can you check with Evelyn? I need to get back to work on that wildlife painting for the Andersons." That meant he'd soon be off to his island, nicknamed Blueberry Island by the locals, where he'd work in his art studio cabin for the rest of the day. On a beautiful day like this, he'd paddle across the channel that separated their islands in his homemade birch bark canoe.

Beth watched him gliding across the water as squawking seagulls soared through the sky. It was time to check on Jason, time for him to get up and do his assigned reading for the day. She homeschooled him on the island throughout the year, although they were considering moving to Houska's Point for the school year next fall so he could attend the school in International Falls.

Chapter Eight

"Mom." A breathless Jason came running down the path towards the gazebo in his pajamas, his hair rumpled as if he'd just tumbled out of bed in a hurry.

"Good morning, Jase," she called out. "You slept in this morning."

"Emily is on the phone, Mom, hurry up." He grabbed her hand, pulling her out of her rocking chair. She tousled his unkempt mop of dirty blond hair and took off right behind him.

It was unusual for Emily to call from Paris this time of the day. Beth was breathless by the time she picked up the telephone and collapsed on the porch swing.

"Good morning, Em. How are you and the baby getting along? Angelique...I love her name."

"We're all fine, Mom. Can't wait for you to meet her. We think she actually looks a lot like you—with a few classic French touches thrown in. You know she was named after Jacques' grandmother. He swears there is a resemblance there also."

"Glad to hear she takes after both of us." Beth smiled. "I'm checking on airfares and can hardly wait. I'll come alone this time, probably sometime after Seth and I spend our anniversary weekend at Kettle Falls."

"That's right. How many years now?"

"Ten years already, and I must say we are blessed, Emily. I could never ask for a better husband."

"I know, Mom. I love him, too. He is so right for you. Ten years... wow! And my little buddy Jason is already ten years old too. How is he doing?"

"You won't believe how he is growing up, Em. He loves exploring the woods, and is into everything, so excited about life. His latest obsession is space exploration. He reads everything about space that he can get his hands on. So tell me what's up over there with you all... aside from keeping busy with your adorable little girl!"

There was a moment of silence as Emily seemed to be hesitating, trying to find the right words.

"Is everything okay?"

"Probably. Just very strange."

"Yes?"

"Well, I got a call from my father that makes no sense. He called to tell me goodbye, that he was leaving the country. Couldn't tell me where he was going, if or when he would be back. Said he was on some kind of secret mission and wouldn't even have access to a phone or the Internet. I can't imagine anyplace in this world like that anymore."

Beth just listened, stunned. That didn't sound like the Rob she had known. He always had to be in contact, in control. "What about the law firm, his career? Surely he has to maintain contact with his partners."

"He quit, he told me. He's on to bigger and better things, but he couldn't tell me what they were. He sounded weird, Mom, like he wasn't thinking straight. Like he was telling me goodbye. He even told me he loved me. Like when has he ever told me that before?"

"He didn't leave you any contact information of any kind, anyone you could call if you needed to get a hold of him?"

"None. I asked a number of times. I asked if he'd be anywhere near Paris. He laughed oddly, somewhat sadly, as he told me that he'd be much farther away than that, as if he was going to the end of the world and wasn't sure he'd be back."

"I don't know what to say or think." Beth sighed, twirling a strand of her auburn hair around her little finger—a nervous habit she'd always had. "Could he be sick or depressed, or maybe suffering from a mental illness?"

"Maybe. I thought about calling his law firm to try to find out what is going on, but not sure I should be checking up on him. Do you think I should, Mom?"

"I would, Emily. Let me know if you find anything out. And please try not to worry, okay? You have little Angelique to care for and to enjoy. I'm sure your father will be fine." Beth tried to reassure her daughter, although she wasn't sure she believed her own words. Something was not right. This was not the Rob she had known.

"Well, at least he shouldn't be bothering you anymore, Mom, not if he's someplace in the far corners of the world." Emily tried to make light of the situation, to reassure her mother that she was not overly concerned about her father's unusual behavior.

Beth smiled to herself. "Honey, I haven't worried about him bothering me since Seth and I got together. He would never consider showing up here after Seth ran him off the island years ago. I'm sure he's moved on to who knows where or what. Or who...."

"Yeah, I'm sure you're right. Just thought I should let you know in case you hear anything from anyone. Love you, Mom, gotta run. Angelique is hungry—again!"

"Love you, too. Hugs and kisses to my grandbaby and to Jacques."

Something didn't feel quite right about this situation. Beth fretted as she did the laundry and chopped vegetables from the garden for her famous chicken vegetable stew. It was one of Seth's favorite meals, Jason's also.

Rob was hiding something, something big. What was he running from? What had he done?

She was stirring the stew, its fragrance filling the cottage, when the phone rang again.

"Mom, you won't believe this. Are you sitting down?"

"I am now." Beth turned down the heat on the stove and settled herself in one of Nana's old vinyl chairs at the kitchen table. Gazing out the wall of French windows, she watched a spotted fawn scampering across the lawn, ignoring the attempts of its mother to lure it back into the woods.

"Dad has embezzled ten million dollars from the law firm and disappeared! The IRS is also on his tail for income tax evasion! Oh my God!"

Beth clutched the phone, shaking her head in disbelief, trying to calm her daughter down, to reassure her that this was not going to hurt her or her family in any way. Her father was not her responsibility.

Rob had apparently disappeared from their lives. He would live out the rest of his days as a fugitive from justice, a man without an identity, without a country. Or he would spend his days behind bars, blaming everyone but himself for his foolish decisions.

Beth was numb, not knowing what to feel, if anything. How could someone she'd known so well and been married to for over twenty years do such a horrible thing? He obviously was not thinking rationally. He was a lawyer. He knew all the tricks. He had defended many high-profile clients who had committed white collar crimes just like this. What was he thinking?

Chapter Nine

"Mom! Dad!" Jason's voice broke through the early morning stillness as his footsteps thudded down the stairs from his bedroom, which was perched high above the rest of the cottage in what they called their "eagle's nest."

Beth sleepily untangled herself from the warmth of Seth's arms, pulling the covers up over them before Jason threw open the door and bounded in. He landed on the corner of their bed.

"What in the world?" Seth sat up in bed, rubbing the sleep from his eyes as he glanced at the clock on the bedside table. "This better be important, son. You know it's only six in the morning. The sun is not even up yet. And what about the knock on the door rule?"

"But this is important, really important, guys! Wait till you hear what I just discovered online!" The boy was continually doing research, fascinated with all he was learning about the world around him. He seemed to absorb a great deal of information, and had an incredible sense of curiosity. This morning his blue eyes sparkled with excitement, enough to make his parents forgive his intrusion into their space.

"Go on, Jason," Beth sighed. "Tell us what you discovered."

"Well, I decided what I'm going to do, what I'm going to be when I grow up. An astronaut! Not only that, I'm going to join the Mars One program and settle on Mars. Really!"

"Wow, that's quite a goal," Beth responded enthusiastically, never wanting to squelch his dreams and his enthusiasm. "Mars is a long ways away, you know—a long way for us to go to visit you."

"Well, that's the only scary part, Mom. You see, it takes three-hundred days to get there; like almost a year, right? And we will be setting up a permanent human settlement there. It's like this—once we get there, we don't come back. I'll miss you guys, but I will be making history and science. And anyway, by the time I'm old enough to go, I bet they will have space shuttles taking people back and forth at lightning speed. Technology is changing the world, you know."

"So you really think Mars is habitable?" Seth asked his son.

"They are finding more evidence every day," Jason enthusiastically replied. "You know about the Curiosity rover up there, right?" He waited for their heads to nod that they knew. "Well, it has found some organic modules and methane up there in the Gale Crater. They think this area was habitable about 3.5 billion years ago! The data Curiosity discovered shows conditions very similar to the ones here on Earth when life evolved here. Can you believe that?"

Beth and Seth exchanged glances, simultaneously raising their eyebrows. Their son sounded like a walking encyclopedia.

Jason could hardly contain himself as he bounced on the bed in pure excitement. "Have you ever seen a picture of Curiosity, Mom and Dad? I'll get my laptop and show you later. It's so cool. It's about the size of a car, with huge wheels and a seven-foot long arm sticking out from the front. It carries ten science instruments and seventeen cameras. Also a laser to vaporize rocks." He finally came up for air, waiting for some reaction for his parents.

"You certainly know a lot about Mars exploration." Seth smiled at the boy.

"I have an idea," Beth chimed in. "How about doing a research paper on Mars and space exploration as a home study project?"

"Yes!" He jumped up to give her a hug. "Great idea, Mom. For some reason, I just love Mars, and I can't wait to go there." He paused a few moments, reflecting seriously on something. A strange look clouded his eyes as he announced, "Maybe I lived there three billion years ago...maybe that's why I really want to go back—back *home.*"

Beth shivered at the thought as Seth just stared into the past. They'd each had enough supernatural experiences to realize that this could actually be an insight into a past life, not just the overactive imagination of a young boy.

"Maybe, you never know." Beth smiled wistfully as she drifted back in time to a past life she'd once shared with Seth out west in the 1840s. A young, recently widowed pioneer woman living alone in the primitive cabin her late husband had built before he was killed, she had gone out to the chicken coop to collect eggs one morning, where she was shocked to discover an unconscious Shoshone Indian brave, Seth, lying on the ground. His faithful horse stood by, whinnying into the frosty morning as if calling for help. She had taken him in and nursed him back to health. They'd fallen in love, learned to speak each other's language, and shared several wonderful years together—before she died in childbirth. The baby also died.

A tear slipped down her cheek this morning as she remembered what she'd forgotten. These memories had somehow come back to life, seeping through the thin veil separating the world of the living from the land of the dead. Seth had been the one to discover their shared past life through one of his visions. He had always been tuned into the spirit world. She was learning.

Yes, it felt like she and Seth had known each other before in another time, another place. She'd never forget the first time she met him in this lifetime and lost herself within those deep, chocolate eyes she'd somehow always known and loved. What was that old saying? "The eyes are the windows to the soul."

"Mom? Are you listening to me?"

"Sorry, Jase, I'm hardly awake. But as long as we are all up, how about some blueberry pancakes for breakfast?"

"Yes!" He bounded back out of their bedroom. They heard him

creak open the heavy wood door and run out onto the porch, down the stairs, and onto the trail leading down to the lake. He loved exploring the island, always looking for wildlife, birds, native plants, and flowers. Who knew what he would bring home with him this morning? He'd be back when he smelled the bacon frying and coffee brewing.

Sure enough, he was soon running back up the porch steps, grinning as he sat down at the kitchen table. He was starving, as always.

"So did you find anything exciting out there this morning?" Seth inquired as he dished up homemade blueberry pancakes and bacon, smothering them with homemade maple syrup. Early morning sunlight filtered into the room through the large wall of kitchen windows, a slight breeze ruffling Nana's homemade lace curtains.

Before Jason could answer, a loud croaking sound filled the room.

"Whoops." He jumped out of his seat, his pocket wiggling. He pulled out a large frog, stroking its back gently. "Isn't he cute? Can I keep him?"

"No, I'm sorry, you can't." Beth shook her head firmly. "You need to take him outside right now. He needs to be back in the lake with his friends."

Noticing the boy's slumped shoulders, his head hanging sadly, she softened her tone. "How would you feel, Jason, if you were a frog and someone captured you and took you away from the lake you loved, where you lived your whole life? Away from your family and frog friends? Would you want to spend your life in a bucket waiting for someone to feed you insects?"

"No, I guess not."

"Good. Now please put him back in the lake where he belongs. You can still play with him and his friends down on the beach sometimes, okay?" Seth added. "Hurry back so your breakfast doesn't get cold."

Jason's returning steps were slower, despite his growling stomach. He was no longer running, no longer excited about his latest discovery.

Sensing the boy's mood, Seth came up with an idea. "How about coming over to the island with me today, Jason? You and Mom. I have some things, some special things, to show you. We can have a picnic.

You can explore while I work on my latest painting. Would you like that?"

JASON SUDDENLY EMERGED from his funk, anxious to accompany his parents to the magical little island across the channel. Who knew what he might discover there? Maybe even some Indian artifacts. He'd been doing some research, and knew that there were Indian burial grounds on some of these islands. His dad had also told him many stories about his ancestors who once lived in teepees around the lake. Sometimes Jason wished he'd lived back in those days. What fun it would be to spear a sturgeon at Kettle Falls. To harvest wild rice. To hunt deer and moose. And in the winter, to sit around a campfire and tell stories, the way his dad did.

Jason loved his dad's stories about the Ojibwe people and their beliefs. The scary ones about the Windigo were some of his favorites. The Windigo was an evil man-eating giant. Huge, he appeared to be a monster with some human characteristics. He grew larger and larger every time he ate someone. In fact, he could grow to be twenty to thirty feet tall! He had jagged teeth, claws, and huge red eyes that glowed in the dark. He was coated in ice, and ice flowed through his veins. People who committed bad sins were turned into Windigos as punishment, his dad told him.

Jason's dad, with his high cheekbones, dark eyes and pitch black hair, looked like an Ojibwe, because he *was* mostly Ojibwe. Jason's mom certainly didn't. She had auburn hair, pale skin, and green eyes. Jason wished he looked more like his dad, but his skin wasn't dark enough, nor was his hair. And he had blue eyes. Maybe when he got a little older, he would look more like an Indian. He hoped so. But he didn't have as much Indian blood in him, he figured, as his dad did. Too bad his mother wasn't Indian. Then he, Jason, would be a real Indian. He could go on a vision quest someday and learn really cool things from his spirit guide—maybe even things about Mars. He wondered if any Indians had ever lived on Mars.

"Beth? Are you okay with spending the day on Blueberry Island?" Seth asked, interrupting her thoughts.

"It's a lovely idea. I'll bring a picnic lunch and a book. Jason, bring your laptop, and maybe you can start on your Mars project."

"Yes!"

Chapter Ten

Blueberry Island had barely changed since Seth first moved in some twenty-five years ago. He'd lived alone in this rustic cabin, creating his beautiful paintings, until he met and married Beth ten years ago. He still used it as his art studio, and spent a considerable amount of time there.

"Your man cave," Beth teased him. She also loved the place. It was nestled amongst massive pines and rocky ledges overlooking Rainy Lake. They could see the place from the gazebo on her grandmother's island.

Today they followed Jason up the winding path to the cabin. He was always one step ahead of them, anxious to find out what treasures his dad was planning to show him today. Eager to explore the island, looking for Indian artifacts. He had found a few old pottery shards and arrowheads earlier this summer. Maybe there would be more.

As they entered the cabin, Seth breathed deeply, closing his eyes, absorbing the spiritual essence swirling around him. He did this every time he entered, as a matter of respect for his elders. Then he would gaze solemnly at his grandmother's portrait, which still hung on the far wall—the one he had painted of her years ago. He felt that she was his spirit guide, watching over him, sometimes casting a subtle warning in his direction, trying to call his attention to important matters.

Today, he lingered longer than usual before her portrait, a frown clouding his face. Something didn't feel quite right...but he couldn't put a finger on it.

"What is it?" Beth whispered after a few moments of silence.

Seth shook his head, somewhat bewildered. "Nothing, hopefully. I'm just getting an uneasy feeling from her today. We need to be vigilant. That's all. It's very vague."

Gently taking his hand in hers, she smiled into his eyes, trying to reassure him. "What do we need to be vigilant about?"

"I don't know. That's all I'm picking up right now. I'll try again later." He gave her a quick hug before heading to his easel in the far corner of the room and beginning to work on a painting of the historic cabin of one of his clients. The tilting log structure depicted in an old photo displayed on the table beside his easel had been in their family for well over a century. They had hired Seth to capture the essence of the place, adding a few wild animals in the forefront.

Beth grabbed her book and beach hat and headed down to the beach, hoping to keep an eye on Jason while Seth worked.

"Keep an eye on that boy of ours, honey," he called out to her as the screen door slammed behind her.

"I will. Don't worry, okay? We will be back for lunch."

With that she was gone and Seth was alone, trying to focus on the old photo as he mixed his palate of paints. He soon slipped into his creative mode, where he would lose track of time and place and any worries that clouded his mind. He was in flow with his work and the universe, almost becoming a part of the scene that was unfolding through his paint brush.

It seemed like only minutes had passed when the door was flung open and Jason came flying in, a bucket of rocks in his hand. "Hey Dad, I got some really cool rocks. Agates. Granite. Some of these could be thousands of years old, you know."

"Probably, son." Seth smiled as he put his brushes away and watched Beth come in, her long auburn hair disheveled from the sun and wind. *She is beautiful,* he sighed to himself. How could he have gotten so lucky? He'd been a confirmed bachelor until she showed up and changed his entire life, in ways he never could have imagined. It was destiny...he sincerely believed that. They'd been together in a previous lifetime, he had discovered, and expected they would be again in a future life someday. For now, they were thoroughly enjoying this time around.

"Time for lunch, guys." She began clearing the table and retrieving food from the refrigerator. Cold fried chicken from last night's dinner, cheese and crackers, and a fruit salad she had tossed together earlier that morning.

The three of them took their usual places at the old wood table. In between mouthfuls of food, Jason enthusiastically told them about his rocks. "I wonder if they have rocks like that on Mars. Maybe someday I will go to NASA and see the moon rocks there."

Seth and Beth exchanged an amused glance. The boy's enthusiasm and curiosity had no limits.

"When I do my paper on Mars, I'm going to google 'rocks on Mars' to find out all about them," he informed them as he gulped down a big glass of milk. "Hey, can we have a campfire here tonight, down by the lake? You can tell us some more stories, Dad," he implored with a hopeful look on his face.

"I like that idea." Beth gazed up at Seth. "What do you think, Seth?"

"Sure. Why not?" He loved sharing stories about his people, his culture, and his spiritual beliefs with his wife and son. It pleased him that Jason was interested, that he wanted to be a "real Indian," as he frequently told his parents.

As he devoured another piece of chicken, Jason chattered about all he had discovered this morning on the island; the doe and her fawn, the fox, and the huge eagle that dove down to retrieve a big fish from the lake. Then he remembered something he'd been too busy to ask about. "Hey, Dad, what were you going to show me here on Blueberry Island?"

"What?" Seth brought himself back from his wandering thoughts.

He'd missed part of the conversation, pre-occupied with unsettling feelings that seemed to be swirling around him. He was, apparently, the only one tuned in to whatever was happening—or about to happen. His sixth sense, he called it—or his connection with his spirit guides.

"Seth?" Beth frowned, her eyes searching his for some sign, silently asking if everything was okay.

"Sure." Seth grinned as he shoved himself away from the table, stroking his wife's arm reassuringly before he disappeared into the back room and came back with a large wood box that he placed in the middle of the table.

"Wow, what is that? It looks really old, like hundreds of years old. What is it?" Jason clamored over to stand beside his father, his blue eyes wide with excitement.

"It is old, son. In fact, it is filled with things that my dear grandmother made well over a hundred years ago."

"Really? You mean Nokomis, that old lady on the wall, whose eyes always follow me around like she's making sure I don't get into any trouble here?"

Beth and Seth laughed together, shaking their heads. You never knew what Jason would say next. At least he'd learned to call her Nokomis, the Ojibwe word for "Grandmother." It was a sign of respect.

The boy could hardly contain himself as his father carefully opened the aging box and began to lift items out onto the table. A little basket made of birch bark and decorated with porcupine quills. A tiny pair of deerskin moccasins decorated with elaborate beadwork—possibly a gift for a new baby? An elaborate jingle bell women's dress that Nokomis had made and worn for years as she danced at traditional pow-wows. Several bowls made of clay. Eagle feathers. A number of beautiful necklaces made of animal teeth and bones. Seth enjoyed showing each piece to his son, sharing stories with him about each one.

There was one more item in the bottom of the box. He held his breath as he reached in and carefully extracted a faded old photo of an elderly Ojibwe woman sitting by a fire in front of a teepee. She held a newborn baby in her arms.

"Who's that?" Jason whispered, his eyes wide, as his mother put her arm around his father's shoulders and moved in closer.

Seth sighed as tears gathered in his eyes. Tears of joy and sorrow. Of missed opportunities. Of regret over never having had the opportunity to know his dear grandmother in this lifetime. Only in the spirit world, where they sometimes connected as she continued to watch over him.

Finally he responded. "That's Nokomis, Jason, on the day she died. She died...," he paused to regain his composure, "...she died just hours after she held this baby in her arms and had this picture taken." He sighed as Beth gently stroked his back.

"Really? Who is that little baby? Isn't she too old to have a baby?"

"It's me." Seth turned away for a moment to wipe a lonely tear from his eye. "You see, I was born the day she died. They say that despite her ailing health, she was determined to live just long enough to see me enter the world and hold me in her arms. Then she left her body and went home to the spirit world."

"Gee, Dad, that's really sad. So is she in Heaven then?"

"I'm sure she is with her ancestors up there in the spirit world, son. Someday we will all be together again, you know. For now, I think she watches over us sometimes. She still loves us...and we still love her."

"Really? So she's kind of like an angel, huh?"

"Yes." Beth hugged the boy close to her. "Just like an angel."

"Okay, gang, it's time to get back to work for a while." Seth's voice broke through the heaviness of the emotions hanging over them all. "Then we will have a nice campfire on the beach just before dark. Deal?"

"Deal!" Jason high-fived his father, grabbed his five-gallon bucket, and headed out the door to see what treasures he could find on Blueberry Island before darkness descended and his family would gather around the campfire. That was always one of their favorite family times together.

Chapter Eleven

An early hint of fall swept through the air that evening as they gathered around the campfire on the beach. A touch of red could be seen on the leaves of some of the staghorn sumac growing along the path that meandered down to the lake. Beds of wild ferns were beginning to turn brown. It wouldn't be long before flocks of Canadian geese gathered nosily, organizing themselves into formation to head south for the winter. Sometimes they seemed to be jockeying for position, as if they were trying to decide who their leader would be.

Tonight the lake was perfectly calm. A full moon rose over the horizon, casting rippling shadows across the waters as loons called out to each other. A perfect evening to relax and enjoy each other's company.

Seth had finished his painting and was pleased with the outcome. Beth and Jason made a nice fire and retrieved jackets for them all. While the adults enjoyed a glass of wine sitting side by side on Seth's old Indian blanket, Jason busied himself making his traditional s'mores. He roasted marshmallows on a stick over the fire, making sure each was done to perfection. His father liked his slightly burned; his mother liked hers golden brown. As for Jason, he ate whatever was left, and usually made several more for himself. He carefully assembled each s'more, placing the roasted marshmallow on a graham cracker, adding part of a Hershey's chocolate candy bar, and topping it all off with another graham cracker. The marshmallow filling would ooze out onto his sticky hands, which he washed off in the lake.

"Delicious, Chef Jason," Beth teased her son as she ate the s'more he'd prepared for her.

Seth was unusually quiet this evening, staring out across the lake, lost in thought as he sometimes tended to be. Nature calmed his soul and brought out another side of him—a philosophical, spiritual side that seemed to balance him throughout his journey in life.

"Penny for your thoughts." Beth snuggled up beside him.

"Just look at those stars," Seth sighed, gazing up at a canopy of brilliant stars twinkling overhead, lighting up the dark sky. They seemed to be dancing to the rhythm of the gentle waves lapping against the rocky shoreline. In the background, the wind whispered through the white pines. They seemed to be singing tonight.

"Reminds me of one of my favorite poems," Seth continued, remembering how many times he'd read these lines while growing up. They had always brought him comfort.

"What poem, Dad? Can you read it to us?" Jason took his place by the fire.

Seth knew it by heart and began to recite it as he continued to stare up into the starlit night.

"This is our language. It is the sound of the waves crashing on the shore, the sound of the wind in the pines, the rustle of the leaves in autumn. It is the sound of the birds singing in the forest and the wolves howling in the distance. This is our language, from which we obtain life, our means of knowing who we are, this sacred gift, bestowed upon us by our creator.

"By Gordon Jourdain of Lac La Croix," Seth concluded.

"That is beautiful, honey." Beth smiled into his eyes.

"Yeah. Pretty cool." Jason stoked the fire with a big stick. "I wonder if you can see these stars from Mars. Or do they have their own stars up there? Their own universe? I wonder how all of this stuff ever got made...the sun, the moon, the whole world."

"Good questions, son." Seth beamed at the boy. "Nobody really knows the answers to a lot of these questions yet. Maybe we are not meant to know everything. But I can tell you a story that my people have passed down over the generations. A story about the creation of our world."

"Yes!" Jason scooted over to sit beside his father, anxiously waiting to hear another of his stories. He loved Indian stories.

"There once was a time before time," Seth began. "Gitche Manitou, the Great Spirit, was sleeping, and he had a dream."

"A bad dream, like I do sometimes?" Jason interjected.

"Hush, let's just listen, okay?" Beth advised.

"Not a bad dream. What he saw in that dream was beautiful lakes like ours, majestic mountains that rose up into the sky, woods filled with beautiful trees, flowers, waterfalls cascading into oceans that went on forever. He saw animals that walked through the forest, flew through the air, and swam in the water. He dreamed of a brilliant blue sky, and clouds that dropped snow and rain to feed the trees and plants."

"That's a good dream, Dad."

"It is. So when Gitche Manitou awoke, he decided that the dream had come to him to tell him that he should create a place just like he'd seen in his dream. So he did just that. He created the earth. He created plants and trees, birds and animals. It was a beautiful place, like a paradise."

"Wow!" Jason moved closer to his father, awed by this miraculous story.

"But," Seth continued," as beautiful as it all was, he became lonely all by himself. So he took soil from the earth and created a man and a woman. He breathed life into his new companions, and told them to take care of Mother Earth and she would take care of them. He told them not to be greedy, and to take only what they needed. And that is how the Ojibwe people came to be."

"That's us, right?"

"That's us." Seth gazed into Beth's eyes, hoping their son would not pursue any more questions about his heritage this evening.

"The great spirit…." The boy pondered this information. "So, is he still up there in the sky someplace? Like in Heaven? Does he ever talk to us or tell us what to do?"

"He's everywhere, and yes, he and our spirit guides do help us. They guide us through our lives if we listen hard enough. And the Great Spirit does have a plan for each of us."

"Really? What is my plan? Do you think he wants me to be an astronaut and go to Mars someday?"

"Time will tell, son." Seth rumpled his hair affectionately. "Timing is everything. We never fully know what his plan is for us, but we do get glimpses of it as we go through life. Sometimes we find out the next steps of our plans through dreams or visions."

"Someday," Jason yawned, "I want to do one of those vision things like you did." The boy was exhausted after a long day of exploring the island.

"We will see when the time is right."

Before leaving the island to head home across the lake, Seth felt compelled to take a packet of sage from his pocket and scatter it into the glowing embers of the fire. As the sage smoke swirled into the night air, he fanned it out across the three of them, across the land. Saying a silent prayer. Asking the spirit guides to cleanse and protect them all, to drive out any negativity and evil influences that could harm them. It was the Ojibwe way. It was his way of responding to the subtle warning that Nokomis had implanted in his mind earlier today.

Chapter Twelve

So near and yet so far. Bob sighed as the moon crawled up over the horizon, casting reflections upon Rainy Lake. He gazed across the choppy expanse of water separating the little island on which he'd been camping from Beth's island. He could see the lights of her cabin glowing in the dark.

Now and then a shadow would cross the expanse of windows. Was it Beth? What would she say, what would she do, if she knew her true love was out there watching her through his night vision binoculars? If she knew that she was about to be rescued after being held a prisoner for ten long years?

Of course, she was a prisoner. What the hell did the guys at the bar in Ranier know? She simply had to pretend she was happy in order to survive her ordeal with Seth. She had to pretend to be happy for the sake of the kid...the kid who never should have been born.

Yes, she was so near, but yet so far. Some nights as he sat here perched on this flat boulder overlooking the lake, it was all he could do to refrain from taking his boat over to her island, peeking into her windows, and barging in to rescue her when the first opportunity arose. But he had work to do first, he realized.

Tonight, as he finished off his last bottle of whiskey and his last peanut butter sandwich, he decided it was time to leave the island. Time to head back to The Arrowhead on the mainland so he could stock up on supplies. There was already a hint of an early fall in the air, and he had lots to do before winter settled in.

Besides, he'd been off the grid for over a week now. He had to find out if the IRS or FBI was on his tail, if they had any clue where he was. Surely they had already contacted his daughter, Emily, in Paris. Hopefully she'd told them he'd left the country. He needed to get onto the Internet soon to find out what was happening. He could do that from his little cabin at The Arrowhead. Hell, the folks there were probably wondering where he'd disappeared to. He'd have to come up with a good story.

"I'LL BE BACK, MY DARLING," Bob whispered early the next morning as he blew a kiss towards Beth's island, shoved the last of his gear into the boat, and began his journey back to Lake Kabatogama.

The wind whipped across the lake, waves crashing along the rocky shoreline as white caps danced wildly through the narrows. Bob slowed down and stayed as close to shore as possible. Rainy Lake could be unpredictable, he knew. Beth's mother had drowned in this lake, after all, as had a number of others.

It was a long harrowing trip back to Kettle Falls, where he would have his boat portaged from Rainy Lake to Namakan Lake. He was hungry and thirsty by the time he maneuvered his boat up to the dock, hiked up the trail, and over the wooden bridge spanning the swamp below. The historic white clapboard Kettle Falls Hotel with its red awnings soon appeared in the clearing in the forest. A welcome sight, indeed.

Bob decided he needed a drink, and headed to the old bar with the sloping floor. He recognized the bartender, Mike, from his last visit. Maybe Mike had some news about what was happening out there in the world. He seemed to be a very knowledgeable guy who kept up with the news and knew a lot about local history.

"Hey there, Mike." Bob saddled up to the bar.

"Bob, right? And Jack Daniels?" Mike grinned at him.

It unnerved Bob a little to think that Mike had, for some reason, remembered him. Why? Maybe he already had him pegged as a guy with a secret, a guy on the run. But then, there were probably a lot of folks hiding out up here in the woods. A lot of people with secrets.

Bob remembered Mike's stories about his grandfather, who had been a bootlegger up here during Prohibition Days, hiding his stills in the woods near the falls. In fact, Mike's Grandpa Bob had been an acquaintance of the infamous gangster Bugs Moran, who had run Canadian whiskey through Kettle Falls. So Mike probably had secrets of his own, right? He probably didn't give a shit about Bob or any of his secrets. Why should he?

People often flocked to Kettle Falls to be entertained with Mike's stories about the good old days. Today was no exception. As Bob nursed his second drink, a houseboat full of vacationers came in, asking Mike to tell them more stories about life at Kettle Falls. Bob began to relax as he also became caught up in stories about the people who once lived here. People like Catamaran, a reclusive character who mysteriously sailed a catamaran boat to Kettle Falls in the 1920s—and never left.

"He was a vagabond," Mike told the growing crowd at the bar. "Yup, I have an old photo of him wearing ragged clothes, a long gray beard and mustache that covered most of his face, and stringy gray hair hanging down below his shoulders. Barefoot. Always barefoot, even in the winter, they say. And he was never seen without his long hand-carved walking stick."

"Where did he live?" one young man asked.

"Well," Mike continued, leaning over the bar towards his guests. "He actually lived in a hole-in-the-ground, a cave he dug out for himself not too far from the old hotel. He built a wooden roof-like structure over his cave to protect it from the elements. He constructed paths and colorful gardens around his cave, grew his own vegetables there. He hunted and fished. Lived off the land for twenty years." Mike grew silent.

"What happened to him?" another guest asked.

"Well, sad ending," Mike shook his head. "Was the winter of 1940 when he decided to try to walk out across the frozen lake to Ash River on the mainland. Wasn't feeling well. Well, he never returned. They found his body just a half-mile from here...frozen to death."

"Very strange," one young lady reflected. "Nobody ever knew who he really was or why he just came out of nowhere to hide out here in the woods?"

"He did offer up another name, Bert Upton, but nobody was ever able to trace that name. Probably just an alias. Yup, he probably was hiding out from someone or something. Happened a lot in those days. Still does. Not a bad place to hide out, eh?" Mike chuckled.

Bob wasn't sure if he should be relieved or concerned by Mike's comment. At least Mike appeared to be okay with people hiding out and keeping secrets. He didn't seem the type to call the cops or FBI anytime he suspected something wasn't quite kosher. Maybe he was okay. Still, Bob decided it wasn't a good time to ask too many questions, to try to find out if anything significant was going on. Besides, the FBI would have no reason to be looking for him up here in the middle of nowhere, right?

As the crowd grew and Mike continued telling his stories, Bob slipped away to wolf down a delicious fresh fish dinner in the dining room. He was famished—hadn't had real food since he left the Arrowhead Lodge. Didn't think he'd ever eat a peanut butter sandwich again in his life. Except, he reminded himself, he and Beth may need to live on them for a while on their journey back into Canada.

As he entered the dining room, he cautiously scanned the room for any suspicious looking individuals. Then he settled into a chair at a table for two by the windows on the veranda. Looking around, he discovered that he was the only one dining alone. As usual.

He studied the faded portraits hanging on the walls, portraits of people who were probably long gone from this world. He wondered if any of them had secrets like Catamaran in the bartender's story. But didn't everyone have a secret of some kind? Secret thoughts, secret desires, secret fears? It was impossible, he lamented, to ever really know anyone. Not completely. There were too many layers of secrets buried beneath the faces we all showed to the world. No wonder we are all ultimately lonely, he mused. Maybe it wasn't possible to truly connect with another human being no matter how much we thought we wanted to. Maybe that's what had happened to him and Beth. Maybe. But it would be different this time, wouldn't it?

After dinner, he hiked along the wooded path down to the falls, where he watched the root-beer colored water cascading over the dam, erupting into kettle-like whirlpools churning with froth. Mesmerized, it almost made him forget his worries. As the sun began to set over the lake, he decided to call it a night and check into his room in the hotel. He'd get an early start tomorrow morning after having his boat portaged to the Namakan Lake side. Then he'd navigate his way back into Lake Kabatogama to his little cabin at The Arrowhead Lodge.

It felt so good to have a real bed to sleep in again, a real shower and toilet.

But it wasn't long before the sound of heavy footsteps infiltrated his dreams. Footsteps slowly walking the halls outside his door, down the stairs, back up the stairs. Getting louder. Closer. Someone was stalking him. Was it the FBI? Had someone recognized him and turned him in? Was he dreaming, or was this for real?

Struggling to escape from the dream that was holding him hostage, heart pounding, he finally regained enough control to quietly slip out of his bed and retrieve the loaded pistol he'd smuggled into his room and hidden beneath the bed. He was well aware that guns were prohibited throughout Voyageur's National Park. Still, a man had to do what a man had to do, right?

Tiptoeing past the antique dresser, he stationed himself behind the door and waited. If that bastard dared to try to open the door, that would be the end of him, Bob decided, FBI or not.

He waited. He listened. But there were no more sounds. Just dead silence. Had he actually heard footsteps? Or was it just a figment of his imagination? Maybe it was a warning that he needed to be more cautious. Hell, who knew what the FBI was capable of doing? They could have surveillance cameras anywhere...probably not here, but maybe back at his cabin at the Arrowhead. Maybe it wasn't safe to spend any more time there after all. He'd need a backup plan.

So much for a good night's sleep, he sighed, as he spent the rest of the night wide-eyed, propped up against the headboard of his bed, gun in hand—just in case. By the time the first rays of sunlight streamed through his window, he heard the sounds of people moving around and smelled bacon frying downstairs in the kitchen.

He ordered a quick breakfast of scrambled eggs, bacon, and toast, washed down with several cups of strong coffee. Thankfully, nobody seemed to pay much attention to him as he buried himself in an old newspaper, pretending to be reading while he cautiously checked out the other diners. Nobody acted suspiciously. Still, he wondered if any of these dudes had been walking the halls past his door late last night. If so, why?

He breathed a sigh of relief once his boat had been portaged over to the other side and he was back out on the lake again. Thankfully, it was a much calmer day on the lake today, no whitecaps. Some of the sumac along the shore was already turning red, he noticed—a sign of fall. He shuddered to think of all the work he still had to do before it was time to rescue his wife and head back to Canada with her.

Chapter Thirteen

While he'd hoped to slip back into the Arrowhead docks pretty much unnoticed, no such luck. Big Billy just happened to be there on the dock, hauling crates of something or another out of his float plane, which was tied up at the dock. *What a pain in the ass.* Bob shook his head. Why couldn't he just disappear and quit harassing him?

"Hey there, Bob, where ya been?" Billy hollered, a big grin spreading across his chubby face.

He's pretty much harmless, Bob tried to assure himself. *Too dumb to be dangerous*...or was he? *Can't trust anyone,* he reminded himself as he pasted a fake smile across his face.

"Hey there, Billy," Bob returned the greeting.

"So did ya catch lots of nice fish?"

"Fair amount. Fried them up for dinner at my campsite."

"Great. So where did ya camp out?"

What a nosey character he was. That was none of his damn business. "Here and there. Found lots of interesting places on several different lakes," he forced himself to respond as he glanced around, looking for any suspicious activity. The coast looked clear. No immediate threats, he decided. Now if he could just get away and check into his cabin, all would be well.

Bob eventually settled into his cabin after carrying in all his gear. His first task was to scope the place out carefully, looking behind the curtains, under the bed, into the closets and cupboards, searching every inch of the place to make sure there were no hidden cameras or recording devices of any kind. Finally convinced that the place was secure, he closed the curtains and locked the door, lodging a big chair in front of the door, just in case anyone else had a key to enter the place. Placing his loaded pistol on the bedside table, he decided he needed a nap after his sleepless night.

The sound of a low-flying airplane overhead startled him from his sleep. He cautiously crept to the windows and peered out. The plane was gone. It didn't return. Glancing at his watch, he was surprised that it was almost dinner time. He'd slept away the entire afternoon. Now he was hungry.

He headed up to the lodge where he was greeted warmly by the owners, who welcomed him back but never inquired as to his whereabouts. Several other guests milled around the great room by the fireplace or were already seated in the dining room. They looked like your typical tourists. A few kids tagged along. Nothing threatening —hopefully.

The prime rib special was delicious, topped off with fresh apple pie a' la mode. The lodge was known for its home style cooking, and Bob thoroughly enjoyed his meals here. Especially after pretty much living on peanut butter and jelly for the last week or so.

After dinner, he drove in to the little store in Kabatogama to stock up on supplies and liquor. He had a list he'd compiled in his journal while camping on the island, and was pleased that he was able to get almost everything there—everything except lumber, nails, a tarp, and other materials he'd need to fix up that old cabin on Rabbit Island. That was where he and Beth would probably spend their first night together, their first night after being apart for more than ten years.

By the time he returned to his cabin, the sun had set and the temperature had dropped. He shivered in his light jacket beneath a canopy of glittering stars. After hauling in his supplies and securing the cabin, he devoured all the newspapers he'd been able to find and purchase at the store. Mostly local news. Nothing at all about him.

That was good, but he needed to get online to find out if there were any news articles about him and his disappearance—about his alleged embezzlement. That was bullshit, of course. He'd taken only what he deserved after all he'd done for that law firm, after all the money he'd made for them. His bastard of a father had founded that firm and coerced him into managing it for all those years. Hell, if he hadn't been so preoccupied with the business and trying to meet his father's demands, his marriage to Beth would have thrived. He was sure of that, the more he thought about it.

The old Rob had been gone a lot those days, he recalled. Beth was probably lonely, he now realized. She didn't understand the demands and pressure he was under, why he had to de-stress himself with alcohol—and, admittedly, sometimes within the arms of another woman. Or two...or three. Hell, it really didn't matter, did it?

But I never loved any of them. Not even the one who got herself knocked up and was determined that he should divorce Beth and marry her. Or else—or else she would tell his wife and shame him in public.

Anger surged through his veins, once again, as he recalled how his old man had insisted that he comply with the girl's demands after she threatened to go public, accusing him of fathering her child. He probably should have gotten a DNA test, but truthfully, whether he wanted to admit it or not, he believed he was the father. The foolish girl had been so madly in love with him that she would not have even considered sleeping with anyone else. DNA results would have most likely implicated him instead of exonerating him.

"Can't you do anything right?" the old man had yelled at him, slamming his fist on his desk, shaking his head in disgust. It didn't matter that the old man had had his share of affairs over the years. "You are hell bent on destroying this firm, aren't you? After all I've done to build this empire, after all I've done for you. You ungrateful bastard!"

"Look," Rob had glared at his father, trying to keep his cool, "This is not going to destroy the firm, Ben. Things like this happen all the time. I'll pay her off. She will go on with her life, and I'll go on with mine."

"Bullshit! Our reputation will be destroyed. Oh no, you're not just walking away from this. You're going to pay, son. You are going to divorce that wife of yours and marry this little tramp. Do you hear me? It's the price you will pay for your foolishness. Next time, keep it in your pants. Do you hear me?" He'd paced around the room, around his son's chair, fury in his eyes, gulping down another glass of whiskey.

"What about Beth?"

"What about her? She was never good enough for our family. Grew up on the wrong side of the tracks, so to speak. Hell, she even has a hard time as a hostess trying to entertain our clients. What use is she to the firm?"

"She's my wife, and I love her. I'm not divorcing her. And that's final!" He had stormed out of the room to the sound of his father's evil laughter.

Late that night, the shrill ringing of the telephone woke him from a troubled sleep. He fumbled to retrieve the phone from his bedside table. "Hello?" he mumbled.

"You WILL divorce her, or I'm throwing you out of the firm. Right now!" his father bellowed in his ear.

Rob grabbed the phone and retreated to his home office so Beth would not overhear the conversation.

"I will destroy your reputation, do you hear me? I will destroy you financially. And you know I can do that, as the major shareholder in this corporation. You will be broke, with no place to go. Think about that before you make a stupid decision. Hell, Beth will leave you anyway. You won't be able to support her. And I'll make sure she knows about your affair. Is that what you want?"

"You wouldn't really do that. You need me in that law firm. Without me, you would not survive. Look what I've done to modernize the firm, all the clients I've brought in—big names, big bucks. Look at the revenue I bring in. You can't do it without me and you know it. Your old way of doing business is history, Ben. You need me."

"The hell I can't. Just try me, son. If you don't do as I say, I will be paying your wife a visit tomorrow morning, and it will all be over. If you agree to divorce her now, I won't divulge your secret affair. You'll be in a better position when it comes to a divorce settlement. Got it?"

"If I comply with your asinine demands, how do you think people will react when I marry that young girl? You think she will be a better hostess than Beth, for God's sake?"

The old man had chuckled that hideous laugh again, the sound of ice cubes clinking in a glass in the background. "It's only a temporary solution to prevent the girl from going public and destroying our reputation. We will keep your impending marriage very quiet. Nobody needs to know anything about her. Move in with her to get her off our backs. String her on as if you plan to marry her later. Timing is everything. We will find a way to get rid of her later, maybe after the kid is born."

Shivers had run up and down Rob's spine as he listened to his father's chilling words. What the hell was he threatening to do to this foolish girl? Would he really tell Beth about this and destroy their marriage? Yes, he would. Knowing what his father was capable of, there was no doubt in his mind whatsoever. What choice did he have? His father held the key to his future. What could he do?

Over the years, Rob had watched his father ruthlessly destroy anyone who got in his way. His usual pattern was to destroy them financially or destroy their reputations. Some of his best-paying clients had organized crime connections and shady dealings that the old man had kept to himself. There had been one mysterious death involved in one of his father's cases. It had never been solved.

Now it was Rob's turn apparently. He had no doubt that the old man would make good on his threats and promises. Reluctantly, he had caved in to his father's demands.

Bringing himself back to the present, Bob angrily paced around his cabin, cursing. "May he rot in hell!" he screamed into the black night. "My life is a pile of shit...and it's all his fault!"

But...I have a rendezvous with death...with death...with death.... A surreal but familiar presence infiltrated his consciousness once again. What the hell did that mean? How and why had someone, somehow, implanted this chilling message into his subconscious mind, over and over again? Was he losing his mind? Who was doing this to him, and why?

The only logical answer seemed to be that someone or something was preparing him for what he needed to do. Maybe the voice was telling him he must get rid of Seth in order to rescue Beth. It was as simple as that. If he didn't do Seth in, Seth would be back. Seth would find them and haunt them forever.

The mere thought of that half-breed with Beth, *his* wife, drove him crazy. She had no right to be involved with another man. *She promised to love, honor and obey me—till death do us part.*

Finally, he calmed down enough to turn on his laptop and mobile hotspot. He grinned, congratulating himself on having the wisdom to use his own private device instead of relying on the lodge's public internet connection. Nobody would ever find a way to tap into any searches he did on his own secure site.

He soon discovered that he had Internet reception as long as he sat at the table by the window overlooking the lake. Of course, he'd already closed the curtains to prevent anyone from peering in. He would, occasionally, peek out from behind the blinds to be sure nobody was there lurking around the corner, waiting to capture him. A full moon shimmered across rippling black waves that seemed to be growing larger and larger as the wind began to howl.

Holding his breath, Bob began searching Chicago newspaper sites. He googled his old name, Rob Calhoun. Did anyone know, or care, that the old Rob had disappeared from the face of the earth? Would anyone actually miss him? Probably not, he sighed to himself. He hadn't had any real friends for years, preferring to keep people at a distance, preferring the company of good old Jack Daniels when he wasn't working. Life was simpler that way. Besides, he had needed time alone to plot his disappearance and the rescue of his wife. He had too many secrets to even think about socializing with others.

But what a brilliant plot he had carefully constructed. He was proud of himself for that. Now all he had to do was implement his plans. Just so the kid didn't get in his way. If he killed Seth and rescued Beth, what would happen to the kid? Did he care? Hell no, not really. After all, the kid was the product of an illicit relationship between Beth and Seth. The product of a rape, no doubt. Beth would never have given herself to that man freely. No way. *Her heart still belongs to me and it always will. Someday she will realize that....*

Just as he began to focus on his Internet search, a bolt of thunder blasted through the heavens, shaking the cabin, startling him. Peering out the window, he watched streaks of lightning flash across the sky. It was good to be back in his little cabin on a night like this instead of camping out in his tent on a remote island. Pouring himself a drink to celebrate his homecoming, he settled back down at the computer.

It wasn't long before a news article popped up on the Chicago Tribute site, along with a photo of the old Rob Calhoun—clean-shaven, nice haircut, dressed in an expensive suit, Rolex watch, looking very professional, very lawyerly. *If they could only see me now,* he chuckled to himself, as he began to read the article.

Rob Calhoun, vice-president and partner in the prestigious Calhoun & Clark Law Firm, has mysteriously disappeared after having allegedly absconded with ten million dollars. The FBI has launched a criminal investigation and is attempting to locate Mr. Calhoun. Leads are currently being pursued in California as well as several international destinations. Pending charges include grand theft and income tax evasion. Anyone with any knowledge as to his whereabouts is encouraged to contact the Chicago FBI Office. A $50,000 reward for information leading to the arrest of this man is currently being offered.

Bob poured himself another stiff drink as he read the article once again. So he now had a bounty on his head. Fifty grand at that. He'd have to be more cautious than ever. Couldn't trust anyone. California and international destinations? He chuckled to himself, pleased at the red herring destinations he'd laid the ground work for before he left Chicago. Of course Emily would have been contacted and told them that her father planned to leave the country. And Bob himself had had a contact in California postmark and mail a letter to the law firm from California. The guy owed him big time after Bob had pulled some strings and paid off a few people to keep him out of prison on a manslaughter charge.

His thoughts were suddenly interrupted by the crash of thunder and the deafening roar of ferocious winds whipping through the large pines surrounding his cabin. Peering out the window, he jumped back as a bolt of lightning struck and splintered a massive Norway pine not far from his cabin. The top of the tree crashed down onto the rocky point jutting out into the lake. The world suddenly went black. Lights out. No power.

Heart pounding, Bob felt his way along the wall to his bed, where he sat down and reached for the flashlight on the bedside table, finally finding it and flicking it on. Thank God he'd made it back to the cabin before this monster storm hit. What if he'd been out there on the island in a tent? Whose *rendezvous with death* was this anyway? His own, perhaps? No, that wasn't possible. He had an important mission to accomplish first. Once the storm let up, he'd be off for Rabbit Island to fix the place up for Beth. It wouldn't be fancy, but it would do until they escaped back into Canada and made their way to their new home at Black Bear Camp in Nestor Falls.

Bob huddled beneath several heavy quilts to stay warm until the power came back on. Finally he drifted off to sleep, with visions of his wife filtering through his dreams. She was lying in bed wearing that sexy black negligee he loved. Her long hair glistened in the sunlight streaming through the window on a lazy Sunday morning. Her eyes sparkled, smiling at him as he brought her breakfast in bed, a single red rose on the tray. Yes, he had served her breakfast in bed almost every Sunday the first few months they were married. Somehow things changed after that. She no longer smiled at him like that, no longer wore sexy negligees.

It won't be long now, my darling, he sighed as he curled his body around an extra pillow.

Chapter Fourteen

"Be a good boy for Grandma Evelyn." Beth hugged her son closely as she and Seth prepared to leave the island for their anniversary getaway at Kettle Falls. "Remember what I told you about always asking her before you go exploring?"

"Yes, Mom." Jason sighed with exasperation. "I'll be good."

"You sure you can handle this, Evelyn?" Seth grinned at the old woman, still spry at eighty years of age. Still, Jason, with his adventurous spirit, was a handful for anyone. It was hard for the boy to sit still for long. There was a huge, wondrous world out there, calling to him. So many adventures. So many places to explore. So much to learn.

Evelyn's aging eyes sparkled as she put an arm around Jason's shoulders. "We're going to have fun together while you're gone. Maybe we will even play a few games of Yahtzee—if you promise not to beat me." She grinned at the boy.

"You're on, Grandma." He high-fived her.

It was hard to believe this was the same woman who had once caused so much heartache and pain in the lives of Beth and her mother. But that was then; this was now. Jake would be happy with the way things had turned out. They were there for Evelyn as he'd asked them to be, and Evelyn was there for them. She was especially good with Jason, thrilled to be a part of his life. He was the grandson she never had.

IT WAS a beautiful early fall day when Beth and Seth launched their vintage boat and began their journey through Rainy Lake to the historic Kettle Falls Hotel. The sun sparkled, dancing on the rippling waves. Now and then they met a boat on the lake, mostly islanders or local fishermen these days. Most of the tourists were gone for now, although some would be back for hunting and snowmobiling later in the season.

It felt good, Beth thought, to have the lake to themselves once again. She had so many fond memories of life here on this lake with her beloved Nana. They'd loved the winter solitude that would soon settle into their little world. Time to sit by the fire, read, play games, and snowshoe through the winter wonderland that surrounded them. To feed the birds and watch the wildlife, especially the deer that stopped by for their daily meal of cracked corn. Beth had loved to feed the deer, to talk to them. They were so tame they sometimes followed her around the island.

Sure, there were some tough times—ice and snowstorms, loss of power, worrying about freeze-up or ice-out, which meant there'd be no way to get to or from the mainland for weeks at a time. Making sure they had enough food and supplies to last the winter. Always having to plan ahead.

Kettle Falls had been a special place for her family for as far back as she could remember. Some of her earliest memories were of Jake and her mother, Sarah, taking her there when she was just a little girl. Jake —her good old Uncle Jake, who had turned out to be her father. Beth sighed. Life sure got complicated sometimes, didn't it? But she was finally at peace with it all, even with Evelyn.

"A penny for your thoughts." Seth leaned over from his captain's seat to stroke the back of her shoulders. She sighed deeply, gazing into his warm brown eyes.

"Just that I'm feeling so blessed the way things have turned out in my life, after all the difficulties in the past." She squeezed his hand. "I'm feeling so peaceful, so happy, so much in love with you." Her eyes met his, melting together as they sometimes did. As if they were one.

"You're the best thing that ever happened to me, Ninimoshe." He stroked her leg. "And we're going to have a wonderful time together at Kettle Falls."

"Yes, we are. Where are we staying? In the lodge?"

"Not this time. I booked the honeymoon cabin at the far end of the rocky point by the lake. We will have some well-deserved privacy—Jason won't be barging in on us this time," he chuckled. "And we have an outdoor hot tub on the deck where we can sit and watch the sun set."

"Whoa! You thought of everything, didn't you? I couldn't be happier."

"You deserve to be happy. Life is good, eh?"

"Life is perfect. I could not ask for anything more. You, me, Jason. We've got it all. And Emily over there in Paris—even a brand new grandchild."

A seagull swooped overhead before landing on a slab of rock in the middle of the lake that was full of chattering seagulls. Beth grabbed her camera to try to capture a few shots as Seth quietly guided the boat closer.

Seagulls held a special place in her heart, ever since the surreal experience she and Seth had shortly after Jake had died. They'd been quietly sitting on the rocky ledge of what they referred to as Sarah's Island, the place where Jake had spent many hours thinking about and talking to his beloved Sarah, trying to communicate with her through the thin veil that separated the world of the living from the land of the dead. Jake had claimed that Sarah sometimes made her presence known to him in the form of a seagull that would land on the rock beside him. She emanated love, a sense of peace and comfort.

While Beth had always figured this was just wishful thinking on Jake's part, she and Seth were stunned that day when two luminous seagulls circled overhead several times before landing on the rock beside Beth and Seth. Surreal waves of love and peace had flowed through her very being. The female gull had stared into her eyes, mesmerizing her, as images of her dear mother drifted through her mind. Time had seemed to stand still as unspoken messages filtered through her mind—messages from Sarah and Jake. Messages that they were together at last, happy. They would always love her and be there for her, in this world and the next.

It had been one of the most profound experiences of her lifetime, and had, in fact, given her a sense of peace and hope in what lay beyond the confines of this world.

Today, she snapped photos of the gulls, remembering her mother and father as tears of happiness filled her eyes.

"You okay? Ready to move on?" Seth broke through her reverie.

"I'm fine. Just remembering, that's all."

He brought her hand to his lips and gallantly kissed each fingertip, a playful grin spreading across his face.

As they neared Anderson Bay, he suggested stopping for a break in their two-hour boat trip. They were soon climbing the meandering wooded trail leading to the very top of jagged granite cliffs that towered over the lake and islands below. It offered one the most breathtaking views one could ever find on Rainy Lake. A photographer's dream, it had, in fact, been captured in the old Hamm's Brewery television commercials years ago.

Huffing and puffing, racing each other to the top, they finally arrived at what felt like the top of the world. Falling into each other's arms, they clung together as they gazed down at the churning blue waters, sprinkled with diamonds of sunlight.

"Remember our Christmas Day hot dog roast down there?" Seth pointed towards a granite spit of an island in the middle of the bay far below.

"How could I forget? It was Emily's first trip back home, her first time on a snowmobile, her first winter adventure in the North Woods—"

"The first time I met your lovely daughter, *our* daughter now. She showed up in high heels, fashionable Paris clothing—and was rather humiliated when she had to put on a very unstylish snowmobile suit, heavy boots, and a helmet," he laughed.

"Ten years ago already," she sighed. "I remember Jake proudly guiding us out here to this special place, showing us all the historical landmarks along the way. And it wasn't long before Emily began to really enjoy herself. Remember how she loved roasting hot dogs on the frozen lake in the midst of a winter wonderland?"

"She did. That's when she and I first bonded, remember? We started talking about art. Two artists who understood the passion that drives us."

"I miss her."

"I know. Me too. You do need to start checking on airline reservations so you can go visit soon and see that new grandbaby. I'm also anxious to visit as soon as I get caught up on the paintings I've promised to finish."

"For now, we'd better get on our way to Kettle Falls. I'm starving."

"Again? How can you eat so much and never gain an ounce? Me, I'd weigh two hundred pounds if I ate like you," he teased her. And she loved it. She usually got him back. They loved to laugh together.

Several miles before reaching Kettle Falls, they passed Rabbit Island. The remains of an old log cabin and outbuildings were tucked away in the dense woods surrounded by rocky cliffs. You could barely see the buildings from the lake. Legend had it that this place was haunted by the eccentric old man who once lived there. He had mysteriously disappeared years ago. The place was abandoned and had fallen into a state of total disrepair. Nobody bothered to stop there anymore since people felt it was haunted, or may have been booby-trapped by the old man who had hated visitors of any kind.

But today....

"Wait, slow down," Beth called out to Seth, pointing towards Rabbit Island.

"What the...?"

Fumbling for the binoculars, Seth slowed the boat down. "That's strange. Looks like smoke coming from the chimney. And...." He focused the binoculars, gazing out towards Rabbit Island. "Something like a brown tarp hanging over a dilapidated shack."

"Let me see. Very strange," Beth agreed as she focused the binoculars. "Looks like a cyclone blew through. Trees down. Overgrown brush. Junk everywhere. I think I see what's left of an old dock. No boat, though. Could someone have purchased the island, thinking they would fix the old place up?"

"Unlikely. I thought it was a part of Voyageur's National Park. If that's the case, it's not for sale to anyone. Maybe the park service is tearing it down. Or, maybe some outlaw is hiding out there."

"Yeah, right. Why would anyone in their right mind want to hide out in a haunted shack with no plumbing or electricity? Maybe some kids are just having fun over there. Or," she paused dramatically, leaning in towards her husband, teasing him, "...maybe the ghosts have moved in."

"Whatever. No idea how anyone could have gotten there, unless they swam a very long way, or someone dropped them off. Still very strange.... But we'd better move on and get checked into our honeymoon suite, eh?"

Chapter Fifteen

After tying their boat up at the pier, Beth and Seth hiked up the wooded trail and across the rustic bridge until they reached the clearing in the middle of the woods. Holding hands, they stopped to admire the historic white clapboard Kettle Falls Hotel with its red-striped awnings. It never ceased to amaze people, no matter how many times they visited, to find this jewel in the midst of the forest on a wilderness lake in the middle of nowhere.

Beth sighed. "So many memories here, Seth. I always feel like I'm coming back home in a way. Knowing that some of my mother's, grandmother's, grandfather's, and Jake's ashes were scattered over these falls, I feel like this place is a part of my roots."

"We will pay them a visit at the falls for sure. Maybe after dinner?"

"Perfect. Let's check in and pick up our key first...and maybe have a drink at the bar before dinner?"

"Welcome back!" The hotel's owner immediately recognized them when they stepped through the veranda and into the hotel lobby. It never changed after all these years...and that was a good thing. The history of Kettle Falls was one of its most important assets. People enjoyed sitting in the lobby beneath the large bear hide hanging on the wall, paging through books filled with photos and stories about life at Kettle Falls over the past hundred plus years.

"Hey, there, it's great to be back, Pete. We're celebrating our tenth anniversary in the honeymoon cabin," Seth informed their friendly host.

"That's what I heard. We have a bottle of champagne on ice in your cabin, as a matter of fact."

"That's so nice of you. Thank you." Beth smiled at her old friend. He'd been there many years, as far back as she could remember.

"Are you joining us for dinner?"

"Absolutely. Say about seven?"

After checking in, they headed for the bar with the sloping floor. Mike was tending bar as usual, entertaining customers with his stories about life at Kettle Falls when he was growing up here years ago. He was pouring a glass of Jack Daniels for a scruffy looking guy at the bar. The guy had a scraggly beard, wild hair, and an old baseball cap pulled down over a pair of mirrored sunglasses.

"Hey there," Mike greeted his old friends. "Haven't seen you two for ages. Rumor has it that you're here celebrating your anniversary?"

"That's right, Mike. Ten years, would you believe?" Seth put his arm around his wife's shoulders.

"Well, Happy Anniversary. Drinks on the house!"

As they began chatting, the man at the bar suddenly bolted from his bar stool, leaving his drink behind untouched, and rushed out the back door.

"Did I say something wrong?" Seth joked. "Haven't seen that guy around before. Is he an islander, new to these parts, or just passing through?"

"Name's Bob. That's about all I know about him. Says he's a fisherman. Stops in now and then and loves his Jack Daniels. Can't believe he walked out before inhaling his drink. He drinks that stuff through a firehose," he chuckled. "Oh well. Tell me what's new with you guys, and Jason."

After a leisurely conversation with Mike they headed to the dining room, where they found a table for two reserved for them on the veranda overlooking the grounds and the path leading to the falls. They could hear the falls roaring through the open, vine-covered window. They enjoyed an excellent walleye dinner, caught fresh that afternoon by one of the hotel's staff members.

The sun was hanging low in the sky, the first streaks of pink and gold shimmering above the lake as they hiked up the rocky trail to the top of Kettle Falls. There they stood in silence, arms around each other, mesmerized by the falls cascading down into churning root beer colored pools of water.

Beth was lost in thought. Lost in memories of her deceased loved ones. Sending silent messages of love to them all. Seth also cherished his memories of Nana and Jake.

Finally, as the sun was setting, casting a warm glow over the lake, she pulled away from Seth and plucked four large red leaves from the nearby sumac bushes. "This is for you, Nana." She tossed the leaves, one by one, out over the falls. "And for you, Mommy, and Jake, and Grandfather. We love you all."

A wistful tear slid down her cheek as they watched the breeze pick the leaves up, scattering them through the air before they drifted into the churning kettles of water below. She nodded at Seth, letting him know it was time for them to leave.

As they began their way back down the trail, holding hands, a loud thrashing noise from the nearby woods startled them both. "What was that?" she clung to Seth.

Gazing intently into the darkening woods, he saw nothing. "Probably a deer, maybe even a bear. But it's gone now."

"Is everything okay?" she asked, picking up on his furrowed brow. She recalled the premonitions he'd felt emanating from his deceased grandmother's portrait several weeks ago. It had been very vague, nothing specific...just a note of caution. He had said nothing about it since then, but she sensed he was more cautious than usual. Especially when it came to Jason.

"Yes, everything is okay." He smiled at her warmly. "Let's give Jason and Evelyn a call when we get to our cabin to make sure all is well there also."

They were soon settled into their cozy cabin, complete with a wood-burning fireplace, a Jacuzzi for two, and the promised bottle of champagne sitting in a bucket on the kitchen table beside a bouquet of flowers that Seth had delivered earlier in the day. Red roses. Her favorite. He never failed to remember on very special occasions like this one. Normally he picked her bouquets of wildflowers. Lilacs were her favorite.

The hot tub on the deck overlooking the lake was warmed up for a romantic evening together beneath the full moon, surrounded by the forest. They would be alone here, far away from the other cabins and the rest of the world.

Seth was already calling home by the time Beth emerged from the bedroom wrapped in a sexy black silk robe. She could only hear his side of the conversation, punctuated with pauses while Evelyn rambled on and on as she usually did.

"Evelyn? It's Seth..... Yes, we made it just fine. How are you and Jason getting along...? Good. Good. No problems then? He is behaving for you...? That's my boy. So he's back home from his explorations and settled in for the night...? Again, thanks so much for being there for him, Evelyn. Will you put him on?"

Once Evelyn came up for air, Jason finally got on the line. Seth and Beth hovered closely together over Seth's smart phone, their bodies touching, eyes melting into each other's. Jason relayed the day's exciting adventures and his discoveries, including what he assured them was an ancient turtle that had to be at least a thousand years old. Thankfully, everything was fine on the home front.

"I love you and I miss you, Jason." Beth told him goodbye as she felt Seth's hand slip beneath her robe, obviously excited to discover that she was naked beneath the flowing silk garment that she'd purchased for this special occasion.

Shutting down his phone after telling their son goodnight, he immediately shed his clothes, leaving them in a heap on the floor. Grabbing the bottle of champagne and a couple of glasses, he led his wife out to the hot tub.

Beneath the light of the moon she casually removed her robe, slowly, teasingly. He was already emerged in the bubbling water, partially obscured by streams of steam emerging into the chill night air, anxiously waiting for her to join him.

"A toast first?" She smiled at him as she joined him in the pool, cuddling up beside him, stroking his thigh.

"Okay," he groaned as he reached over to pour them each a glass of champagne, trying his best to wait until she was ready. "To the most beautiful, sexiest woman in the world, the woman I will always love with all my heart and soul." He clinked his glass against hers, caressing her breast with his free hand.

Trying to contain her growing excitement, she whispered huskily, "To the only man I ever have or ever will love, the one who turned my life around and has made my life worth living. I will love you forever."

"Happy anniversary to us."

They gazed deeply into each other's eyes, clinking their glasses together. Ten years and that spark was still there. Sometimes shimmering quietly in the background, sometimes exploding with desire, but always a surreal connection when their eyes met, as if their souls knew and had always known each other.

Their whispered words echoed across the still waters of the lake below. They were more than anxious to fall into each other's arms, to make love beneath the glittering canopy of stars hovering overhead.

Consumed with growing waves of passion spiking and surging through their bodies, they had no idea that a boat idled there in the cove, hidden in the darkness. No visible lights. Just watching...and waiting....

No idea...until they were startled by the sound of a boat gunning its engine and roaring out of the cove into the darkness of the big lake.

"What the hell?" Seth jumped out of the hot tub, grabbed his flashlight and a towel, and headed down towards the beach.

But the boat was long gone, disappearing into dense banks of fog descending upon Rainy Lake.

Chapter Sixteen

"The only man she ever has or ever will love?" Bob shouted after making his way out of the sheltered bay and into the wild waters of the narrows. Fury surged through his veins as he roared across Rainy Lake, oblivious to the buoys marking protruding rock formations that could easily take out the lower unit of his motor. He didn't give a shit. Not anymore. Didn't matter that white caps were rolling across the black fog-enshrouded lake, tossing his boat around like a toy as waves crashed over the bow. Didn't matter that he was soon drenched, shivering in the chill of the night.

What the hell was she talking about? Why would she say such a thing? It was a lie. Bob knew, deep within his heart and soul, that she still loved him, not Seth. She was obviously brainwashed. He would need to set her straight once he rescued her from that bastard.

Beth was and always would be *his* wife. How could she tell another man that she loved him? Images of the two of them together, naked, in that hot tub flashed through his mind again and again. *How could she? What about me?* Fists clenched, speeding recklessly across an angry Rainy Lake, Bob began to sob, tears streaming down his face, blurring his vision. *What about me? I'm the one she loves.*

How could she have sex with another man? How could she? What evil power did he have over her to make her give in to him? Had he put a curse on her or drugged her?

He had to get rid of the Indian, no doubt about that. He'd already found several convenient places to dispose of the body. *I have a rendezvous with death,* he reminded himself, *Seth's death.* The very thought made him smile through his tears. Justice would prevail. It was his responsibility, after all, to avenge his wife's honor; to take out the man who had raped her, taken her hostage, and forced a kid upon her.

He'd come close tonight, sitting out there in his boat, hidden from their view, watching them having sex through his night vision scope of his loaded gun—something no loving husband should ever have to endure. Just waiting for the right moment. Heart pounding wildly, he'd waited for the two of them to separate long enough for him to get a clear shot at Seth, without hitting Beth instead. But they'd been inseparable.

He'd been ready to explode, trying to control his shaky trigger-happy finger. Just waiting for the perfect shot. But the rising steam from the hot tub obscured his view. Then an eerie bank of fog settled over the lake, making it impossible for him to see anything.

He'd seen enough. He roared off into the night, promising himself that there would be another opportunity, no doubt about that. Seth had to be eliminated from the picture. It was the only way that Beth would come to her senses and realize that it was Bob, the old Rob, she really loved.

On second thought, maybe it was time to implement Plan B instead of waiting any longer for the perfect shot at Seth. Eventually Seth would have to go, of course. But Plan B might help to expedite the process. It would certainly give him more leverage. Plan B would surely create a crisis, and put Beth and Seth into panic mode so he could make his move more easily. He didn't have a lot of time to waste, after all, not if he and Beth were going to get back to Canada before winter set in.

Tonight would be the night to make his move, Bob decided as he docked his boat at the secluded cove on the back side of Rabbit Island.

Thankfully, the lake was settling down a bit and the fog was beginning to lift. Stumbling up the rocky, overgrown path to the shack where he'd been hiding out and stockpiling items he'd need, he decided this place was no longer safe. Too close to Kettle Falls, especially now that he knew Beth and Seth were there and were, in fact, well known there.

Even Mike, the friendly bartender, knew them. That had sure as hell been a close encounter at the bar earlier this evening. Seeing his wife there with another man had been more than he could handle. His first impulse had been to throttle the Indian right there, grab Beth, and escape. Enraged, he'd stormed out of the place before he did something stupid.

What if Mike had picked up on something he'd said or done while they were bullshitting at the bar? He'd been careful not to say much of anything, but what if he'd left a hint of some kind after belting down a few too many drinks at the bar? Couldn't trust anyone these days, especially when you had secrets that you must guard with your life.

It was time to move out of this hell hole on Rabbit Island, he decided, patting himself on the back for having already set up a temporary camping site at a secluded spot on the Canadian side of Rainy Lake, just an hour or so from this dump. It would do for now. It would have to.

He began hurriedly stashing his supplies in garbage bags and hauling them down to his boat. Then he carefully loaded the little duffle bag he kept under his boat seat with the important items—his guns, ammunition, smart phone, matches to start a fire, bottled water, candy bars, plastic gloves, an extra pair of boots, towels...and a bottle and a small vial of chloroform.

Kicking the rickety old door shut for the last time, he retrieved a flask of whiskey from his pocket and took off in his boat. Liquid courage, he laughed to himself, as he headed up Rainy Lake towards Beth's island.

The moon had taken refuge beneath hovering clouds by the time he arrived at Beth's island, shut off the boat lights, and slowly guided his boat towards the secluded landing place where he had previously docked while exploring the island and familiarizing himself with the layout of the cabin. He shut off the engine and let the boat's momentum drift it into shore.

The last time he was here, he'd been planning to rescue Beth. He would still do so, of course…later. For now, the nature of his mission had changed.

The world seemed to be wrapped in a shadowy blanket of sleep-induced solitude as he crept up the path to the cabin. Thankfully, the place was quiet. No lights on in the cabin. After overhearing the conversation between Beth and Seth in the hot tub at Kettle Falls, he figured that the old lady must be there somewhere with the kid. Hopefully, she was sound asleep and hard of hearing. Didn't matter though. She wouldn't be a problem. He was too smart to let an old lady infringe on his plans.

Bob pulled on a pair of plastic gloves and clutched his duffle bag to his chest. He couldn't screw this up. He already knew where the kid's bedroom was—way up in the alcove above the main room. He'd have to be very quiet creeping up the stairs. First, he made his way around the perimeter of the cabin, peeking in the windows to make sure the coast was clear.

Peering into the screened porch, he was startled to see the kid, fast asleep on the day bed. Grinning to himself, Bob realized this was going to be much easier than he had imagined. Holding his breath, he retrieved the small vial of chloroform, doused the towel with it, and snuck in through the unlocked screen door.

A glimmer of moonlight suddenly slipped through the layer of clouds, shining upon the face of the sleeping child. His left arm was curled around his pillow. A book lay open on the floor beside him.

Bob was suddenly jolted by a flashback, back to the days when he was a kid about the same age as this one. He had always slept with his left arm curled around the pillow, just like this kid. And he'd always fallen asleep reading one of his books, usually about space travel and the universe. He had dreamed of exploring space, going to the moon, to Mars. But his father had discouraged him, made fun of him for his stupid and unrealistic dreams.

"Grow up, son. You'll never be an astronaut. That is not a realistic goal for someone like you." He shook his head, a look of utter disgust playing across his face—a look of deep disappointment in his only son.

"But why not, Father? I'm really good at science and astronomy. It's what I love. And I could make a difference in the world. Someday we will have to settle colonies on another planet if we want to survive. I want to help make that happen. I know I can do it."

Bob would never forget his father's reaction to the heartfelt unveiling of his dreams, or his father's cruel laughter echoing throughout his office. Laughing at him. Laughing at his dreams.

Tears had filled Rob's eyes as his father finally quit laughing and began to lecture him.

"You're nothing but an unrealistic dreamer, son. Reading too much science fiction, perhaps? Wake up, kid. You're old enough to get over your childhood fantasies and live in the real world. Besides, you already have your career path laid out for you. You will become a partner in my law firm. Someday the business will be yours. What more could any kid want in life? Money. A nice house. Travel. Prestige. That's what it's all about."

"But...but...that's fine for you. But that's not what I want, Father." Rob had mustered up his diminishing courage to speak up, staring at the swirling patterns of the old rug on the floor, afraid to look his father in the eye.

"Who the hell do you think you are? You're just a young punk who has no clue about life. And you are one of the most ungrateful kids I've ever known," the old man had snarled at him, pacing around his office, circling his trembling son. "Hell, you're not smart enough to be an astronaut. Maybe you're not smart enough to be a lawyer either, but at least I will teach you and help you out along the way."

His eyes filling with tears, Rob had turned away so his father would not see him crying. He had never been allowed to cry in front of him, not even as a little boy.

But the old man had not missed the tear slipping down his son's cheek. "Crybaby," he had scoffed in disgust. "And you think you are a big enough man to go to the moon someday?" Shaking his head, he'd poured himself another glass of whiskey, glared at his son, and simply said, "Dismissed."

Ten-year old Rob had scurried out of his father's office, thankful that his father hadn't cuffed him on the side of the head this time. His mother was nowhere to be found, as usual. She was never there to comfort her son. Probably out partying with her friends or in the arms of her latest lover. It didn't really matter whether she was there or not. She simply didn't give a shit.

Little by little, Rob's big dreams for his future, his self-confidence, and his self-esteem had eroded at the hands of his dysfunctional parents. He began to question whether he was competent enough to explore space or pursue his own destiny.

In later years, he'd made up for his insecurities by mustering up an attitude of arrogance and extreme self-confidence. That was the face he displayed to the world, but it wasn't the real Rob. Nobody had a clue as to the demons that possessed him.

Bringing himself back to the present, still watching the sleeping boy who was unaware of what was about to happen to him, Bob couldn't resist reaching down to pick the book up off the floor. Holding it up to the moonlight streaming in through the window, he was shocked to read the title. *An Earthling's Guide to Outer Space,* by Bob McDonald. What the hell? He impulsively stuffed the book into his duffle bag.

He shifted his gaze back to the sleeping kid. The kid who never should have been born. At least he would serve a useful purpose now. He was soon to become Bob's bargaining chip and his hostage in negotiating an exchange for Beth.

It was time to make his move. Bob retrieved the towel and the vial of chloroform from his duffle bay. He sized the kid up, assuring himself that he probably weighed about seventy pounds, typical for a ten-year-old boy, just as he had figured. The dosage he'd calculated should be perfect—just enough to knock him out for six to eight hours. Not enough to kill him.

No, getting rid of the kid would not be in anyone's best interest, despite the complications his presence may present down the road.

Besides, he didn't need a murder rap on his back. He had enough problems to deal with, enough agents on his tail for other alleged crimes. Crimes that were, in fact, not really crimes at all if one knew all the facts and reasons behind these alleged crimes. The problem was that most people, including the FBI, were too ignorant to understand. Besides, they were out to get him, to destroy him. That's why he'd had to take matters into his own hands. To hell with the rest of the world! All he needed was Beth and their cozy little hideaway in Canada.

Fast asleep, the kid barely moved or made a sound when Bob carefully placed the chloroform soaked towel over his nose and mouth. Just one sharp intake of breath, blue eyes popping open, a shocked expression on his face, and moments later, his body went limp.

Bob picked him up and carefully carried him out the door, listening intently for any sound from the old lady who had to be sleeping close by. Hell, she'd probably taken her hearing aids out for the night, he laughed to himself. Even if she heard anything, it would be too late. They would be long gone by the time she managed to get out of bed and check things out. Glancing over his shoulder, he carried the kid down to his boat where he put him into a sleeping bag, laid him on the back seat of the boat, and quietly paddled the boat away from the shore before starting the engine and heading out across Rainy Lake. By the time the kid came to, they would be in Canada and settled into their camp.

Good job, Bob patted himself on the back. He couldn't wait until Beth and Seth discovered that their beloved son was missing. They deserved the hell they would surely go through. After all, they had betrayed him. Nobody betrayed the old Rob and got away with it. Beth should have known that before she took up with this loser. And had a son with him! Yes, they deserved to pay, especially after that sex scene in the hot tub at Kettle Falls. What Bob had been able to see, through the fog and steam arising from the hot tub, sickened him and made his blood boil. Yes, he must get rid of Seth. It was the least he could do to avenge what the bastard had done to his wife. "My wife!" Bob shouted into the waves.

Now, all he had to do was arrange a private meeting during which he would return the kid in exchange for Beth. Tricky, but he could do it. He could and would do anything if it meant Beth would be his once again.

For now, he was stuck with the kid. A kid who was the product of his wife's infidelity. Exactly what was he going to tell the kid when he woke up? At least they'd be far enough away from civilization, in a foreign country with no way to escape.

The sun was just beginning to creep up across the horizon as they entered Canadian waters, heading towards the Rat River where they would begin their journey upstream and into the Seine River, where their campsite was hidden in the woods. Bob was super vigilant now, keeping an eye out for Canadian patrol boats in the area. He had all the necessary permits and fake ID's for himself, but how would he explain the kid passed out in a sleeping bag in the back of the boat?

Chapter Seventeen

Rousing herself from a blissful night's sleep after the perfect anniversary celebration last night, Beth reached out for Seth, wanting to cuddle up in his arms and watch the sun peek through the window. But he wasn't there. That was strange.

"Seth? Honey?" she called out as the early morning light began to creep through the shadows.

No answer. That was strange. Where was he? Why was he up before dawn, especially on their special getaway weekend?

"Seth?"

No response once again. Maybe he was preparing a special breakfast for her as he liked to do on special occasions. Sometimes he served her a breakfast tray in bed, complete with a vase of wild flowers he'd picked. Throwing on her robe, she stumbled into the living area. He wasn't there. Where was he? No sign of breakfast. Not even the aroma of coffee filling the air.

"Seth?"

Finally, she heard his muffled voice coming from the porch outside. What in the world was he doing up so early and on the phone? Stumbling out onto the porch, she found him anxiously pacing back and forth, a frightened look upon his normally calm and serene face.

"Evelyn, please pick up now!" he was barking into his cell phone. "This is really important. I've left you several messages. This is important! Call me back right away. Please...." Shaking his head, he shoved his smart phone into his pocket and resumed angrily pacing back and forth across the porch.

"What in the world?" Beth touched his shoulder from behind, startling him. "What is going on?"

"I don't know." He shook his head back and forth. "She won't answer. Something's wrong. I know it."

"Honey, it's too early for them to be up. She probably left her cell phone on the charger downstairs. I'm sure everything is just fine. Come on back to bed." She rubbed his tense shoulders, but gazing into his eyes, she knew everything was not fine. She knew he had an uncanny sense about danger. And she saw fear lurking in his dark eyes.

"We'd better pack up and get the hell out of here. We need to get home ASAP."

"But—"

"But nothing. Something's wrong, really wrong," he barked at her, something he never did.

Backing away from him, she stood her ground gently. "That is not like you, Seth. What is going on? I need to know."

"I'm sorry, Beth." He rubbed his hand through his disheveled black hair, obviously frustrated with himself over his outburst. "Jason is in trouble, that's what's wrong. My grandmother came to me in a dream. I don't know what has happened, only that we need to get home right away. And damn it, Evelyn won't answer her phone." He pounded his fist on the porch railing just as his phone rang. Evelyn's ring. "Evelyn? Evelyn? Is everything okay? What? What's wrong?"

Standing close, Beth could hear uncontrollable sobbing coming from the other end of the line.

"What is it? You need to calm down enough to tell me what's wrong."

"He's...he's...gone. I've looked...everywhere."

Beth and Seth both froze for a moment, stunned, unable to respond.

"He's gone," Evelyn continued to sob.

"Maybe he's out exploring," Beth offered hopefully, trying to calm the situation down a bit, trying hard to believe that there must be a logical explanation for this. Inside she was trembling, terrified that something was indeed very wrong. Just like Seth had told her. The look on Seth's face told her that he wasn't buying her optimistic suggestion. He knew that Jason was not out exploring. The sun wasn't even up yet.

"Evelyn, you need to calm down and tell us exactly what happened." Seth forced himself to speak slowly, calmly, trying to conceal the fear that surged through his body.

"I...I got up to go to the bathroom and decided to look in on him. He was sleeping on the porch like he always likes to do. And...and he was gone. Not in his bed. His clothes and shoes were still there on the chair. He must have left in his pajamas."

"Did you look around, try to find him?"

"Oh yes. I took my flashlight and I've been all over the island. I've been to all his favorite places. The boat is still tied up at the dock. But he's gone." She began to sob once again. "I...I'm so sorry. I don't know how he got out or where he went. Or how he could get off the island without his boat. It's all my fault. I should have checked on him earlier. I should have done something. Anything—"

"Evelyn, it's not your fault," Beth interjected. "We will find him."

"We're on our way as soon as we can throw our things into the boat," Seth broke in. "Gotta go. We will see you soon. Call if you find him in the meantime."

"Oh, I will. I'll keep looking. I'm so sorry...."

"It's okay. We will find him," Beth tried to reassure both Evelyn and herself.

THE BOAT TRIP back to their island home seemed to take forever, despite the calm water and high speed they were traveling at. Beth's eyes filled with tears as she stared straight ahead into the rising sun, trying to believe that Jason was all right. He had to be out exploring somewhere. Maybe he'd fallen asleep in one of his favorite hiding spots. A new hideout that Evelyn had no clue about.

Seth reached out to hold her hand, to brush away her tears. He was obviously trying to maintain his composure. He was not about to share the full extent of his worries. That would only upset his wife even more than she already was.

"What's our plan?" she finally asked him, knowing his mind would already be reeling with their next steps once they hit shore.

"First, we search the island. Then...."

"...*if* we don't find him?" she completed his thought for him, emphasizing the "if."

"We will get the sheriff's department out there. We will find him, Beth, come hell or high water." His jaw was clenched with fierce determination.

Once they finally docked the boat on their island, they jumped out, leaving everything behind.

Evelyn was waiting, pacing slowly back and forth on the beach, tears in her eyes, shaking her head. "No luck. Still no luck," she whispered. "He's gone. He's just gone."

"Evelyn, you look exhausted." Beth gave her a hug. "Go on up to the cabin and stay there, in case he shows up. We'll start searching and stay in touch by phone."

The old woman reluctantly headed back up to the cabin, head hung low, crushed at the loss of the boy.

"Jason! Jason!" Seth and Beth each cried out, over and over again, as they separated and began searching every nook and cranny of their little island. Their cries echoed through the stillness of the early morning, alerting fishermen within range.

"Everything okay?" One local fisherman finally pulled up at their dock as Seth came down the path once again, retracing his steps. The old man said he hadn't seen anyone around since he got out on the lake just before sun up. He offered to cruise around the neighboring islands just in case the boy had somehow gotten off the island. Unlikely without a boat, but it wouldn't hurt. Seth had agreed.

Seth decided to boat over to Blueberry Island and search there, just in case. Jason loved to explore this island. Maybe, somehow, he was there. Maybe he'd fallen asleep. Maybe he was in the cabin, paging through some of Seth's old history books. He especially loved reading about the Indian culture and beliefs. Seth phoned Beth to let her know that she should stay there and continue searching while he checked out Blueberry Island.

Bleary eyed and numb, she continued to walk the familiar paths that Jason had walked. Nothing felt real. This had to be a dream. A nightmare. Jason couldn't really be gone.

Could he have possibly swam over to Blueberry Island? In the dark? That made no sense. No more sense than any of the other scenarios that flashed through her mind. She held at bay the really ugly possibilities, refusing to let them seep into her troubled consciousness. He had to be okay. *Please let him be okay,* she prayed to God. *Please bring my boy back home.*

But the hours droned on endlessly with no sign of Jason. Seth finally returned, shaking his head. "Nothing. He's not there," was all he could say. Pulling Beth into his arms, his own tears finally began to fall, mingling with hers as they held each other close. It was time to bring in the sheriff's department.

Chapter Eighteen

Two boats and four armed deputies soon docked at the island, sober looks on their faces as they expressed their condolences at the disappearance of the boy. While several began immediately searching the premises, the sheriff and one of his deputies escorted the family back into the cabin. Seated in Nana's old rocking chair in the front room by the fireplace, he began asking them all questions, including a trembling Evelyn.

Did Jason have access to another boat, or any way he could have gotten off the island? Any recent signs of bear or coyotes on the island? Was he a good swimmer? Was he unhappy or depressed? Any reason he'd want to leave home? Had he ever disappeared before? Had he ever dabbled in drugs? Who did he hang around with? Were they good kids, bad kids? Any problems the sheriff should know about?

"Jason is a good kid," Beth pointedly assured the sheriff, wiping her tears. "He was never in trouble. He has nice friends. He never would have left this island."

"That's what I thought." The sheriff attempted an assuring smile at the boy's distraught mother. "I need to ask these questions, just in case they trigger any information that we may not have already covered. I'm sorry. I know this is difficult."

Seth put his arm around his wife, holding her close, trying to comfort her as best he could.

While they were all being interviewed in the cabin, Beth could see the sheriff's deputy and chief investigator out there by the sleeping porch taking photos and looking for evidence. Treating it almost like a crime scene.

Has someone taken our boy? That was the lingering unspoken question that haunted both Beth and Seth. If he had not disappeared on his own, then someone had to have taken him. But who? And why? Stunned, in shock, they had no possible explanation to share with the sheriff.

Or could he have possibly drowned in the big lake, like Beth's mother had? That made no sense either. He was an excellent swimmer, and certainly would not have gone swimming in the middle of the night. Still...the sheriff was determined to do a search around the lake, just in case.

The darkness of a cloudy evening soon filtered through the cabin where they all sat waiting—waiting for something, for anything that could shed some light on the boy's disappearance.

"Sheriff," the investigating deputy suddenly appeared, poking his head through the door from the porch. "Need to talk with you privately."

The sheriff excused himself, leaving the family alone, facing their growing fears in the dark. Shadows seemed to drift through the room, haunting them as they waited. For what? Seth finally flicked on a light and began pacing back and forth before the cold fireplace.

Finally the sheriff and deputy returned, serious looks clouding their faces.

"I'm sorry to have to tell you this." Sheriff Olson cleared his throat. "But we do have reason to believe the boy was taken from his bed on the porch."

"That can't be," Evelyn wearily protested. "I would have heard him. He would not go with anyone without making plenty of noise. I would have heard him. I know I would have."

"That may be true, ma'am, but you all need to know that we found large boot prints outside the porch. We've made casts of them. We've wiped the place down for DNA and will be doing an analysis at the lab." The sheriff paused before continuing. "We did find a trace of what we believe is chloroform, a drug that can be used to temporarily render one unconscious."

"What? Oh my God," Beth cried out, as Seth reached for her hand once again. "So someone may have drugged him and taken him? Why?"

"That's what we *will* find out, I assure you. You also need to know that we followed the footprints through the woods and down to the hidden cove on the back side of the island. Only one set of footprints. There was an indentation on the beach that was probably made by a boat landing at the site. Whoever took your boy must have landed there during the night, made his way through the woods and up to the cabin, where he found him sleeping on the porch. No signs of a struggle of any kind. Your boy was probably passed out and carried to the boat."

"But why? Why in the hell would anyone take our Jason?" Seth demanded.

The sheriff sighed, shaking his head. Seating himself again in the big rocker directly across from the sofa where they sat, he leaned in towards them. "I need to know if you can think of anyone, anyone at all, who may have taken your boy."

They shook their heads in unison.

"Whoever did this may contact you offering to bring the boy home if you give him what he wants. Any idea what that could possibly be?"

"Money? We're not rich. What else could they want from us?" Beth replied.

"Men," the sheriff interrupted her, nodding at his deputies. "This is now an active crime scene. A missing person. Probable kidnapping. I want you out there ASAP to initiate a search party. Report back to me as you go. And bring in the dogs. Got that?"

"Yes, sir," the deputies replied in unison.

"First, we need some of the boy's clothing, something he's worn recently."

Beth managed to get up out of her chair and up the stairs to retrieve Jason's favorite pajamas—the blue flannel PJs decorated with planets and space ships. He'd worn them the night before they'd left for Kettle Falls. Holding them close to her cheek, eyes closed, she inhaled the scent of her missing son before handing them over to the deputies. They nodded and immediately left to begin their search.

Sheriff Olson turned his attention back to Beth and Seth, moving his chair closer and staring at them intently. "Now, I need you to think hard. Go back in time if you have to. Is there anyone, anyone at all, who may possibly have it in for any of you? Anyone who may want to harm you? Anyone who has caused problems for any of you in the past?"

Beth and Seth exchanged a guarded look, holding their breaths, as if they were debating whether or not to reveal a secret of some kind, a look that the sheriff recognized. One he'd seen many times before in his long career. People had secrets they didn't always wish to reveal. Sometimes they had no choice. Not if they wanted the situation resolved.

"All right," he began firmly. "If you want your boy back, I need your full cooperation. Withholding any possible motives for this abduction will not help. Believe me." Then he waited, glancing back and forth between Beth and Seth.

Seth finally began. "This probably has absolutely nothing to do with this situation. But...." He glanced at Beth for reassurance. "Beth's ex-husband harassed us, even tried to take her away from me once. But that was ten years ago."

"I'm sure he has moved on," Beth continued. "We've heard nothing from him in years." She began to relax a bit. There was no reason to delve further into other aspects of Rob's possible involvement in the boy's life long ago. Besides, Rob had already fled the country, according to Emily.

The sheriff pulled a notebook from his pocket and began making notes—Rob's name, birth date, previous address.

Beth even shared Emily's discovery that he had apparently absconded with money from his law firm and was wanted by the FBI.

The sheriff's eyes widened at that, making a note to follow up, just in case. He also wrote down Emily's contact information, indicating he planned to give her a call in Paris the next day.

Finally, Sheriff Olson called it a night. "I'm sorry you have to go through this. We will do everything possible to bring your boy home safely. I need to check on my men now and get this investigation going. I'll be in touch. And let me know if you think of anything, anything at all, that may help us find Jason."

He took a recent photo of Jason with him, one that he'd post on the law enforcement missing children's website and would also use for posters that would soon be all over Ranier, Kettle Falls, International Falls, even Ontario, Canada.

"We will do our very best to find him," he repeated himself, tipping his hat at them as he disappeared into the night.

Chapter Nineteen

Papa's old grandfather clock continued to tick, loudly, in the silence of the front room, marking time. Apparently unaware that time had pretty much stopped for Beth, Seth, and even for Evelyn, who continued to rock furiously in Nana's old chair, her knitting needles flying, as if trying to knit her way out of this surreal situation.

Finally realizing that none of them had bothered to eat all day, Beth retreated into the kitchen to make sandwiches for the three of them. Evelyn would stay. She was too distraught to go home and stay alone. Besides, nobody wanted to leave the island, just in case Jason came home.

Tears began to flow once again as Beth slathered mayo and mustard onto slices of bread before piling on a layer of Swiss cheese and roast beef. Somehow they had to keep themselves nourished, to keep their strength up so they could think straight and do whatever they could to bring Jason home.

After forcing down a few bites of her sandwich, she decided she'd better call Emily to let her know what happened, before the sheriff called her tomorrow inquiring about her father. As usual, it was the middle of the night in Paris when a sleepy Emily answered the phone.

She'd just finished nursing little Angelique, and was badly in need of some sleep.

Stunned, Emily listened in silence as her mother tried, in between her sobs, to relay what had happened. Seth also got on the line when Beth was too distraught to continue.

"Oh my God! This can't be for real! Who could have possibly taken him?" Emily wiped away her own tears before it hit her. "Oh my God," she repeated herself. "You don't think *she* could have done this? After all these years? After abandoning him? How could she have even found him?"

A chill slithered up and down Beth's spine. Emily's suggestion was totally absurd, right? At least highly unlikely...wasn't it? Still, was this something they needed to share with the sheriff? And if they did, what were the legal ramifications? What would happen to their little family once this long-held secret was revealed? A secret that even Jason had no knowledge of... one that could shatter his little world.

"Mom, are you there?"

"Yes, I just...I don't know. I just don't know."

"What do I tell the sheriff when he calls me?"

"He's calling you about your father, Emily, although from what you've told us, there seems to be little chance that he could be involved in this in any way, right?"

"Not if he's left the country like he told me. With the FBI searching for him, it wouldn't make sense for him to be hanging around. But...should I tell them about *her?* What do they need to know?"

"For now, I wouldn't say anything." A trembling Beth crumbled into Seth's arms. "Seth?"

He grabbed the phone from her. "Emily?"

"Seth, what am I supposed to do? We need to find Jason. We can't withhold any possible leads if it will help us find him. But...then what? What will happen? Seth?"

"Sorry, I'm trying to think this through. Maybe we do our own little investigation to try to find out where *she* is, what she's doing.

Maybe we can rule her out as a suspect without having to say anything to anybody."

"I can do that. I'm a pretty good cyber sleuth, you know." Emily tried to lighten the conversation with a touch of humor. "For some reason, I actually kept her contact information and a few old photos. I'll get on it right away."

"Thanks, Emily. Let us know anything you find out. We will find him, okay?

"Seth? Please put Mom back on for a minute and keep an eye on her. She sounds like she's not doing well…who would be?"

Beth took the phone. "I'm doing fine, Emily, under the circumstances. I don't want you to worry. Please. Just find any information you can. Take care of yourself and your darling little girl. We love you all."

"Love you, too, Mom, and Seth, and our dear Jason," Emily choked back her tears. "Mom, I think I need to get on the next plane."

"Absolutely not, Emily. What about the baby? You're nursing, and you can't take her on a long trans-Atlantic flight. Not at her age. She needs you there. We have things under control here. The sheriff's department has launched an investigation, out searching with their dogs. We will find him and bring him home soon."

"But—"

"No buts. Please. If things change and we need you, we will let you know."

"But this is my fault. I started it all. If I hadn't…. You know. I just want to help."

"It is not your fault! No way! You did the right thing, Em, and we all love you for it."

Chapter Twenty

"H*e's okay. Okay…okay….*"

These unspoken words echoed, over and over again, through Seth's dreams that night as he and Beth thrashed about in a fitful sleep, coming together through their tears, tearing themselves apart as they dealt with their own private fears, startling at the slightest noise. Was it Jason? Where was he?

Where were the words in his dreams coming from? And what did they mean? Was he really okay?

Down the hall, Evelyn's sobs could occasionally be heard. "It's all my fault," she wailed into the depths of the night.

Staring out their bedroom window, a wide-eyed Seth watched the first blush of a new day creep up over the horizon. Swirls of pink and gold cast their shadows over Rainy Lake, as if this was just another day. Jason would already be up, taking it all in, waiting to get out and explore the island. But Jason wasn't here…not anymore. Instead, search teams and their dogs were spread out, searching Rainy Lake, looking for their missing son.

Was it too early to call the sheriff for an update? Maybe he shouldn't bother him or disrupt him from the search. He had, after all, promised to call with any news. Waiting, however, was hell on earth.

What could he do? Pacing around the cabin, hour after hour, wasn't an option. He had to do something. Go someplace. Search some more.

Blueberry Island was calling his name as Seth crept out of bed, trying not to wake Beth. She had finally drifted off into a troubled sleep after tossing and turning most of the night. He tiptoed into the kitchen to make a pot of coffee, poured himself a cup, and settled down on the bed in the sleeping porch, gazing out into the forest that surrounded their little cabin.

He needed to get in touch with Nokomis as soon as possible. She may have the answer to their prayers. But why had she waited so long? Why had she not bothered to alert them so they may have prevented Jason's abduction? *Why, Nokomis?* He blurted out his frustration. *Why?*

"Seth?" A bleary-eyed Beth suddenly stumbled through the kitchen and into the sleeping porch, disrupting his thoughts. Pale, disheveled, with bags beneath her swollen red-rimmed eyes and wild hair, she looked like she'd been through hell, and had every reason to look that way, given what she was going through.

"I hope I didn't wake you." He pulled his obviously distraught wife into his arms.

"No news?"

"Not yet. I...I just need to get over to Blueberry Island. I need to find a way to communicate with Nokomis, to see if she can help us."

"Oh Seth, do you have to go? Shouldn't we be out looking for Jason? Waiting for him to come home?" She clung to him, tears filling her eyes.

"You need to stay here, Beth, in case anyone calls. In case Jason comes home. That's what the sheriff told us, you know. But I am being called to my island. Nokomis may have some insights for us. You know she has come through in the past...although I admit I am not happy that she didn't warn us about this in advance."

"If she knew. Maybe she didn't," Beth sighed. "Maybe she still doesn't."

"But it is worth trying, isn't it? Anything is worth trying to get our boy back home."

He gathered her up into his arms, holding her close, before trekking down the path to his boat that would take him across the lake to Blueberry Island. He hoped to find answers there to this dilemma. If only Nokomis had some answers, some guidance for them

He drove slowly around Nana's Island first, his eyes searching the shoreline for any hint of his son. Then he crossed the bay and circled Blueberry Island. No signs of Jason. He did see several patrol boats slowly cruising around neighboring islands, binoculars in hand. He could hear other members of the search party and their dogs stomping through the woods.

"Jason! Jason!" their voices echoed across the still lake.

It was time to pay Nokomis a visit, a respectful visit. It wasn't fair to blame her for Jason's disappearance, he realized. Still...if only she had warned them. But maybe she had, and for some reason, he had not picked up on it.

Looking back, he remembered that uneasy feeling emanating from her portrait several weeks before he and Beth went to Kettle Falls to celebrate their anniversary. Maybe they should not have gone. Maybe, if they'd been at home with Jason, this never would have happened.

In her defense, Nokomis had, after all, come to him at Kettle Falls, urging him to check up on Jason their first night there. He had, and all was well. Early the next morning, she'd slipped into his dreams to alert him that Jason was in danger and they must get home right away.

Too little, too late. He kicked several rocks out of his way as he hiked up the path to his artist's cabin. The old door creaked and groaned as usual when he entered. Flicking on the light, he stood gazing up at his grandmother's portrait on the wall. He felt nothing aside from his own lingering anger. Anger and frustration that was probably preventing her spirit from coming through to him, blocking any communication between his world and hers.

Maybe it was time to burn some sage and do a little smudging ceremony. That should help to cleanse the place from any negativity and drive out the evil spirits. It could also help him to calm down and get rid of his anger, opening himself up to the spirit world and any messages from Nokomis.

He retrieved the herbs from the jar in the cupboard and placed them in the smudge dish on the table near her portrait. He lit the herbs on fire. Closing his eyes, he inhaled deeply, and began gently fanning the smoke around the room, breathing slowly, deeply, in and out, in and out, letting go. A sense of peace finally began to seep through his soul, displacing his negative emotions. Finally, he was ready.

Opening his eyes, he focused his gaze on his grandmother's portrait, waiting to feel her presence, for her thoughts to drift into his mind, for her wisdom to make itself known.

"Boozhoo, dear Nokomis," he spoke softly. "I come to you for your help in finding my boy."

No response. He waited patiently, his eyes boring into his grandmother's eyes on the portrait he'd painted of her long ago. Timing was everything in the spirit world. He knew that. He must be patient. He must remain peaceful, breathing deeply, opening himself up to any messages that may come through.

Finally, a chill swept through the room. He sensed that she was there in spirit, listening, absorbing the pain he was trying to hide from her. A gentle breeze suddenly caressed his cheek, bringing tears to his eyes. Nokomis was there, caring about him, trying to help.

"Daga," he pleaded. "Please help me find Jason. What can I do?"

Her thoughts begin to infiltrate his mind. Wordlessly she informed him that Jason was, in fact, all right, and that she was watching over him.

Do not be afraid, my dear grandson, for all will end well.

"But, where is he? What has happened? What can I do?" Seth's words tumbled out. He needed more from her, something concrete. He needed to know where Jason was, with whom, how and when they would find him.

Know that Gitche Manitou, the Great Spirit, is also watching over him to be sure he is not harmed. Your boy has been called to fulfill an important mission, one he signed up for before he was born into this lifetime. He has something to accomplish before he returns to you. But he will return when the time is right. It will not be long.

"But he has been kidnapped, Nokomis!"

While that appears to be the case, there is more happening here than any of you realize. This is pre-destined.

"But I can't just sit and wait for him to come home when the time is right!"

Of course not. You will continue to search, to help put the pieces of this puzzle together. But you must trust that he will be found when the time is right. I believe the Ontario Provincial Police will assist in this search.

"Canada? Are you telling me he has been taken out of the country?"

I believe he will be found in a remote area of Canada, not all that far from here. He will be found once he accomplishes his mission.

"Where in Canada? I need to know." Seth began to plead with his grandmother as her presence began to fade away. "Don't leave me, not yet!"

I must go now, but you must keep the faith, dear Seth. Know that your boy will not be harmed. He is okay. I must leave you now to watch over him.

With that, Nokomis's presence floated away.

"Miigwech," he called after her, thanking her for her words, for being there for him. However, her words left him more perplexed than ever. Jason was on a pre-destined mission? Really? Still, he felt somewhat reassured that Jason was being watched over and would come home again. He must trust the words of his elders, especially that of his dear Nokomis.

For now, he at least had one piece of information to share with the sheriff's department. The boy may be in a remote part of Canada. How was he going to deliver this information to them without sounding like a crazy person? And wasn't Canada a country of millions of remote acres? Still, Nokomis had indicated he wasn't all that far from here. He prayed that she was right.

Chapter Twenty-One

"It's all my fault...all my fault." A distraught Evelyn rocked furiously in the old rocking chair where Nana had once spent so many hours rocking back and forth. Nana, Beth's deceased grandmother.

Evelyn had miraculously found her way into Beth's life and become a part of their family after Jake, Evelyn's husband of sorts, had died. Good old Jake, who was in fact Beth's father. That had been a well-kept secret for many years. Beth never knew the identity of her father until she was grown.

Shivering, Evelyn sighed, staring into the cold ashes of the massive stone fireplace. Cold—just like Jake. She rarely thought about him anymore, but today he was on her mind for some reason. Old memories began to flash through her mind. A few good ones. Some bad ones. He had betrayed her, after all.

Good old Jake had fallen helplessly in love with Beth's deceased mother, Sarah; soulmates, they'd called themselves. Evelyn had done her best to keep them apart, to make life as difficult for them as possible. It had taken many years, and the death of her husband, before Evelyn had made amends and actually became an important part of Beth and Seth's family. She doted on young Jason. She'd learned to forgive and to move on with her life. Until now. Now what?

She was grateful for having become a part of Beth's family. This was the only family she had left in this world. At least they had been like family...until she'd allowed Jason to be kidnapped. *They may not want to have anything to do with me anymore,* she lamented. *Not after what I've done to destroy their family.*

But maybe, maybe she could find a way to find Jason. Could Jake help them all out? After all, Jason was his grandson.

"Jake? Can you hear me? We need your help to find Jason!" she cried out into the stillness of the early morning light that was beginning to waft through the drafty old windows.

Clad in her flannel pajamas, hair uncombed, eyes puffy, sluggish after a sleepless night, she startled when someone emerged from the kitchen. She'd thought she was alone at this ungodly hour of the morning.

"EVELYN?" Beth stumbled into the great room. "What are you doing up so early? Talking to Jake? My father? What does he know about any of this?"

"That's what I'm trying to find out," Evelyn sighed.

"But he was *my* father!"

"So? He was also *my* husband, you may recall!" Evelyn glared at her as Beth threw a pillow onto the floor and began to retreat to the kitchen. "At least he was until your mother stole him away from me!"

"What the hell? This is not the time to bicker over the past, Evelyn. Jason is missing and we need to find him!"

"Of course." Evelyn's tears began to fall once again. "I'm sorry. I don't know what got into me—or into you, for that matter."

"We're all on edge, I guess." Beth shook her head.

"You know, it's all my—"

"Stop. Just stop! I do not want to hear you say it's all your fault ever again! It is *not* your fault, Evelyn. Let it go and help us find Jason.

Try to get in touch with Jake if you can. I'll also try. So...here's the plan."

Beth moved in, reluctantly giving Evelyn a hug. The old woman was not really at fault, and she was obviously suffering. None of them were at their best as they each struggled with their emotional reactions to Jason's abduction.

"Here's the plan," Beth repeated herself. "You are to stay here, answering the phone if the sheriff's department or anyone else calls. Or if Jason comes home. Seth and I have our cell phones with us. You need to call us immediately with any news, do you understand?"

"Got it." Evelyn perked up, relieved to learn that she still had a mission, a purpose, in all of this. "And where will you and Seth be?"

"He's already over on Blueberry Island," Beth sighed, her jaw tightening, "thinking he can find some answers there. As for me, I'm heading out to the gazebo and to explore the island, once again, just in case our boy is here somewhere. Just in case we missed any evidence."

"Good luck, Beth."

Beth trudged down the familiar path to the gazebo which was perched on a cliff overlooking the lake. Along the way, she stopped to inspect every nook and cranny for any clue, anything that could lead them to Jason. Where was he? Was he all right? Was he warm enough? Did he have food to eat? Dear God, where was he?

The sun was beginning to rise over the lake, penetrating a layer of fog, as she slunk down into her wicker rocking chair in the gazebo. She could see Blueberry Island across the bay. She knew Seth would be sitting in the cabin by his grandmother's portrait, concentrating hard, trying to connect with the old woman, trying to glean any information she had about Jason. While Seth's relationship with Nokomis was rather mysterious and difficult to understand, Beth had learned to trust it. It was an important part of the man she loved. Besides, there had been times in the past when Seth had gained some valuable insights from Nokomis, insights that seemed to flow through the veil that separated their worlds.

Sipping yesterday's strong black coffee from her travel mug, she began to pace around, unable to sit still. She had to be doing something. She wandered into the family graveyard that surrounded the gazebo, pausing to wipe the dew off the headstones of Nana, Papa, her mother Sarah, and her father Jake.

"Please help us find Jason," she pleaded, staring at her father's grave. She would never forget how Jake had been able to communicate with Sarah after she'd drowned in Rainy Lake. He would spend hours sitting on a rock, waiting for her presence to make itself known, sometimes in the form of a seagull that would perch on the rock beside him.

Maybe she should try to sit still and wait for one of them to come through to her. That was pretty much what Seth was doing over on his island. She finally settled down in the gazebo, closed her eyes, and waited. *Dear God, please bring Jason home. Please keep him safe.* She repeated her heartfelt prayer over and over again.

Waking with a start, realizing she'd fallen asleep on the job, she chastised herself. How could she fall asleep when Jason was missing? What was wrong with her?

She suddenly heard the sound of a motor boat approaching. Squinting into the sunlight, she saw the familiar logo of the sheriff's department on the side of the big boat. The sheriff waved as he passed the gazebo, heading for the boat landing on their island with no expression on his face. What did that mean? Good news? Bad news? No news?

Heart pounding, she began running down the trail to the dock, arriving just as the sheriff tied his boat up. Seth's boat came roaring up behind him. He'd obviously seen him approaching from Blueberry Island.

Seth jumped out of his boat and shook the sheriff's hand as he passed him on the dock. He then ran to Beth's side, putting his arm around her protectively. They anxiously searched the sheriff's expressionless face for answers.

"Any news?" Beth cried out, unable to stand the suspense.

"I'm sorry, folks." Sheriff Olson shook his head. "No sign of the boy yet. We've brought in the FBI, our dogs, and law enforcement officers from neighboring departments. Set up a command center, searching around the clock. Rainy Lake is huge, as you know. We have a lot of territory to cover."

"No sign...." Beth's tears began to flow as Seth held her close.

"Could he have been taken into Canada possibly?" Seth carefully brought up Nokomis's thoughts, trying not to disclose why he was suggesting this possibility.

"That's certainly possible," the sheriff nodded. "As you know, we're not far from Canadian waters. It would make sense for the kidnapper to try to get out of the country by boat. We are, in fact, already in contact with the OPP, Ontario Provincial Police. They have pictures of Jason, and a Rainy Lake map pinpointing your island and other possible locations. They are on it."

Seth sighed with relief. They were already on it. Thank, God. "But, the Canadian side of Rainy Lake is so remote, so isolated."

"Whoever has your son is most likely hiding out in a remote area. We are combing the brush. We will find him. Believe me, we will find him. You've obviously not had any contacts, phone calls, notes, any possible leads?"

"None," Beth and Seth replied in unison.

"Typically in cases like this, the kidnapper will try to contact you to get what he wants in exchange for the boy. Keep your phones on you at all times. Check your mail, your email, Facebook, whatever you use."

"Mail...we need to get into Ranier to get the mail," Seth reminded himself.

Once the sheriff left, trying to put an optimistic spin on this horrible situation, Seth decided to take the boat into Ranier to pick up the mail, just in case there was a letter. Unlikely. Jason had been gone less than two days. It felt like an eternity, however.

"No, you need to stay here with Evelyn," he told Beth firmly, before she could even ask the question. Of course, he was right, she realized. While he was gone, she'd get online to check email and Facebook for any possible clues or messages.

Seth soon returned from Ranier, grim-faced. Nothing. No mail. He had, however, seen all the missing child posters plastered around the little village, posters with Jason's beaming face. The villagers he ran into all expressed their concern, sent their love to the family, and assured him they were also searching for any sign of the boy.

Darkness soon descended upon the island—another lonely night without their beloved son. The three of them prayed together, then stared silently into the flames dancing in the fireplace, lost in their private thoughts.

Seth gently tried to relay some of Nokomis's messages, although he was still puzzled as to what it all meant. He stressed the parts about Jason being okay, that he would be found and come home again soon. That Nokomis and her people were watching over him. He didn't get into the part about Jason fulfilling a mission he'd signed up for before he was even born. That would upset his wife, probably Evelyn as well. Best not to go there, not yet anyway.

THE GRANDFATHER CLOCK chimed twelve times, then once, twice, as Beth and Seth lay side by side in bed, awake, staring into the dark. The wind howled outside as raindrops began to splatter against the window panes.

"Shit," Seth finally spoke. "That's all we need with Jason missing. Where is he? Is he warm and safe, or out in this weather?"

"My thoughts exactly. I can't sleep when we don't know where he is or if he is okay."

"I keep remembering what Nokomis said," he began carefully. "She says he is okay and will be home soon."

"But...but how does she know? What if she's wrong? How can a dead person, a spirit, do anything on earth? How can she possibly watch over him? How can she keep him safe?"

"I hear you, but there are things we will never really understand here on earth—not until we cross over someday."

She shook her head sadly. "I can almost see him out there in the rain, alone, or with some horrible person. He is wet and cold and hungry." She began to sob.

"Look, it doesn't help to expect the worst to happen. You need to have hope, to have faith. If we both expect him to come home safely, that might even help trigger a better outcome. The power of positive thinking." He stoked her back as she cried in his arms. "He will be okay," Seth tried to reassure her, trying to reassure himself as well.

"How can you be so sure? Just because Nokomis told you he would be fine? Is there more? Are you hiding something from me, Seth? We never hide anything from each other."

He hesitated.

"What is it? I need to know everything. Anything. We've never kept secrets from each other before."

"Just that our boy will be found soon. He may well be in Canada."

"What?"

"And...although this is still confusing to me, she thinks he may be on a mission, something he needs to accomplish while he's gone. I know it doesn't make a lot of sense."

"That's for sure." She tensed up, her body rigid.

"I don't want to upset you, honey. Maybe I shouldn't have told you."

"So you're trying to tell me that someone kidnapped our son so he could perform some kind of a mission?"

"I know...." He shook his head sadly, "I don't quite understand this either, despite knowing the beliefs of my people about visions and missions. Let's not talk about this anymore. I never should have brought it up. I'm sorry. I didn't mean to upset you."

"I'm sorry, too." She turned to face him, folding herself into his waiting arms. "Just hold me, Seth, and never let me go."

Chapter Twenty-Two

The kid was still knocked out in the back of the boat. He'd have no recollection of anything that had happened, according to the research about chloroform that Bob had done. That was good. He reached back to check his pulse now and then, to make sure he was still breathing.

Cautiously gazing around in all directions, he searched for any boats. All he needed was a patrol boat to stop him. Maybe he should move the kid into the fish box, just to be safe. For now, he decided to cover him with an old tarp.

He was getting closer, could even see the mouth of the Rat River ahead. That's where they'd get off the big lake and into safer territory as they made their way up river.

Before they got too close to shore, he took off his big boots and stuffed them into a heavy duty bag, along with the plastic gloves he'd worn. Then he weighted the bag down with a heavy concrete block and threw it overboard. The bag sunk down into the depths of Rainy Lake, where it would remain forever.

Putting on a pair of new boots, he congratulated himself on being one step ahead of them all. No possible evidence to link him to the crime scene. His plan could not fail. He'd thought of every possible angle, although the kid had managed to mess up his original plans. He'd had to improvise in the end.

He'd made his move almost a week earlier than planned. He'd been in a blind rage last night after the sickening scene he'd witnessed at Kettle Falls. *His wife* with another man!

Soon, the sheriff's department and their investigators would be crawling all over Beth's island, looking for any possible evidence. "Good luck!" he cried out as he began to laugh out loud. Hell, they were amateurs, rednecks, up here in the woods. Nothing like the investigators and private detectives he and his law firm had worked with back in Chicago. He'd learned one hell of a lot from those guys, things he was putting to good use now in his new life on the other side of the law. Who'd have ever thought the honorable Rob Calhoun would end up as a fugitive? It was all Beth's fault, of course.

He could almost see her sobbing, frantic, searching for her missing son. A twinge of guilt rippled through him, but was soon replaced with a sense of justice. She deserved this, didn't she? If she hadn't left him, her rightful husband, for another man, and had a child with him, none of this would have happened. She deserved to suffer the consequences for her betrayal.

Someday he would find it in his heart to forgive her—after she'd paid her dues and was living happily with him in his Canadian cottage. But...what to do with the kid? The plan was to exchange the kid for Beth. But would she blame him forever for taking her son away from her? Or would she finally understand that he was a bastard child, conceived with the help of the devil? The kid was probably just like his evil father, Seth. They belonged together.

Lost in thought, he was shocked to hear a loud noise overhead. They couldn't be on his tail already, could they?

What the hell? A small yellow float plane came into view, flying closer and closer, tipping its wings in greeting. Big Billy, the Minnow Man, flew in close enough for Bob to see his chubby face grinning at him through the pilot's window. He waved hello, then he was gone.

Bob couldn't believe it. How could that idiot keep showing up, wherever Bob happened to be? Could he be watching him? Still, he didn't act like anything was wrong. In fact, he had that stupid grin on his face as usual. It was uncanny, spooky, the way he was always there.

Billy and the others would soon hear about the missing kid. And although there was no evidence to connect Bob with the kidnapping, Big Billy would know that Bob was last seen on Rainy Lake heading towards the Rat River in Canada. He'd have no way of knowing, however, that they'd soon be heading up the Seine River towards Seine River Village.

People may start to wonder what happened to the fisherman named Bob Johnson, the one who had stayed at the Arrowhead Lodge and spent time drinking in the bar at Kettle Falls. They may wonder why he disappeared without a word, never bothered to check out of his cabin at The Arrowhead. In fact, his SUV was still there by the cabin. He was paid up for another month at least. People would think he was just out exploring the lake and doing some fishing—for now.

No sense in working himself up about it, he decided, as he maneuvered his boat into the entrance of the Rat River. It was shallow in these parts, with wild rice beds nestled along the wooded shoreline. He'd read that the local Indians would soon be harvesting the crop.

Massive trees spread out over the river, forming a canopy in some places that almost blocked out the early morning sun. The river twisted and turned to the melody of birds chirping. An eagle perched high in a tree, ready to dive into the river to retrieve his breakfast of fish. An otter playfully splashed not far from the boat. And the kid slept on, oblivious to anything that was happening.

As the river narrowed and became shallower, he slowed down and raised the motor. The last thing he needed was to hit a sunken log or abandoned beaver dam. He took a deep breath. Not a soul in sight, thank God. Even the yellow float plane had disappeared. Before long they entered the Seine River, headed toward the Seine River Village, a tiny community (population 271) that was a part of the Seine River First Nation Band of Ojibwe Reserve.

Yup, he'd found the perfect spot to hide out and set up his camp in the woods, not all that far from the Indian Reserve. Close enough so he could make his way up river to purchase a few supplies, liquor, and gas at the little general store there. He'd scoped the place out earlier in the summer before he decided to set up his camp here. Seemed safe enough, he'd decided. Just a bunch of ignorant Indians, right? Indians...like the bastard who had stolen his wife away from him.

Squinting into the rising sun, he had to carefully scope out the shoreline on his left to locate the boulder he'd placed along the shore to mark the entrance to his campsite. There it was. Just beyond the marker, he maneuvered the boat into a hidden alcove that could not be seen from the river. From there, he had cut a little path through the woods leading to his campsite. He had no idea whose property he was on, and he really didn't care. It most likely belonged to the Indians. But it was so remote, so far away from civilization, even from their little village, that nobody would know he was there.

After tying the boat up to a tree, he plopped himself back down in the boat, exhausted after no sleep all night. Maybe he'd shut his eyes for a few minutes, basking in the warmth of the sun that was now filtering through the trees. The kid should still be out for hours. Still, it probably wouldn't hurt to tie him up, just in case. He removed the tarp that covered him, tied his hands together with a piece of rope, and attached the rope to the handle of the fish box.

Waking with a start at the sound of crows cawing overhead, Bob was disoriented at first. Where the hell was he? Then he remembered. He'd done it! He'd made it this far with his hostage. Negotiations would begin soon.

But first, it was time to haul all his gear and supplies up the trail to the tent that he'd already set up in a small clearing he'd brushed out in the woods. Thankfully, he'd stocked it pretty well with sleeping bags, pads, a camp stove, a portable heater—everything they'd need until he could negotiate the exchange for Beth. Soon the two of them would be on their way to their honeymoon cabin in Nestor Falls. A second honeymoon, he grinned to himself, fantasizing about finally being with her once again. So close...yet so far.

But first there was work to do. He trudged back and forth, up and down the trail, carrying gear, food, supplies, and a duffel bag that contained well-worn maps and his secret journal, detailing his plans to execute the most important mission of his lifetime.

Behind his campsite, he'd cut another trail leading to a small clearing where he'd hidden the old trusty, rusty pick-up truck he'd purchased with cash from a local in a nearby village. Once he had Beth here with him, they'd load all their gear into the truck and brush out another short trail that would take them directly onto Canadian Highway 11. From there, they'd be on their way to their new life in Canada.

Once he had Beth here.... He sighed. He could hardly wait.

For now, he made one last trip down to the boat. He untied the unconscious kid's hands, scooped him up into his arms, and stumbled up the path to the campsite. There he shoved him into one of the sleeping bags he'd set up in the tent.

The kid was still out, and had never moved. That was good. As he watched him, he couldn't help thinking about how easy it would be to get rid of him. After all, this bastard child should never have been born. Bob could feel the anger rising from the pit of his stomach. It was all he could do to restrain himself from hurting the kid. He walked out of the tent and began angrily pacing around the campsite.

He hadn't quite decided exactly what he was going to tell him when he woke up. He'd rehearsed a number of scenarios and conversations in his head, but wasn't sure which one he'd use. He only knew he had to treat him like a human being. If he couldn't bring himself to do that, the kid might try to escape. Where would he be if his hostage disappeared?

He really didn't like the idea of having to keep the kid tied up, but he may have no choice if he tried to escape. He would have to keep a close eye on him. Who knew how he was going to react when he woke up in a tent in the middle of nowhere with a stranger?

Chapter Twenty-Three

"Mom? Dad?"

Screams of utter terror erupted from the tent, startling Bob as he sat outside on a tree stump beside the campfire. Night was setting in, and an early fall chill was in the air as a full moon rose slowly over the distant lake. A pot of stew simmered in a cast iron kettle propped up over the fire.

Stuffing his flask of whiskey back into his jacket pocket, Bob rose and stoked the fire, bracing himself, reminding himself he had to remain calm. He had to be nice, regardless of his feelings.

Jason stumbled out of the tent, still a little woozy. His eyes darted around frantically, trying to figure out where he was and what was happening. He stopped dead in his tracks when he caught sight of a large bearded man standing beside a campfire.

"Mom? Dad? Where's my mom and dad? Where am I? Who are you?" The kid shrieked, darting one way, then another, as if trying to decide if he should run, and if so, where to? This wasn't the island he called home. Where was he?

Bob moved in slowly, trying to make sure he didn't scare the kid away. He forced a smile upon his face as he touched the boy's quivering shoulder. "It's okay, kid. You are safe. Your parents will be here soon." *Like hell they will.*

"But...but...who are you, and why am I here?" Jason backed away from the stranger.

"Your parents didn't tell you before they left?"

"Tell me what? Where are they? Who are you?"

Bob shook his head thoughtfully. "Hmm...maybe it's supposed to be a surprise for you. You know they're at Kettle Falls, right?"

"Yes."

"Well, they called me and asked me to pick you up and take you to meet them here. Wanted you to join them for a little camping trip after they'd celebrated their anniversary at the falls."

The kid continued to frown, perhaps softening just a bit at the thought that this guy at least knew where his parents were. He was still not about to trust anyone or anything out here in the woods, alone with a stranger. It looked like he was wondering if he should run or not.

"Who are you? I don't know you!"

"I'm Bob, an old friend of your folks. Been gone for a while. Just moved back to Rainy Lake and got back in touch with your mom and dad. We were good friends for many years—before you were even born."

"Bob...," the kid repeated. "Bob. So if that is true...." He straightened up, trying to act like a man, trying to be brave. "So if that is true, why didn't they tell me about you? Why would they ask someone I don't even know to pick me up? They wouldn't do that! I know they wouldn't!"

"It's okay, kid. I get it. You're upset because you've forgotten some things. You don't remember."

"I never forget. I remember everything!"

"Maybe, but not after you hit your head. I bet you don't even remember getting here, do you?"

"Well no. How did I get here? My head is just fine." He ran his hand over the back of his head. "I just have a headache. That's all."

A side effect of the chloroform, Bob recalled.

"A headache? Yes, that's to be expected after a fall like that. Sit down by the fire, kid. I'll get you some stew and tell you more. You know, you haven't eaten in a day. You've been unconscious. That's why you don't remember."

Starving, Jason approached the fire, keeping himself a safe distance from this guy called Bob, whoever he was. He watched as Bob ladled a big bowl of stew and handed it to him along with an old spoon. Unable to help himself, he began scarfing the food down. He even accepted and devoured a second bowl of stew, eating in silence as the stranger watched from his stool by the fire.

"So…." The kid finally put his spoon down and gazed at Bob, his eyes searching for answers.

"So, it's like this. I got a call from your mom, my old best friend. She missed you and wanted you to go camping with them. Isn't some old lady, what's her name, taking care of you?"

"Evelyn?"

"Of course, Evelyn. Well, your folks were worried that Evelyn wasn't up to taking care of you for much longer—and she sure couldn't take you by boat to the camping site they'd picked out. So they were wondering if I could bring you. They knew I was headed out this direction on a fishing trip anyway. I know these lakes and woods like the back of my hand."

"So you came and picked me up?" Jason frowned, not sure if he believed any of this or not.

"Well, yes, I came and met you. Evelyn packed a few things for you. You don't remember any of that?"

Jason shook his head.

"Of course not. Not after you took that fall and hit your head."

"What fall? I don't remember anything! How can I not remember—if you are telling me the truth?" With that, the kid backed farther away from the fire and the stranger, as if trying to decide if this guy could be trusted or not. None of this made any sense. Should he run? But, where? He had no idea where he was.

"It's okay, kid." Bob rose and moved closer to the trembling boy, forcing a warm smile upon his face.

"The name's Jason! And I'm not a kid!"

"Okay, Jason, you fell and hit your head on a big rock when we stopped at an island for lunch. We were already too far away from your island, or from Kettle Falls, to go back. I checked you out carefully, and although you were unconscious, I knew you were fine. You see, I am a doctor. I figured I'd just get us to the designated campsite, keep an eye out for any complications, and let you sleep it off. I wanted to be sure we were here when your folks arrived." Bob could almost see the conflicting emotions swirling through the kid's head. Smart kid. He waited for a response, then continued. "In all my years of practice, I've seen a number of cases like yours. It's not unusual that you don't even remember meeting me or our trip to get here. It will come back to you after a while."

"So, Doctor Bob," Jason finally spoke. "I need some proof. Where's the things Grandma packed for me?"

Shit. Too smart of a kid. Then he remembered the space exploration book that he'd found on the floor of the sleeping porch and thrown into his own duffle bag.

"Come on, I'll show you." He led the way back to the tent, where he found a flashlight, opened up his duffle bag, and retrieved the book that had piqued his own interest. One thing he had in common with this kid.

Jason hovered at the entrance to the tent as if he was not sure he should go in.

"Here you go, one of your favorite books, right? Your folks thought you'd like to read it on your camping trip. Evelyn gave it to me. You know, I've always been fascinated with space. Once thought I'd like to be an astronaut when I grew up."

"Really?" Jason beamed, finally beginning to almost warm up to this stranger. "That's what I'm going to be!" He grabbed the book from Bob's hands and held it close. Maybe things were going to be all right after all. "You decided to be a doctor instead? Why?"

"It was my calling in life after all. I decided I needed to help people, especially kids like you. Always loved children." *Bullshit…but whatever it takes, right?*

"Do you have any kids?"

Bob cleared his throat, watching the boy. Somehow the kid almost reminded him of himself when he was a young, curious, adventurous child. Yes, Bob had kids of his own—kids he barely knew, one of whom he had no idea where he was.

"Yes, a grown daughter…and a boy about your age, probably."

"So where is your boy?"

"With his mother. Haven't seen him for a while. Enough of that. Now we need to get you settled in here."

Taking charge, he changed the subject and began showing the boy around the place. He gave him the duffle bag he'd stuffed full of kid-size clothes, a pair of boots, even a warm winter jacket in case the weather turned. Then he showed him the makeshift outhouse in the woods—a hole in the ground covered with a tarp hung on four log poles. Piles of brush were stacked along three sides to provide shelter from the elements.

Later that evening, they sat outside by the fire. Jason read his book by flashlight while Bob took an occasional nip from his flask, writing in his journal and planning his next move. He'd survived round one. At least the kid hadn't tried to run.

"When will my mom and dad get here?" Jason finally broke the silence.

"Thought they'd be here by now," Bob lied. "But there could be some weather moving in that is delaying their arrival."

"Really? The sky here is clear, no wind. The moon is bright, and so are the stars. Should be a perfect night for travel."

"Yup, but I hear a storm may be moving in farther to the south where they are coming from. So let's call it a night, and maybe they will arrive and wake us during the night."

A wolf howled in the distance as the full moon shone through the trees. Something suddenly shimmered, rustling the leaves at the edge of the forest. Bob and Jason both heard it, glancing towards the sound.

Jason's eyes widened as he jumped up. "Wow, did you see that? Who is that?"

Bob couldn't see a thing. What if someone had already found

them? Was there really somebody out there in the woods, watching them? He fingered the pistol in his jacket pocket, hoping he wouldn't have to use it.

"Can't you see her?" Jason whispered, tiptoeing closer to the edge of the clearing.

"See who? I don't see anyone. Jason, don't get too close. Come back!"

"But...she's nice. She's here to help us. She won't hurt us."

"Who? What does she look like?" *Beth? Could it be Beth, looking for her son?*

"She's...an old Indian woman. But...." He paused, his eyes wide. "She...she just disappeared. She's gone."

There was no more movement in the forest, no shimmering light, no rustling trees. Whatever it was had mysteriously disappeared.

Smart kid, Bob mumbled to himself, *but what an imagination*. "It was probably just reflections of the moonlight through the trees."

"But I heard something...and I saw her."

"Time for bed." Bob yawned and led the kid back to the tent.

Later that night, the two of them lay side by side in the big tent, a row of duffle bags and supplies between them. Neither one spoke. Finally Jason whispered into the night, "Do you think my mom and dad will be here soon?" His voice was tinged with a note of sadness, of fear and loneliness.

"Probably not until tomorrow. Too dark and late for them to be out there on the lake. Best they take their time and arrive safely, eh?"

"I guess so," Jason sighed.

Bob remained awake, vigilant, for most of the night. He had to make sure the kid didn't sneak out and run away. That would ruin everything. Sipping his whiskey, he finally dozed off.

Chapter Twenty-Four

What the hell? Bob woke with a start, focusing his gaze on the kid's sleeping bag. It was empty. *Can't you do anything right?* His dad's familiar words echoed through his mind once again. Bounding out of his sleeping bag, he threw on his boots and jacket and bolted out of the tent. The sun was already high in the sky. How could he have slept this late? Where was the damn kid?

Heart banging in his chest, bleary-eyed from too much whiskey, he stumbled around, trying to be quiet so the kid wouldn't hear him. He'd need to sneak up on him, grab him, and haul him back where he belonged. But what if he was gone?

He noticed small footsteps near the fire pit, almost as if someone had been trying to restart last night's fire. A new log had been placed on the cold ashes. The footsteps headed down the trail towards the lake. Bob followed quietly until the lake was within view.

There, on the edge of the lake, the kid sat on a large rock skipping stones into the water. He apparently didn't hear Bob approaching until Bob bellowed, "What the hell do you think you are doing out here by yourself?"

Jason spun around, his mouth hanging open, a look of shock upon his face as he backed away towards the lake and away from this angry guy. "I...I just woke up and went out to explore this place—to wait for my mom and dad to get here."

Unable to control his anger, Bob grabbed the kid by the shoulders and shook him. "Don't you ever do that again, do you hear me?"

Tears filled Jason's eyes. "What did I do? What's wrong with exploring this island, or whatever this place is? I always do that at home. Besides, I need to look for Mom and Dad."

"You ask too many questions, kid." Bob took a deep breath, trying to settle down. Still, he needed to teach him a lesson. "I'll tell you why. I'll tell you why you will never again disappear on me like this. Do you hear me?"

Jason nodded, wiping the tears from his eyes, staring down at the ground.

"Look, I'm responsible for keeping you safe. That's my job. This is not a safe place for a kid to be out exploring on his own."

"Why not?"

"Because this place is known for bears, hungry bears. Wolves. This is the wilderness out here. There are also some bad people, even wild Indians, that don't like people like us."

"Wild Indians? But I like Indians. My dad is mostly Indian, and one of the best men ever. And that makes me part Indian. Someday I'm going on a vision quest like a real Indian. Do you know what a vision quest is?"

Bob took a deep breath. *Seth? One of the best men ever? Bullshit!* He restrained himself from replying to that comment, shaking his head. Did the kid ever quit asking questions?

"Do you promise not to ever again disappear on me, Jason?"

"Yes, sir."

"All right then. Sorry I yelled at you. I just don't want anything to happen to you. Now, let's get back to the campsite and make ourselves some breakfast."

Jason followed Bob back to the campsite, shuffling his feet, staring down at the ground with a worried frown on his face. "Doctor Bob? When will my mom and dad get here?"

"Soon, I'm sure. Doesn't help to keep asking. Won't make them get here any faster, you know."

Bob had the kid haul a few logs and sticks to the fire pit. He lit the fire and hung a coffee pot over it, desperately in need of coffee to clear his hangover. Then he boiled oatmeal, throwing in a handful of trail mix.

Relieved that the kid had not escaped after all, he decided on a project they would tackle today. They would build a fence made of cans hanging on a rope around the campsite. That would alert him if Jason tried to escape again—or if any unwelcome guests showed up.

As they ate their breakfast by the fire, he told Jason about the plan.

"Why do we need a fence made of cans?"

"To keep the bears out. This way we will hear them if they try to get in."

"Oh…okay. Where will we get enough cans to do that?"

Good question. The only answer was to hike down the nearby road towards the Indian village. There was a little general store there that also served as a smoke shop, liquor store, and post office, with a big dumpster in the back. They would retrieve all the beer cans that Bob had noticed when he was scoping the place out last week. Besides, he had to mail a very important letter today.

After breakfast, Bob put on a pair of plastic gloves and retrieved a piece of paper and envelope from his duffle bag. "I have to write an important letter before we go get the cans," he told the curious boy.

"Why are you wearing gloves to write a letter?"

"Because. Just because. Do you have to ask so many questions?"

Jason retreated back into the tent to retrieve his space exploration book. Seating himself on a log across from Bob, he kept glancing around as if looking for any sign of his parents, then glancing back at Bob.

"Why do you keep looking at me?" Bob scowled, putting his pen down.

The kid shrugged his shoulders. "Why are your hands shaking? Is it from drinking too much whiskey? Why do people drink?"

He'd hit the nail on the head, but Bob was not about to admit that.

The shaking would stop soon. It always did. He just glared at the boy and continued writing his letter, trying hard to steady his hand. He printed in large bold letters, unlike his usual handwriting.

With the letter tucked into his jacket pocket, Bob grabbed several large garbage bags. "Let's go," he nodded at the kid. The two of them hiked down the winding dirt road towards the tiny Indian village. Bob glanced around often, worried that someone could come by and think it strange to see him with a kid in tow. Several of the Indians had seen him before, by himself. He'd bought liquor at the store. But how to explain the kid?

"It's best not to talk to any Indians we meet," he cautioned the boy. "I'll do any talking we need to do. Got that?" His tone was firm.

"Yes, sir."

As they approached the village, they saw a few tiny clapboard homes scattered along the wooded trails that served as streets. Not many people were around—more dogs than people.

Finally they arrived at the ramshackle building that served as a store and post office. They walked up onto the sagging porch, dodging several rotting boards about to give way beneath their feet. Bob pried open the torn screen door that was falling off its hinges and entered the store. As he approached the mail slot in the corner, he took a deep breath before dropping his letter in the mail. Only then did he take off his plastic gloves and discard them in an overflowing garbage can.

The boy opened his mouth, ready to ask another question. After noticing Bob's piercing gaze, he shut his mouth again.

A stern-faced Indian man approached them, nodding at Bob as if he recognized him. "Welcome. What do you need today?"

"Nothing today, but we do need some empty cans for a project at my place. Can we check out the dumpster?"

The elderly man looked puzzled. "Why, yes. Take all you want. Saves us from hauling them away." Gazing at the boy, he asked, "Your son?"

"No, just the son of a good friend, waiting for his parents to come pick him up."

With that, Bob and Jason headed out to the dumpster. Standing on a pile of logs and old blocks, they reached in and began retrieving cans —mostly beer cans—and stuffed them into their garbage bags. It didn't take long to fill the bags. Soon they were headed back to the campsite.

Bob breathed a sigh of relief when they were safely back to the campsite. No incidents. Nobody should have any suspicions about either one of them. The village was so remote and out of touch with the rest of the world that nobody would have a clue as to who they were. Nobody cared. They minded their own business.

Bob got out his chain saw and cut up a few small trees to use as fence poles, installed the poles around the perimeter of the site, then strung a rope between the poles. He called the boy over to start tying the cans along the fence line. Then he settled down by the fire pit with his journal. He had a lot of thinking and planning and tweaking of his plans to do.

He watched the boy hard at work on the fence project. At least it would keep him busy and out of his hair. The kid was a pain in the ass —always there, always asking questions. Didn't seem to be a bad kid, but he had sure as hell screwed up his plans. It would have been so much easier to simply do away with Seth and rescue Beth.

Rendezvous with death. The familiar words that had haunted him for so long crept back into his mind as he stoked the fire. *Rendezvous with death…with Seth…with death.* Something was telling him that Seth must be eliminated. He deserved to die—his sentence for what he'd done to Beth and for stealing her away from her rightful husband.

But if he knocked Seth off, what about the kid? Bob sure as hell didn't want a package deal—Beth, and the kid who was a product of her infidelity. Maybe the kid would have to fend for himself, or someone would adopt him. Maybe it didn't matter. It sure as hell wasn't his responsibility.

Every time he looked at the kid, he was filled with rage and disgust. All he could think about was Beth having sex with another man. Images of her in the hot tub at Kettle Falls cycled through his mind over and over again. He felt like he was going to throw up, just thinking about the sickening scene he had witnessed from a distance.

Seth's slimy hands crawling all over her body. The way she touched him, leaned in to him. The sound of their moans and groans echoing across the lake.

If it hadn't been for the fog moving in and obscuring his vision that night, he would have fired the gun, killing Seth. Then he could have rescued Beth and taken off for Canada. Maybe kidnapping the kid hadn't been the smartest move. Maybe. Maybe not. It was what it was, and he'd have to deal with it.

Focus, damn it, he chastised himself. He had to quit thinking about what Beth had done and his plans to kill Seth. First, he had to plan his next moves. The letter was in the mail, on its way to his contact in California who would re-mail it to Ranier, Minnesota, no questions asked.

By the time Beth got the letter, Kettle Falls would be closed for the season. The place would be empty—perfect for their rendezvous.

Jason interrupted his thoughts as he came back to warm up by the fire. Fall was moving in entirely too fast. The leaves were beginning to turn into vibrant shades of gold and red. Hopefully, the weather would hold until their meeting at Kettle Falls.

"I'm done," Jason proudly informed him, "and I'm hungry."

"Good. Good job," Bob forced himself to say. Maybe he'd been a little tough on the kid today. He didn't want to scare him away, that was for sure. "Here." He retrieved a loaf of bread and a jar of peanut butter from the cooler. The boy dived in, making himself two sandwiches.

"Don't you think my mom and dad should be here by now? Could they be lost? Should we look for them?"

Bob pulled a smart phone from his pocket, pretending to check his messages although he was well aware that he had no reception in this remote area. He'd already tried from multiple places, even the Indian village. Nothing.

"Hmmm.... So that's the problem...that's why they aren't here yet."

"Why? What happened?" Jason's eyes grew huge.

"Well, there is a big storm moving in. Severe wind, huge waves, for almost a week. They are stranded at Kettle Falls. Not safe to venture out on the big lake."

Jason's shoulders slumped. He looked like he might cry. "So we have to wait here for a whole week?"

"I'm afraid so. We have no choice. It's not safe for us to try to get to Kettle Falls either."

THE DAYS PASSED, slowly, mostly in silence. Even Jason quit asking his endless questions as he dragged himself around, keeping an eye out for the big storm that never came. He huddled by the fire or snuggled in his sleeping bag to keep warm. Now and then, he thought he saw the old Indian woman watching him from afar. Somehow, he felt comforted when he saw her. She only stayed a few minutes each time before disappearing into thin air.

Chapter Twenty-Five

Beth bolted out of bed the moment the phone rang early one morning. Maybe it was the sheriff. Maybe they'd found Jason. *Dear God, please let it be good news,* she prayed silently.

"Hello? Yes, this is Beth. What? A letter for me?"

Seth rushed into the room, leaning into the phone beside her so he could hear the conversation.

"It's the post office." She mouthed the words to him before turning back to the phone in her hand, listening intently to the postmaster on the other end of the line. "No return address, you say? What's the postmark?"

A puzzled look spread across her face when she learned it had been mailed in California. That was strange. Still, they needed to check this out right away, just in case it had anything at all to do with Jason's disappearance.

"We will be right there. Thanks so much for letting us know."

Seth threw his clothes on, grabbed a jacket, and was almost out the door when she called him back. "Wait, I need to go with you. I can't stand waiting here by myself, Seth. Just give me five minutes."

He shook his head in frustration, but decided it wasn't worth an argument. They'd had far too many of those recently. Endless days of worry about their son was taking its toll on both of them.

Seth fired up the boat and the two of them were soon off, headed for the post office in Ranier. Neither one spoke. They were each lost in their private worlds of fear and anxiety as various good and bad scenarios played through their minds. The sheriff had told them it was very possible the kidnapper may contact them in some way. Maybe this was it. Maybe not.

Hiking up the road from the boat dock to the post office, they met a number of their neighbors who all inquired about the boy and expressed their hope that he'd be back home very soon. Posters with Jason's smiling face were still plastered throughout the little village. The whole world had become surreal, like a bad movie that never ended.

Finally they retrieved the letter. The handwriting on the letter almost looked like a child had scrawled Beth's name and address in big block letters. Beth clutched it to her chest as they walked back down the street to their Ranier cottage.

Once inside they sat side by side on the sofa as Beth carefully opened the letter, holding her breath. Seth put his arm around his trembling wife as they leaned in together to read the short note:

I've found your son, Jason, and am taking good care of him. He is fine. Do not worry. I will bring him to you next Thursday, 1 p.m, at the Kettle Falls Rainy Lake landing. It is important that you and Seth come alone, for reasons I cannot disclose. I am serious. If you bring in the cops or anyone else, I will be forced to take the boy with me. No cops! If you want your son back, do as I say. Sincerely, The One Who Saved Your Boy

Beth's tears began to flow. Seth held her tight until she regained control of herself.

"He's fine...he's fine...." Beth repeated the words over and over again.

"We don't know that, Beth. All we know is that this guy says he found him and will bring him to us at Kettle Falls. But something is weird here. Why all the secrecy? Why no cops? We need to call the sheriff. He will know how to handle this." He reached for his phone.

"What?" Beth jumped off the sofa, a look of horror upon her face. "We need to do this by ourselves, Seth! Or…or…we may never see our son again! If this guy catches wind that anybody but us is there, what will he do?"

"Calm down. Please. This guy is up to something. Why else would he set this meeting up at Kettle Falls? The place is closed for the season, you know that. We'd be all by ourselves out there. Who knows what he might do if there's nobody there to protect us? He could be some kind of psychopath."

Beth paced back and forth through the living room, trying to clear her head. "He said he found him and is taking good care of him."

"Sure, that's what he said. You can't believe what he wrote in that letter, no matter how much you may want to believe it. Look, the sheriff needs this letter. We can't withhold evidence, Beth."

"Wait…just please wait. I need to think."

"There's no time to waste. Thursday is the day after tomorrow. We need to form a plan now." With that he picked up the phone to make the call. "Beth? Are you okay with this? We need to find our boy."

She nodded quietly. There were no easy answers, as much as she wished there were.

The sheriff arrived at their cottage within the hour.

"Thursday at 1 p.m." Sheriff Olson scratched his head after reading the note several times and putting it into a plastic evidence bag. "Okay, here's the plan. The two of you should arrive at the boat landing shortly before 1 p.m. There will be no sign whatsoever of me or my deputies. We will get dropped off there the day before, and will hide out in the old hotel until the guy arrives with your son. We will have security cameras hidden around the boat landing and other strategic places on the island so we can keep tabs on him. Once the guy shows up and you have Jason, we will move in."

Before he left, the sheriff tried to reassure Beth that everything would be fine. He had their backs, no matter what may happen. Maybe he was right, she thought to herself. Maybe Seth was right after all.

At least she and Seth had each other. Sometimes they disagreed and struggled these days, torn apart by the ordeal they were going through. But in the end they always came together, their love stronger than ever before.

Chapter Twenty-Six

"Where are my mom and dad? They've been gone forever." Jason poked a stick into the ground as he sat beside the fire across from Bob. "There's no bad weather here. How can it be so bad for so long over there when there's no storm here at all?"

"You don't know this lake, kid," Bob began. "But I think I have a plan, after checking out the weather. It is clear now almost all the way to Kettle Falls. Tomorrow we will leave and get as far as we can. We can camp out at an old cabin on one of the nearby islands, and spend the night there. And Thursday we should be able to get to Kettle Falls. Your folks will be there waiting for you about 1 o'clock."

Jason perked up, a smile spreading across his face, then a frown. "But what if my folks are heading this way and we miss them? They won't know we have gone to find them at Kettle Falls."

"No worries. I've already taken care of that. Got a message through to them this morning before you got up."

"I wish I had my phone so I could text them."

"Well, you will be seeing them real soon. Now, let's get the boat packed up so we can get an early start tomorrow morning. Maybe we will even do a little fishing around the islands."

"Really? I love to fish! I can't wait to get to Kettle Falls!"

Bob couldn't help smiling at the kid's enthusiasm. He'd been moping around for days, missing his parents. Strangely enough, it felt good to see him smile again.

That night, after Jason went to bed, Bob sat out by the fire thinking about Beth. He'd have her back soon, and he'd finally be rid of the kid. He had to admit, however, that the kid had somehow wormed his way into his heart, despite the circumstances of his birth. Bob realized that he might even miss him, just a little. What a crazy thought! Maybe it had something to do with the fact that he never had time to spend with his own daughter as she grew up. And he'd never known the baby son that his second wife disappeared with shortly after his birth. Maybe he'd missed out on something that was more important than his all-consuming career. Well, that was water under the bridge now. Gulping down a mug of whiskey, he stared into the dancing flames of the fire, trying to imagine what it would be like to see Beth, to finally make love to her again after so many years.

Tomorrow could be a little risky. He sure as hell hoped they wouldn't meet any boats, especially patrol boats, out on the lake. And hopefully not that crazy Minnow Man again. Otherwise, he felt he had things under control—as long as Beth had received the letter. She certainly should have gotten it by now. His plan was to move to Rabbit Island tomorrow, the day before the scheduled meeting, early enough to keep an eye out for any sheriff's boats trying to sneak in early.

THE NEXT MORNING they were on their way before the sun broke through the early morning fog. A chill was in the air as they navigated the winding river and headed out into Rainy Lake. Winter was coming, possibly sooner than Bob would have liked. The kid was full of anticipation, chattering about his parents, about fishing.

Thankfully, they never met another boat all the way to Rabbit Island. Most of the tourists were gone now. Kettle Falls was closed for the season. The year-round islanders were busy preparing for a long winter—cutting wood, putting up supplies, winterizing their cabins.

Bob parked the boat in the hidden cove on the back side of the island, his usual docking place. They trudged up the path to the lop-sided old shack, kicked the door open, and settled in with their supplies. Then they headed down to the other side of the island with their fishing gear. From this point, Bob could see any boats headed for Kettle Falls. While the kid fished, and actually caught a few nice fish, Bob got out his high-powered binoculars and scoped out the area.

"What are you looking at?" Jason finally asked.

"Just the birds. Sometimes you see white pelicans out here. Some-times a moose along the shoreline."

The coast was clear. No signs of any activity around Kettle Falls. Hopefully Beth and her bastard husband were taking his advice and coming alone tomorrow. Hopefully she wouldn't protest too much when he took her away. If she did, he had rope and duct tape in his duffel bag, along with his trusty bottle of chloroform. Even a few sleeping pills. He also had his loaded guns carefully concealed in the fish box, just in case Seth should try anything.

The lake was calm, the bright sunshine warming the day. They spent most of the day down by the lake. Jason was actually having fun, his eyes sparkling as he reeled in another fish. He devoured a few sandwiches that Bob had made them for lunch. As Bob watched him, his mind drifted back to his own screwed-up childhood. Would things have turned out differently if he'd had a home and family like Jason had? A home that Bob was about to destroy. Was that a twinge of guilt seeping through his veins? He shook his head. What the hell was happening to him? He had to stay focused. Beth belonged to him and he needed to bring her back. Nothing else mattered, right?

By late afternoon, Bob was feeling quite hopeful and confident that the cops weren't going to show up after all. If they had any brains, they'd have already settled in at Kettle Falls instead of waiting until Thursday. Still, he felt compelled to take a closer look, just in case.

"Hey Jason, let's take the boat out and do a little fishing across the lake. Sometimes those big ones really bite right before dark."

"Yes!" Jason cried as he gathered up his gear and followed Bob back up the trail, past the cabin, and down to the boat on the other side of the island.

Bob's plan was to get as close to Kettle Falls as possible, especially the remote areas where someone could try to land and hide their boats. He knew the place well, having scoped it out as he was planning his rescue operation.

They cruised slowly around Kettle Falls. No boats. No sign of any activity whatsoever—until Jason suddenly pointed towards a wooded area above the Rainy Lake boat landing. "What's that?"

Bob strained to see what the boy was pointing at—maybe another imaginary old Indian woman? Grabbing his binoculars, he zoomed in to find a man hanging something in a tree. A badge glittered in the receding sunlight.

Shit! The cops! The deputy had obviously seen them. While Bob was tempted to gun the boat and race away, he knew that would only make him look suspicious. Besides, if one cop was there, there were probably more crawling all over the place. Damn her, how could she defy his orders to come alone? Well, she'd pay for this!

Trying to act casual, he slowly steered the boat away towards the opposite shore. There they stopped and cast a few lines into the lake. If they were being watched, there was no crime in fishing, right?

Five minutes later, he told Jason to reel in his line. They would try another fishing hole farther down the lake.

"But why? We've only been here a few minutes."

"Because I said so. That's why."

"Isn't that Kettle Falls where we saw the guy in the woods? Aren't my mom and dad supposed to be there?"

"Not until tomorrow as long as their plans don't change."

"Why would their plans change?"

Exasperated, Bob sighed. "How would I know? Let me check my phone for any messages, to be sure they are on schedule." He retrieved the phone from his pocket, pretending to pull up his messages.

"Oh no. It's Evelyn."

"What about Evelyn?"

"She's in the hospital in International Falls. In bad shape. Not sure she's going to make it. Your mom and dad are there with her. They send you their love...." Bob almost choked on the words he felt he had to say to try to reassure the kid.

"So...so what are we supposed to do? Can you take me to the hospital?"

The kid was too smart for his own good. Bob struggled to come up with an answer that would satisfy him. He glanced back down at his phone as if reading more messages. "Your mom says Evelyn is in the ICU and no kids are allowed. So...okay...she wants me to take you back to our campsite for now."

"What?" Tears formed in Jason's eyes. He turned away, wiping his eyes, hanging his head.

A strange feeling surged through Bob's gut, compelling him to reach over and give the boy a hug. What the hell? What was he doing to this poor innocent kid who had never asked to be born? What kind of a bastard was he? Beth's words from long ago rang in his ears. *"You are just like your father, Rob! It's always all about you!"*

"It's going to be okay, Jason. I bet Evelyn will recover soon. Then your mom and dad will meet us at the campsite and take you back home."

"I miss them, Doctor Bob," Jason trembled, finally giving way to his tears as Bob held him close.

Doctor Bob. That's what the kid called him, an undeserved sign of respect for the phony doctor who had abducted him. As he held the crying boy in his arms, he kept an eye out towards Kettle Falls. No boats. No sign of anyone watching them. That was good. But they needed to get the hell out of there as soon as possible.

Stopping at Rabbit Island to pick up their gear, they put on their winter jackets and ventured out across the lake in the dark. Jason was quiet at first, but finally began to come around as he gazed up at the black sky filled with brilliant stars. He pointed out various constellations and talked a little about Mars, one of his favorite subjects.

Bob listened, almost beginning to enjoy the boy's company.

Almost. Somehow the kid seemed to have a peaceful, calming presence about him. Bob actually found himself relaxing a bit, despite the fact that his Plan B was now shot to hell and he needed to come up with another plan. What he really needed after today's foiled adventure was a good stiff drink.

Finally they arrived back at the campsite, turned on their flashlights, and began hauling their gear up the wooded trail and back to the tent. They hadn't even had dinner yet.

"I can make the fire," Jason volunteered as he began gathering small twigs, dry leaves, and pine needles and assembling them into a tinder bundle that he placed in the center of the fire ring. He stuck a long piece of kindling into the ground above the tinder and began building a tent of kindling.

Bob watched in amazement as the boy lit the fire and it immediately flared into action, burning brightly, as Jason added a few logs. "How did you learn to make a fire like that?"

"My dad taught me."

Before long they were warming themselves by the fire while Bob fried up the fish Jason had caught earlier that day. He boiled water and made the kid a cup of hot chocolate before pouring himself a big glass of whiskey. Ahhh...he really needed that tonight. His last bottle of whiskey. They'd have to hike into the village tomorrow to replenish his supply.

"Why do you drink so much?" Jason finally broke the silence.

"What? What do you mean?"

"I'm just wondering why people drink alcohol. Does it make you happy?"

"Hmmm....maybe to forget," Bob confessed, already feeling pretty wasted after belting down a full glass of straight whiskey on an empty stomach. He was probably talking more than he should be. But he didn't really care anymore. Not about anything.

"Forget what?"

"Well, maybe to forget things that I don't like to think about."

"Like?"

"Like people I loved and who are now gone, disappeared from my life."

"Oh…like your kids? Is your wife dead?"

Bob almost choked on that one, and took another swig of his drink before answering. "Yeah, I miss my kids—and my wife. She's not dead. In fact, I think she will be coming home with me again someday soon."

"So you live all by yourself? Don't you get lonely?"

"Not really. I'm too busy," he lied. Hell, he'd been lonely all his life, unable to really connect with anyone in a meaningful way. Not even Beth. Things would be different this time around.

"Well, I'm glad you are friends with my mom and dad. You are my friend, too, Doctor Bob. And I hope you come see us lots. You could come over for dinner. My mom is a really good cook."

Bob almost laughed out loud. Sure, he could almost see them all seated around a table having dinner together. Fat chance of that. His mind drifted back to the days when Beth cooked for him, not Seth. She made wonderful Italian spaghetti. He could still see her in that sexy black dress she wore the first night they'd made love in their Chicago penthouse suite. He'd walked in after work to the heavenly smell of homemade spaghetti sauce bubbling on the store. The table was set with fine china. Candles glowed in the darkened room as romantic music played in the background. It had been a night to remember.

"So, do you want to come over for dinner sometime?"

"Maybe. Does she still make good spaghetti?"

"Yeah, that's my favorite."

"Mine, too. Does she still love red roses?" What the hell made him say that? Old memories, of course. She'd loved it when he sent her a dozen red roses, something he'd done quite often, especially when he was feeling guilty about an affair or the way he was treating her.

"Why would you think she loved red roses?" A note of suspicion crept into the boy's voice.

"Your dad told me, I guess. Does he buy her roses?"

"Well, no. He always picks wildflowers for her. Lilacs are her favorite. Sometimes I pick flowers for her too. That makes her happy."

Bob brushed a tear from his eye. A real tear. Before he could stop himself, he blurted out, "Anyone would be proud to have you for a son, Jason." Where had that come from?

The kid beamed at him, tugging at his heart strings. "So what else do you try to forget?"

"Well, maybe things I've done that I shouldn't have done. Lies I've told. I think we all make mistakes in life and wish we'd done things differently. Haven't you ever done any bad things or gotten into trouble?" He turned the focus back to Jason.

Jason began to giggle. "Well, I sometimes get into trouble for running around exploring the island when my parents don't know where I am. And sometimes I catch critters and bring them into the house. One time my pet rat got loose and hid behind the refrigerator. Mom wasn't happy."

Bob chuckled to himself. "So, tell me about your parents. Are you all happy together?"

"I have the best mom and dad in the whole world," he boasted. "We do things together, like having campfires like this one at night. My dad tells us stories. I want to be just like him when I grow up."

That hurt, but Bob needed to know more. "So how about your mom? Is she happy? Is your dad good to her?"

"Yeah, she says she's happier than she has ever been since she moved back home to Rainy Lake. She and my dad are always doing yucky things like kissing and holding hands. I'm never going to kiss a girl!"

Ouch! "You may change your mind someday, Jason."

Once the soup was ready, they quit talking and began slurping the soup until it was all gone.

"So," Jason finally resumed his questioning. "If you drink to forget, don't you remember what you were trying to forget when you quit drinking?"

"You probably have a good point there."

"Maybe...." Jason leaned in towards Bob, looking him directly in the eye. "Maybe you need to let go of the past, forgive others, and forgive yourself for anything you did wrong. Then you can move on with your life and you won't need to drink anymore."

Bob's eyes opened in amazement. What the hell? Where did this kid come up with these words of wisdom? He was just a young boy. "Where did you come up with that?"

"I don't know," Jason stammered, shaking his head as if he was thinking the same thing. "I don't know. The words just came out of my mouth somehow." He glanced off towards the woods and smiled. Doctor Bob didn't need to know that the old Indian woman was there, sending peaceful vibes their way, almost putting words into his mouth. He liked her. And he liked Bob.

That night Jason crawled into his sleeping bag and stared into the darkness, unable to sleep. The lonesome wail of a loon suddenly pierced the silence. "Doctor Bob?"

"Hmmm?"

"Did you know that loons have four different calls? This was a wail because the loon is probably trying to find a lost chick." A tear slid down his face.

"So they have other calls too?"

"Yes." Jason perked up, always anxious to share information. "There's the tremolo, or the laugh that they use to greet other loons. Then there's the yodel, a loud angry call that male loons make to keep other loons out of their territory."

Guess I'm a yodeler, Bob thought to himself. *Get out of my territory, Seth, damn you.*

"And sometimes they hoot back and forth just to stay in touch with each other."

"You are a wealth of information, young man," Bob grinned, a touch of warmth creeping into his voice.

All was quiet once more as Jason's thoughts turned once again to his mom and dad. Where were they? Shouldn't they be here by now?

Dear God, he mouthed the words silently, not wanting Doctor Bob to hear. *Dear God, please let my mom and dad come real soon. Please keep them safe. And God? About Doctor Bob. Please help him. He's a good man. I know he is. But he needs your help. He needs you to shine your light on him. Thank you. Amen.*

Chapter Twenty-Seven

Beth paced back and forth on the Kettle Falls dock, waiting for Jason to arrive, continually glancing at her watch. It was one o'clock. They should be here soon. Seth stood on the end of the dock with his binoculars, a loaded pistol in his pocket, just in case. Prohibited or not, this could be a matter of life and death.

The minutes crawled by slowly. No sign of a boat. No sign of anyone. The sheriff had alerted them earlier that they were in position, some holed up in the hotel, several hidden in the woods just above the landing. Beth and Seth were unable to detect any motion, any sign of the deputies. Thank God.

The minutes stretched into hours. No sign of Jason or anyone else. Beth's mind reeled with possibilities. Was the letter a hoax written by some sick person? Why would anyone do something like that, getting their hopes up and then cruelly destroying them?

Seth stood beside her. She felt his pain merging with her own.

"Oh Seth, what are we going to do?"

He shook his head helplessly. "It's been four hours. I think one of us needs to go up to the hotel and ask the sheriff what we should do. Do we wait? For how long?"

"You go. I need to stay here."

"Are you sure?"

"I'm fine. Well, not really. But I'm covered, you know. There are several deputies hiding in the woods up there."

He kissed her goodbye before hiking up the road. He nodded at the silent deputies hiding in the woods as he passed them, crossed the bridge, and arrived at the hotel.

Sheriff Olson was seated on the big leather chair in the lobby, his laptop open, when Seth arrived. Several deputies and a scroungy looking guy (undercover FBI, he soon learned) were stationed around the hotel monitoring the situation.

"How long do we wait, Sheriff? What is this, a hoax of some kind?"

The sheriff shook his head sadly. "I'm sorry, but I think we need to call it in another hour or so. I don't think anyone is coming. We need to pursue other leads."

"Other leads?"

"Fingerprints on the letter from California for one. FBI just got a match on the fingerprints on the envelope—a guy who did some time for drugs in Minnesota nine years ago. Also acquitted on manslaughter charges six years ago."

Seth collapsed on the sofa. "Oh my God. So a convict may have my son?"

"We don't know that. All we know is that someone mailed this letter from Laguna Beach, California. The FBI is looking for him as we speak. Strange thing is that there are no fingerprints at all on the letter itself. Strange, unless the letter writer was someone different, someone trying to conceal his fingerprints, maybe wearing gloves. Maybe the letter was simply re-mailed from California."

Seth shuddered. "If that's the case, the letter writer sounds like he's up to no good, right? Why would someone be careful not to leave their fingerprints on a letter, especially if he actually found my boy and was planning to bring him home to us?"

"I know. Good question. We will have answers, Seth. It may just take a little more time. You better get back to Beth. Tell her we will pull the plug in another hour."

"They're not coming, Beth." Seth pulled her into his arms when he returned to the dock. "The sheriff's department is moving out in an hour and following up on other leads."

The two of them clung together, their tears mingling, hearts broken.

"Jason, we love you," Beth whispered. "Please God, please bring him home to us."

Chapter Twenty-Eight

Jason couldn't sleep that night. He laid awake, tossing and turning, listening to Bob snoring up a storm. "Doctor Bob, are you awake?"

No response. He tried several more times. Finally he decided the coast was clear. He put on his jacket and grabbed his flashlight, along with the little duffle bag that Bob kept his papers and writing materials in. Then he quietly unzipped the tent and slipped out.

Missing his mom and dad, he decided he needed to write them a letter. Somehow he had a feeling that Bob would not like that, so he would do it tonight while Bob was passed out. Tomorrow when they went to the village store, he could sneak over to the mail slot and mail it. Bob would be too busy picking out his booze and the supplies they needed. Their food supply was getting low.

He settled himself on one of the logs by the fire pit. Only a few glowing embers remained. It was cold. His fingers were already getting numb. He needed to write fast.

Dear Mom and Dad,

I really miss you and can't wait for you to come and get me. I hope Grandma Evelyn is better. Our camp site is cool, not far from that little Indian village—

Sein River Village, or something like that. I like your friend, Doctor Bob. He loves space and planets too, even Mars. We went fishing today on the way to meet you at Kettle Falls. I felt bad that you couldn't come because of Grandma. But we are doing good. Miss you and see you soon. Love you, Jason

He hurriedly addressed an envelope, stamped the letter with a stamp he found in the duffle bag, stuffed the letter in his jacket pocket, and quickly tiptoed back into the tent. He replaced the duffle bag exactly where he'd found it. As he turned to zip the tent back up, he was amazed to see brilliant green sheets of light swirling across the sky.

"Doctor Bob, wake up. It's the Northern Lights!"

Bob bolted upright to find Jason standing beside him, dressed in his jacket. "What are you doing up?"

"It's the Northern Lights. Come quick!"

Bob threw on his warm clothes and followed the boy out of the tent. They stood together closely in the dark as shimmering curtains of green and red pulsated and danced across the sky.

"Wow! How cool is that?" Jason was so excited he could barely control himself. His enthusiasm was contagious.

Bob soon joined in oohing and aahing as a sense of peace washed over him. Just seeing a spectacle like this could change one's perspective on their place in the universe. Maybe we, and our problems, are not as significant as we think they are, not within the big picture of the cosmos.

Finally, the lights receded and darkness once again descended over their campsite.

"That was so cool!" Jason threw his arms around his new friend.

Bob hugged him back, struggling with feelings he had maybe never experienced before. What the hell was happening to him? What was this kid doing to him?

"My dad and my mom always give me a hug before I go to bed," Jason whispered softly, gazing up into Bob's eyes. Bob melted, pulling the boy into a bear hug, holding him close. Then they trudged back into their tent together.

The wind whistled around the tent as they lay side by side in their winter weight sleeping bags in the dark.

"Doctor Bob?"

"Hmmm?"

"Do you know what it means when the Northern Lights come out?"

"Well, I know that they come out when a solar flare penetrates the earth's magnetic shield and collides with atoms in our atmosphere."

"I know that," Jason sighed. "But do you know what some of the ancient people thought it meant?"

"Not sure I do. Do you?"

"Yup. They thought the northern lights were spirits who have died and are trying to communicate with their loved ones on earth."

"How do you know so much, Jason? You never cease to amaze me."

"My dad knows lots of things that he tells me about. Know what else? Some of the Indian tribes believe that the lights come out when Nanahbozho makes a huge fire in the sky. He's the one who created the earth, you know, like God. Know why he makes such beautiful fires?"

"I'm afraid I don't."

"Because he wants to remind people that he remembers them and is watching over them." With that, Jason yawned a big yawn and fell silent.

Bob lay in the dark, a smile upon his face. Something very strange seemed to be happening to him. That inner rage that had consumed him for so long seemed to be dissipating.

EARLY THE NEXT MORNING, Bob and Jason crawled out of their tent to begin their hike into the village. Snowflakes were beginning to fall lightly around them. Too early for this, Bob grumbled to himself.

"But it's beautiful, isn't it?" Jason stuck out his tongue to catch a snowflake.

While Bob gathered up a few supplies and several bottles of Jack Daniels, Jason wandered around the store, making sure he was not being watched. Then he deposited his letter in the mail slot, heaving a sigh of relief. His parents should be very happy to hear from him after all this time. They would be here soon. Maybe Doctor Bob could come over for dinner after they got back home. He probably didn't cook much all by himself, at least not the kind of meals that Jason's mother cooked for her family.

Chapter Twenty-Nine

"Doctor Bob?" Beth's hands trembled so badly she dropped the letter on the floor.

"Who the hell is Doctor Bob?" Seth retrieved the letter, reading it again, trying to make some sense of it all. "It is Jason's handwriting. There's no doubt about that."

"I know, and he sounds like he is fine, almost enjoying his time with whoever this Doctor Bob is. I don't get it."

"Unless Jason was coerced to write the letter. Still, he has given us some clues. Sein River Village."

"Unless Sein River Village is also a false lead." Beth slumped down onto the sofa, her head in her hands.

There was a loud knock on the door. Seth let Sheriff Olson in and immediately handed him the letter. The sheriff read it carefully several times before settling his large frame in the rocking chair by the fireplace.

"So your son could very well be with the guy who wrote the other letter. And if what your son says is true, they probably aren't far from Kettle Falls and—" The sheriff's phone rang, interrupting his words. "Sheriff Olson here. Yes! That's great news! Get on it right now. Contact Chief Kabatay at OPP. Thanks." A hopeful smile spread across the sheriff's face as he cleared his throat. "We're on it. Contacting the Canadian authorities right now to check out a Seine River Village in Ontario. It's a tiny village, part of the Seine River First Nations Rainy Lake band in Ontario."

Beth and Seth breathed a collective sigh of relief.

"Of course, there is no guarantee that this is accurate, that this is actually where your boy is, but it does look like a very promising lead. You know we're working with the FBI as well as Ontario Provincial Police, since this is becoming an international case."

"Of course," Seth replied. "How far away is this place?"

The sheriff consulted his phone, then announced, "Only about seventeen miles from Kettle Falls. So yes, this is a definite possibility. Gotta get on it. I'll stay in touch." He tipped his hat and was gone.

Beth and Seth sat together on the sofa holding hands, staring into the dying embers in the fireplace.

"Maybe Jason mailed the letter without Doctor Bob's knowledge?" Beth suggested.

"That's possible. I'm really confused about his reference to Evelyn being okay, as if he thinks she is not. He also says they are waiting for us to come and pick him up."

"I'm afraid someone is filling his head with lies, manipulating him. But at least hopefully he is okay and we will find him soon." She snuggled up against her husband, needing to feel his warmth, his comfort.

"I have a strong gut feeling that he is there, somewhere, and we will find him soon."

"Are you just saying that to make me feel better?"

"I'm saying that because I believe it is the absolute truth. Something, someone, is injecting these thoughts into my mind."

"Nokomis?"

"I believe so." He pulled her into his arms and held her close.

The next day, as Beth was making lunch and Seth was out chopping wood, the phone rang. She grabbed it, her heart in her throat, praying for good news.

"We're quite sure we've found him," Sheriff Olson proudly informed her.

Beth collapsed in a kitchen chair, overwhelmed with gratitude.

"The FBI is now taking over, in cooperation with OPP. They will need your help, you and Seth, to identify your son. FBI Agent Will Zolinsky will contact you soon to make arrangements to move in and bring your boy home."

"Seth," she screamed, flying out of the kitchen to the wood pile where he was furiously swinging an ax, taking his frustration out on the logs.

The moment he saw her face, he knew. Throwing his ax to the ground, he ran to her, scooping her into his arms.

"They think they've found him. He's coming home, Seth! He's coming home!"

Chapter Thirty

Bob awoke to excited shouts from Jason, forced himself to crawl out from the warmth of his sleeping bag into the cold tent. The temperature had obviously dropped last night. Frost lined the interior walls of the tent. The flap was already open and an excited Jason stood just outside the opening.

"Snow, Doctor Bob! It snowed last night. Look at all the snow!"

Poking his head out the door, Bob was engulfed within a winter wonderland—and at least six inches of fluffy white snow on the ground. *Way too early for this,* he frowned. This could really mess up his plans—the plans he was still struggling to formulate into anything that made sense.

As he zipped up his jacket, put on his boots, hat, and gloves, and stepped outside, a snowball whizzed past his head, splattering against the side of the tent. A grinning Jason quickly lobbed another snowball at him, slamming him in the chest.

Before he had time to think, Bob joined in, tossing a snowball at the boy who darted around in the snowbanks trying to avoid being hit. Bob threw another one, this time hitting him on the leg.

"This is fun! Catch me if you can!" Jason danced around as Bob chased him. Jason threw a handful of snow in his face and tackled Bob's legs. They tumbled down onto the ground laughing.

"I haven't had a snowball fight since I was a little kid," Bob laughed as he got up, brushing himself off.

"Fun, huh? But I am really hungry, and the fire pit is full of snow."

"We will need to shovel it out and get a fire going if we are going to stay warm out here." He grabbed a shovel that he'd stored outside the tent and began shoveling a path to the fire pit.

Once they got the fire going, they warmed up and cooked some oatmeal.

This is not good, Bob thought to himself. They couldn't stay out here in this kind of weather much longer. The river could begin to freeze over soon if the temperatures didn't rise considerably. Of course, he had his old truck stashed back in the woods and could get back on Highway 11 if they needed to. But where would they go? Plans A and B were exhausted. He needed a Plan C.

To be honest, his mind was beginning to reel with lingering doubts about his master plan to rescue Beth. Did she even need or want to be rescued, or was that just a figment of his own twisted imagination? If he took Beth away from Jason, what would that do to Jason? And if he took Beth and Jason away from Seth, how would Jason feel about that? He obviously loved both of his parents and had a happy home with them. Did Bob really want to destroy all of that?

It had not occurred to him before to wonder, or to care, about how the kid would feel. Did it matter? Maybe it did. Maybe he had been so blind and focused on his own desires and his need to control his ex-wife that he wasn't exactly thinking straight.

Somehow Jason had crept into his mind, into his heart, and changed him. Now he wasn't so sure what he should do. Shockingly enough, he felt like he actually wanted what was best for this young boy. He wanted him to have the childhood and loving home that he had never had.

So what should he do? Confused and surprised at his sudden change of heart, he began scribbling his thoughts and options in his journal. The more he wrote, the clearer it became to him. Jason belonged with Beth and Seth. That meant that he would need to give up his dream of a life with Beth. He could do that. He could forgive and move on, just like Jason had advised him. Strange. Stranger still that it took a ten-year old boy to get through to him and help him see the light.

Maybe he needed to take Jason back home. If the weather cleared up before freeze-up, he could take him by boat and drop him off at their island home. If not, he could risk taking him by truck, across the international border at Fort Frances to Ranier, where he could drop him off and have someone call Beth to let her know he was there. Hopefully the border agents wouldn't find Jason hidden in the back seat. He'd have to hide him since he had no authority to transport the child—no passport, no official authorization from the boy's parents.

He could do that, he sighed to himself. But would he ever see the boy again? Somehow the idea of Jason disappearing from his life really hurt. Jason was almost like the son he never had—maybe a replacement for the one who had disappeared years ago with his mother, Bob's foolish young second wife. He wondered what had happened to the two of them. Not that it really mattered. Jason was what mattered to him now.

The snow was beginning to fall once again as Bob closed his journal and stuffed it back into his duffle bag. He made them sandwiches for dinner, along with canned stew that they warmed in a kettle over the fire. Jason kept throwing logs on the fire and stoking it to generate some heat.

It was going to be a frigid night. Time to get out of there, Bob feared. Maybe they'd make their move tomorrow morning in the truck. First he'd need to fire up his chainsaw and cut a few small trees and brush blocking his truck from access to Highway 11. Maybe he'd better do that tonight yet, in case the weather was even worse in the morning.

"Where are we going?" Jason asked as he tagged along behind Bob and his chainsaw.

"Weather's moving in. Your folks may not be able to get here,

Jason. There's an old truck back in the woods that still runs. I think we will need to take that to get you back home."

"Really?" His eyes widened. "We can drive back home from here? Why couldn't Mom and Dad drive here then? I thought you needed to take a boat to get here."

Before Bob could try to come up with an answer, they arrived at the truck hidden in the brush and Jason continued with his questions.

"I never knew there was a truck here. Why do you need that chainsaw?"

Bob pulled the starter on the chainsaw several times before it roared to life, emitting a cloud of blue smoke. He began cutting brush. Jason automatically pitched in, picking up pieces and hauling them off to the side of the path. He was a hard worker. Once they'd cleared a bumpy path to the road, they headed back to the campsite and began hauling all non-essential supplies to the truck. Bob felt Jason's questioning eyes on him as they trudged through the falling snow in silence.

Finally they were done, ready to crawl into their sleeping bags to try to stay warm. Bob decided they'd make some hot rocks to tuck into their sleeping bags. He'd heard about it in one the survivalist magazines he'd read before this adventure.

Jason found several large rocks that they heated over the campfire, turning them with a stick. Then they pulled a pair of heavy socks over their hands, reaching their fingers down to the toes, grabbed the rocks, turned the socks inside out, and wrapped them. They carried the hot rocks back into the tent and placed them in their sleeping bags.

"Time for a good night hug?" Bob tried to force a brave smile as he reached his arms out to the boy.

Jason immediately gave him a big hug, then looked up into his eyes. "Why are you sad, Doctor Bob?"

Bob brushed a tear from his cheek and hugged the boy one more time. "I'll miss you, my little friend. You've made a big difference in my life, and I'll never forget you."

"But we will still see each other, right?"

"I hope so. Now for a good night's sleep before you go home to your mom and dad tomorrow."

They climbed into their sleeping bags, warmed by the hot rocks as the wind began to howl outside.

"Good night, Doctor Bob. I love you."

"I love you too, Jason," Bob whispered.

Chapter Thirty-One

Bob lay awake in the dark, listening to the boy's soft breathing. This was not the outcome he'd envisioned and carefully planned over the last years. But then, he sure as hell was not the same man he'd been back then. He wasn't sure how, or what, had happened. Had someone put a curse on him? His inner rage was gone. Hell, his nightmares had even disappeared. The chilling words that had haunted him in his sleep, *"Rendezvous with death. Seth,"* were also gone. Somehow the time he'd spent with Jason had changed his entire perspective on life. For once, he actually cared about something or someone more than himself and his own greedy desires.

Now that he'd made his decision, he needed to figure out how he could safely return the boy, border crossing and all, without getting caught himself. Maybe he'd claim that he, now a Canadian citizen, had found the lost boy and was returning him to his parents in the United States. Would they buy that? Or would they already be on the alert for a kidnapped child? The FBI was probably also on his tail for embezzlement and income tax evasion. Maybe he'd have to pay for what he'd done. Maybe he deserved to pay the price.

Just as he was finally beginning to dose off shortly before dawn, he was startled by the sound of cans clanking around the perimeter of the campsite. Heart pounding, he crawled out of his sleeping bag, grabbed his loaded gun, and threw on his boots and jacket. Something had set off their fence of cans. A bear? Wasn't it time for them to hibernate for the winter?

Cautiously unzipping the door flap of the tent, he peered out into the bleak grey of an early winter's morning. A layer of misty fog hovered over the ground. He saw nothing. Heard nothing. Was it only the wind? Not likely. He sensed the presence of something or someone close by.

Pulling his gun from his pocket, he quietly stepped out of the tent, walking slowly towards the fire pit. His eyes darted around in all directions, trying to see anything he could. All was eerily still until a deep harsh voice hollered, "Drop the gun! Now!"

Bob spun around, throwing his gun into the snow, as someone grabbed him from behind, knocking him to the ground and handcuffing him. Looking up, he was stunned to see the stern face of Wee Willy, the crazy Minnow Man's brother.

"FBI. You're under arrest for kidnapping," Will growled at him.

Bob started to laugh. "Are you crazy? You? FBI? Bullshit! Is this some kind of sick joke? You know me, Willy. Bob Johnson from The Arrowhead."

Will flashed an FBI badge and identification card at him. "I know you all right. I've been on your trail for a while now."

"If you're so smart, you should know that you're not in the United States anymore. You have no legal jurisdiction here in Canada, even if you think you are some hot shot FBI agent."

"But we do." Several figures emerged from the woods. "Ontario Provincial Police," Chief Kabatay announced, flashing his badge as he grabbed Bob by the handcuffs.

"Where's the boy?" one of the officers barked at him.

Just then Jason cautiously stepped out of the tent. "Leave Doctor Bob alone! He's my friend. He's a friend of my mom and dad. He didn't do anything wrong!"

Jason ran towards Bob and clung to him.

"You okay, kid?" Will stooped down to the boy's level to search for any signs of injury or abuse.

"Yes, I'm okay," he began to sob. "Why are you doing this? Doctor Bob was just going to take me home to my mom and dad. Because they couldn't get here. Because it was snowing. And we've been waiting for them a long time."

"It's okay, kid." Will patted the boy on the shoulder as he nodded to another police officer. "Bring them in now."

Bob watched several shadowy figures emerge through the fog along the path from the lake. As they got closer, he gasped. It was Beth and Seth. He turned his head away and stared down at the ground, his jaw clenched. The officer tightened his grip on Bob's arm.

Jason looked up, broke out into a huge smile, and ran into his mother's arms. Beth stooped down and gathered him up in her arms, holding him close, sobbing with tears of happiness.

Seth's gaze was drawn to a figure hovering at the edge of the woods. "Nokomis!" he whispered as she suddenly disappeared. Shaking his head in wonder, he turned his attention back to his son and wife, enveloping them both in a close group hug.

One of the OPP officers cleared his throat, touched by the reunion playing out before him. "Beth and Seth, right? And you are Jason's parents?"

They nodded, looking up at the officer and the scruffy looking handcuffed man who was being held by another officer.

"We need to ask you some questions. First, do either of you know this Doctor Bob?"

"We do not know anyone named Doctor Bob. Who is this guy?" Seth demanded.

"What's your full name?" the officer barked at Bob.

"Bob Johnson," he whispered, not wanting the others to hear him speak.

"Speak up!"

"Bob Johnson," he spoke louder.

Beth gasped, her mouth hanging open as she clung to Seth for support.

"ID?" the officer continued.

"In my pocket." Bob nodded towards his jacket pocket.

The agent extracted the ID card and read it carefully. "Bob Johnson, resident of Nestor Falls, Ontario, Canada." Then he turned his attention back to Beth and Seth.

"Oh my God!" Beth cried out as she slumped down onto a log by the fire pit.

"What is it? Do you know this man?"

Jason looked as if he was totally puzzled. "Isn't he your friend, Mom and Dad?"

"It's okay, son." Seth held him close.

Beth tried to compose herself. She could not speak at first as she kept staring at her ex-husband. Of course, he no longer looked like the Rob she had once known. He sported a scraggly beard and wore dirty old jeans. He was in disguise. But she had no doubt whatsoever. She had heard his voice. How and why had Rob kidnapped Jason? What did he know?

"Ma'am?" Will sat down beside her. "I realize this is a shock for you. But we need to know if you know this man and who he is?"

Beth and Seth exchanged worried glances.

She nodded. "He is…he is Rob Calhoun, my ex-husband."

Bob hung his head, unable to look at her or Seth—or Jason. What had he done?

Will's eyes got huge. He shook his head. "Rob Calhoun of Chicago, of the law firm of Calhoun & Clark?"

She nodded.

"Wow! Okay. Well," Will turned to Chief Kabaty, "looks like we've just solved two crimes here. Once you get through with him, I will need him extradited to the United States. He is also wanted on embezzlement and income tax evasion charges."

"Mom? Dad? What is going on?" Jason began to cry. "Why are they doing this to my friend? Doctor Bob is really nice. He was going to bring me home to you today because it was snowing too bad for you to get here. Really…we even packed up the truck last night."

One of the officers gently asked Jason a few more questions. The boy led them to the truck in the woods, where the officers began going through things and taking pictures.

As they all returned to the tent site, one of the OPP officers began leading Bob away. Bob's shoulders slumped, his eyes focused on the ground.

"Doctor Bob!" Jason ran after his friend, grabbing onto his legs. "I love you."

Bob stopped and looked down at the boy who had changed his life. "I'm sorry, Jason," he whispered. "I love you too, son. Remember that."

Seth retrieved the boy and held him close as Doctor Bob was escorted through the woods to an OPP car that would transport him to the jail in Fort Frances.

"Be good to my friend," Jason called out after them. Then he began to sob, his tears mingling with those of his mother, who held him close.

Chapter Thirty-Two

Jason was home—finally. Their little family was together again at last.

Despite the trauma they'd all experienced, Beth and Seth were determined to try to keep life as normal as possible. Jason didn't need to know some things that would merely upset him. This wasn't the time to correct his impressions.

It was all right, they decided, for Jason to keep on thinking that "Doctor Bob" was a nice man and his friend. Beth still struggled with the knowledge that Jason felt he loved Rob, and Rob—or Bob now—had apologized to the boy and told him he loved him too. How could they have bonded so quickly? Rob had never bonded like that with his daughter or with anyone, including Beth.

Their first night home, Beth made Jason's favorite spaghetti for dinner. Then they made s'mores at the fire pit by the gazebo. Jason was unusually quiet, his tears spent. It would take some time for him to get back to his normal self.

"What will they do to Doctor Bob?" he finally asked as he roasted a marshmallow over the fire. "I'm so happy to be home, but...but I miss him, and I hope he will be okay."

"He will be okay," Seth replied slowly, trying to balance the truth with some comfort for the boy. "They will take good care of him in jail until he goes to court. That's when they decide if he did something wrong. And if he did, they will decide what needs to be done."

"But he was good to me. He's a nice man. Really he is."

"Maybe he made a mistake. We are responsible for what we do in life. There are laws that we all have to follow, son. If we don't, we need to pay a price of some kind."

"And then," Jason thought hard, "and then, we need to let go of the past, forgive ourselves, and forgive others, so we can move on with our lives, right?"

"Wow, how profound. Where did that come from?" Beth registered a look of surprise.

"That's something I learned when I was with Doctor Bob," Jason sighed. "That's what he is going to do. I just know it."

After tucking an exhausted Jason into his own bed, Beth and Seth sat by the fireplace, trying to make sense of all that had happened. The most important thing, of course, was having Jason back home again. Maybe that was enough for now.

Just then the phone rang. It was the FBI special agent, Will Zolinski, calling to see how Jason was doing and to let them know that Bob was in the Fort Frances jail. He would not be released anytime soon. Once the Canadians were through with him, he'd be extradited to the United States. They did not need to worry about him getting out and causing any trouble for anyone.

"I do want to close this phase of the case out ASAP," Will advised. "To do that, I will need a certified copy of Jason's birth certificate. Proof of his return to his rightful parents."

Seth almost dropped the phone, unable to reply.

"Seth?"

"Yes, I...I'm not sure we have one."

"No problem. It's easy to get one." Will began reviewing the procedure.

Seth wasn't listening. He was panicking. "I'll get back to you," he replied quietly, and hung up the phone. Shaking his head, running his fingers through his hair, he paced back and forth by the fireplace. "What are we going to do?" he kept asking Beth.

"I don't know. My God, I never thought it would come to this. Maybe we need a lawyer."

"Before we do that, I think we need to get ahold of Emily and get any documentation she has. She's going to need to tell her story. We have no choice."

"But what's going to happen? To us? To Jason?"

Finally, they decided to call Emily in Paris, waking her, as usual, in the middle of the night.

Emily was thrilled to hear that Jason had been found safe and was back home again, but totally shocked to hear that her father had been the one who'd kidnapped him.

"Does he know?" she asked.

"We have no idea, but the FBI needs a birth certificate for Jason."

"Oh my God!"

"We're going to need all the documentation you have, Emily," Beth sighed. "Anything, any notes, any recollections of what happened, dates, you name it."

"I can do that." Emily's voice began to shake. "I will write it up right now. How could I ever forget? I can figure out dates, places. Then I will get on the next plane."

"Honey, you don't need to do that. You can mail it or email it or something."

"No way. I insist. They will have questions for me. You know that. I need to run. Angelique is hungry again, and I need to book my flight. Love you all. I'll be there soon."

With that, the phone went dead. Beth was relieved that Emily was coming after all, but terrified over the predicament they were all in. Would anyone understand why they'd done what they'd done?

Chapter Thirty-Three

"Look...." An impatient Will Zolinski stared sternly at Beth and Seth across a massive mahogany desk at FBI headquarters. "You need to level with me. I'm sorry for whatever you are going through, but I need to do my job here. *You* can't produce a birth certificate for the boy, and *my* staff is also unable to locate one, despite the connections we have. What gives?"

"My daughter is flying in from France," Beth spoke quietly. "She has information to clear this up."

"That's fine. But for now, if you don't have a birth certificate or even adoption papers... is that it? Is the boy adopted?"

"No."

"Well then, we're going to need DNA swabs from the three of you to determine paternity. To prove that you have legal rights to this child."

"You know he is happy and well cared for," Beth pleaded. "You know he's been with us for his entire life. We are his parents!"

Seth took her hand, trying to calm her down. "Can't we wait until Emily gets here?" he tried to stall.

"We will probably need to hear her story, if she has one, but regardless, we will need the DNA. That's the law. I'll send someone out to your island to collect the swabs early tomorrow morning."

With that, Agent Zolinski stood, shook Seth's hand, and escorted them to the door.

"It's time to get a lawyer," Seth announced as they left FBI headquarters. She nodded as he checked his phone contacts and called an attorney he'd previously worked with. Mr. Carlson agreed to meet with them in an hour at his office in International Falls.

After a lengthy discussion, during which Beth and Seth revealed secrets they'd never before shared with anyone, Mr. Carlson agreed to represent them. He would be there when Emily told her story to the FBI.

Beth and Seth picked Jason up from Evelyn's home and returned to their island just as the sun was setting over the lake.

Early the next morning, a boat arrived at Beth's island. A polite young woman calmly collected the DNA samples while joking with Jason to put him at ease. Of course, the boy had no idea what this was all about. And of course, he asked.

"Just a routine test to make sure we are all okay—after you being gone and all." Seth tried to come up with a simple answer.

"That doesn't make any sense," Jason mumbled.

"Maybe not, but that's the way it is. Hey, how about going fishing today?"

"Yes!"

Before long, the three of them were out on the lake, trying to pretend all was well when their world was, in fact, crumbling apart around them.

They didn't answer the phone the next morning, recognizing Will's phone number. He left a message. "I'm sure this is no surprise, but there was no match with the DNA samples we collected. You are obviously not Jason's biological parents. I will need you back in my office on Friday at 10 a.m. This needs to be cleared up ASAP. If you are not there, we will need to issue a warrant."

Once again, Beth collapsed in tears as Seth held her close. Thankfully, Jason was out exploring. He didn't need to hear or see any of this.

The phone rang again. This time it was Emily, letting them know that she'd be arriving at the International Falls airport that evening. Thank God. The three of them would meet her there and have dinner someplace before boating back to the island.

Chapter Thirty-Four

Emily spent the long flight from Paris to St. Paul/Minneapolis making notes about all that had happened ten long years ago. She fought back her tears now and then, blaming herself for this mess. If only she had done things differently…if only they had all done things differently. Now they would pay for it. What about Jason? What would happen to him?

After a two-hour layover in St. Paul, she boarded a smaller plane for International Falls where her family would meet her. As much as she would have loved to bring Angelique, it was not recommended to bring a three-month old baby on an overseas flight. And who knew what Emily would have to do while she was here? She may end up testifying in court. Maybe she'd end up in jail. She had reluctantly decided she simply had to leave her baby at home with Jacques and a live-in nanny.

"Emily! Emily!" An exuberant Jason flew into his big sister's arms once she got off the plane and down the corridor.

She scooped him up, holding him close. "Oh Jase, I'm so happy to see you, so happy you are home." She held his hand as they walked towards Beth and Seth, who were waiting for her with big hugs.

"I'm starving. Let's eat," Jason announced once they were in the car.

"It's Emily's pick this time," Beth smiled. It was so good to have her daughter back home, even under these circumstances.

"How about The Thunderbird?"

"Got it," Seth grinned as he headed for the lodge and restaurant overlooking Rainy Lake. They settled at a table with a great view of the lake.

After catching up and looking at photos of little Angelique, they enjoyed a delicious prime rib dinner. It was getting dark by the time they got to the Ranier cottage, parked their car, and loaded Emily's suitcases into the boat.

For Jason's sake, they all tried to act as if everything was normal. They never mentioned the pending meeting with the FBI agent that was set for the following day. Now and then, Emily stole a worried glance at her mother, trying to figure out how she was coping with all of this. Beth would smile back, trying to reassure her daughter that they were surviving this ordeal.

Sighing deeply, an exhausted Emily almost enjoyed the beauty of the night as they motored their way back to the island. The moon shimmered across the black water. Jason pointed out Venus and various constellations. It was so good to have her little brother back. Now if they could just ensure he'd be there with them forever. They had to find a way.

"Emily? Now that you have a little baby, what does that make me?"

"That makes you Uncle Jason!" She hugged him.

"Wow! I'm an uncle already? And I'm not even eleven yet! Uncle Jason. I like that!"

AFTER DROPPING Jason off at Evelyn's on Friday, the rest of the family was off to FBI Headquarters.

Emily nervously played with her notes, going over them in the car on the way. "I'm afraid I will do or say the wrong thing," she confessed.

"You will do fine, honey. All we have left right now is the truth. There's no place to hide. And we shouldn't have to. We all did the right thing for Jason. That's what matters."

"Still, I'm glad your attorney will be there with us."

Mr. Carlson was already waiting in the reception area when they arrived. He smiled reassuringly at Emily as he went over a few things she needed to know. He would be there at her side to keep things on track.

They were soon escorted into Agent Zolinski's office. He shook hands with them all, welcomed Emily, and introduced his transcriber, who would be taking notes. They took their assigned seats.

"So you've just flown in from Paris, I understand?" He was apparently trying to put her at ease.

"Yes, sir." Emily wrung her hands in her lap, attempting a half-hearted smile. What if she screwed this entire thing up? She glanced at the lawyer seated beside her. He patted her arm reassuringly.

"Cup of coffee?" the assistant offered. They all shook their heads. Then Emily reconsidered. Maybe she needed some caffeine to get through this ordeal. She took a few sips.

"Try to relax, Emily," Will advised her. "All we want is the truth, whatever that happens to be. We need to understand whatever happened here before anyone passes judgement or takes any kind of action. We know that your mother and Seth are not Jason's biological parents. We need to know who his parents really are and how this all came about."

She nodded her head.

"So, whenever you are ready, we want to hear your story."

Taking a deep breath, she began, her mind flashing back to that fateful day over ten years ago now.

"I was studying art in Paris at the time and had come home for a visit," she began. "First to Chicago to visit my father—"

"Your father's name?" the agent inquired.

"Rob Calhoun."

"Go on."

"Well, I found out that my father and his young wife were no longer together. Wanda and the baby, Jason, had disappeared. And my father didn't even know where they were. Didn't seem to care as long as they were out of his life. He had questioned whether the boy was even his at one time. She was a piece of work, I must admit, and I was embarrassed to introduce her to anyone as my stepmother, of all things."

After taking a sip of coffee and relaxing a bit, Emily continued. "So, after a short visit with my father, I was planning to head straight up here to stay with my mom and Seth for a while. But I couldn't quit thinking about my baby brother and worrying about him. Was Wanda taking good care of him? I didn't trust her. So I decided to find her and see how Jason was doing."

With that, Emily teared up and stared down at the floor. It hurt to relive the scene she had encountered once she did find Wanda and the baby.

"Take your time," Agent Zolinski spoke softly.

"Thanks." She took a deep breath and continued in a few minutes.

Emily's search had led her to a rundown apartment complex in a bad part of town. Not the kind of place anyone would consider visiting at night. So she'd waited until the next morning, about ten o'clock, to be sure Wanda would be up and about.

She made her way to Apartment 11 through filthy hallways that had vulgar words and drawings scribbled upon them. She knocked on the door of the apartment—no response. She knocked louder until she finally heard footsteps approaching and the wail of a baby in the background.

"What the hell do you want?" A tattooed man with dirty long hair inched the door open, wearing nothing but his shorts. The pungent scent of marijuana filled the air. Maybe she shouldn't have come alone.

Trying to peek into the apartment, Emily announced, "I'm looking for Wanda and her baby. I'm Emily, the baby's sister."

"Come in, then." He shrugged as he opened the door. She stepped into what looked like a disaster scene. Clothing and dirty dishes were strewn around the place, garbage was reeking in the kitchen, dust was everywhere, holes were punched in the wall, and drug paraphernalia was prominently displayed on a busted-up table in the middle of the room.

The man stared at her, his eyes crawling up and down her body. When she backed away from him, he laughed at her. "So you're not looking for a good lay then?"

"Where is Wanda?" Emily stood her ground. "Wanda?" she called loudly.

"What the hell do you want?" a sleepy, drugged voice responded from a back room. The baby wailed in the background.

"It's me, Emily. I'm here to see the baby."

Wanda emerged from the bedroom, looking like hell, wrapping a torn, dirty robe over herself. Her hair was wild, her eyes dilated. *She's on drugs,* Emily thought to herself.

"So you're here to see the little shit who has destroyed my life." Wanda stumbled into the kitchen to light up a cigarette.

"What? Where is Jason?"

"Back there." She gestured to a closet adjacent to the bedroom.

Emily ran down the hall towards the crying baby. She found him lying in a filthy diaper, a rash spreading across his thin body, lying on a dirty mattress—no sheets, no blankets. He appeared to cringe when she approached. Scooping him up in her arms, she tried to comfort him, tears in her eyes. What had they done to this darling little boy?

"Where are his diapers?" she demanded.

"Probably out of them. Kid won't quit shitting and pissing all over everything. I've about had it with him."

After searching through piles of clothing and debris scattered throughout the closet, she found a clean diaper, took him into the bathroom to wash him off, and changed his diaper.

"He's hungry. I'll feed him," Emily offered.

"Hell, he's always hungry," Wanda replied. She slumped down on the lumpy sofa and obviously had no intentions of getting up to feed the baby. She puffed on her cigarette, blowing smoke across the room. The guy stood there in his underwear, running his hand beneath

Wanda's robe. They made a few crude comments to each other, then laughed.

Emily finally found a can of formula, washed out the only bottle she could find, and fed the starving baby. He began to coo, looking up into her eyes.

"I felt like he was trying to tell me, 'Save me, please save me.' " Emily looked up at the agent with tears in her eyes. He waited for her to regain her composure.

"Go on," he said softly.

"So, I asked her what she planned to do with Jason, if she still wanted him. She told me, 'Hell no. I might drop him off on the doorstep of the church down the street. Don't want anyone to know he's my kid. I don't want no responsibility for him. Never asked to get knocked up, you know. It's all your father's fault.' "

"What about my father? He should know about this before you do something that drastic," Emily had told her.

"Screw your father. He didn't want me or the kid. Never did. All he ever really cared about was your mother and you." That had been a shock for Emily to hear.

The baby clung to Emily. He wrapped his little hand around her finger as if he never wanted to let go. The poor little guy. He deserved so much more than this. That's when Emily made her decision. She was not leaving without the baby. She would find a better life, a better home for her little brother.

"Are you shittin' me?" Wanda laughed when Emily suggested taking the baby and finding a nice home for him. "He's yours. Good riddance. Just make sure he never shows up on my doorstep."

Emily scooped the baby up in her arms, threw a blanket over him, and walked away. Wanda never bothered to tell her son goodbye. She never got up off the sofa. Emily could hear her and the guy laughing as she walked out with Wanda's son, slamming the door behind her.

What should she do now? The only thing she could think of was to take the baby home to her mom and Seth. They'd help her to decide what to do.

"The rest is history," Emily concluded her story. "My mom and

Seth loved him as much as I did. They insisted they'd be happy to raise him as their own son. They've given him the best home anyone could ask for, a loving home. They are his real parents, and they always will be. Jason would be crushed if, somehow, he was taken away from them."

Beth rose to give her daughter a big, tearful hug. "Thank you, Em. Thank you for bringing this bundle of joy into our lives."

Agent Zolinski cleared his throat. "That's quite a story, and I do understand why you did what you did. Still, there are legal ramifications here. No parental rights. No adoption papers. Nothing. Why, may I ask," he turned his attention to Beth and Seth, "have you not, in all these years, taken care of this situation?"

"Because," Beth stammered, "my ex-husband was threatening me. We were hiding from him and could not risk his finding us, let alone finding his biological son. Rob was an abusive alcoholic, certainly not able, or willing, to care for the boy."

"I see. So, to be clear, Rob Calhoun is allegedly the father of this child. And Wanda—what's her last name?"

"Calhoun. She was my father's second wife. They were together for less than a year, until she left," Emily replied.

"Wanda Calhoun is the child's mother?"

"Yes."

"So where is Wanda now?"

"She's dead." Emily dug into her file to produce a copy of an obituary. "Died of a drug overdose three years ago."

Beth heaved a sigh of relief, then reprimanded herself for being insensitive to the death of a young woman addicted to drugs. Still, this should make an adoption proceeding easier, if that's what they had to go through.

"We will need to do a DNA analysis on Rob, or Bob, to determine paternity. We will proceed with that before we go any farther."

"Do we have to? If he is actually Jason's father, then what?" Beth shook her head. "If he has parental rights, he may not want to relinquish them. As it is, I don't think he knows Jason is his son, the one he abandoned as a baby. I'd rather he never knows."

"And after kidnapping the boy, he sure as hell shouldn't have any rights!" Seth stood up angrily.

"That act, the kidnapping, will certainly give us some leverage," the lawyer spoke up. "We will discuss all of this later." He nodded at the family as he stood, signaling it was time to leave.

"I'll be in touch." The agent rose from his chair, shook hands all around, and escorted them to the door.

Chapter Thirty-Five

"DNA test? What for?" Bob grumbled from the lumpy cot in his jail cell, not that he had much of a choice about anything these days—one long, lonely day after another. He had a lawyer now and, with his own legal background, was quite involved in preparing his defense. Still, the crimes against him would be difficult to get out of completely—kidnapping, embezzlement, income tax evasion. He'd probably end up doing time and getting a hefty fine. He'd need to pay back much of the money he'd taken and had socked away. Someday he'd be free and would settle into his little cabin in Nestor Falls. Without Beth, he sighed. He'd have to find a way to move on and start a new life for himself.

He thought about Jason a lot. It was uncanny the way the two of them had bonded, how a young boy could somehow change his life for the better. Bob realized he was a different person these days, thinking more clearly, no longer consumed with revenge and delusional thoughts. What had happened to him was a mystery beyond his comprehension. But it was a good thing, a very good thing. If only he could see Jason again and spend some time with him someday in the future. The kid had said he loved him. That had warmed his heart, healed his soul. And deep in his heart, he felt almost a fatherly kind of love for this kid. Whoever would have thought?

As for his defense on kidnapping charges, hopefully Jason could be called for private testimony. He would certainly attest to the good times they had together. He'd tell the court that Bob was good to him, even that he was his friend and he loved him.

Several days after the DNA test results were in, his lawyer paid him an unexpected visit, a look of amazement upon his face.

"What's up?" Bob rose from the hard straight-backed chair in his jail cell where he spent a good part of his days reading, when he wasn't doing his assigned chores.

"You'd better sit down."

"That bad?"

"Bad, or perhaps good."

"Go on."

"Your DNA results are back, Bob, or Rob. You are Jason's father!"

"What the hell? That's not possible. How could that be?" Bob shook his head in amazement. "He's not Seth's son?""

"No, he is not. Were you ever married to a Wanda, a younger woman who had a son shortly before you split?"

"Oh my God! Jason is *my* son?" Tears filled his eyes. "I never knew. Wanda left with him when he was just a baby. Never saw him again—until now. Oh my God, I can't believe it." He hesitated, a frown spreading across his face. "But how did he end up with my Beth, my first ex-wife?"

"No clue at this point."

Bob lapsed into silence, trying to absorb what he'd just learned. Then the wheels in his head began to spin. "So that means that I, as his biological father, have parental rights, don't I?"

"You do, of course. And Wanda is dead if you didn't already know that."

"That's too bad," he mumbled, trying to show a little sympathy. He felt nothing. After all, if it hadn't been for Wanda and her pregnancy, he never would have left Beth. But on the other hand, if none of that had happened, Jason would not have been born.

"So," he went on, "that means I could legally take the boy and raise him. But...I'll probably spend some time in prison first. And...and...." He sighed, shaking his head. "I really can't take him away from Beth and Seth. It would destroy him, all of them. Still, I really want to be a part of his life any way that I can."

"Are you thinking what I am?" His attorney winked at him.

"Probably so. Maybe we can make a deal. I could grant them an open adoption allowing me extensive visits with Jason, in exchange for them dropping kidnapping charges against me. Yes, let's get on it." He pulled out his legal pad and the two of them huddled together, plotting out their strategy to accomplish this.

Chapter Thirty-Six

Emily couldn't sleep that night. She lay in bed trying to figure out if she should pay her father a visit in the Fort Frances jail. If she did, what would she say? Could she control her anger over what he'd done, kidnapping Jason and putting them all through hell? Still, he was her father, messed up as he was. Could he possibly learn anything from this experience after spending time in jail, and probably a prison sentence as well?

More importantly, she needed to try to find out what he planned to do if and when his DNA results came back indicating that he was Jason's father. She suspected he had no idea that the boy he'd kidnapped was actually his son. He'd probably been trying to get back at Beth by stealing Jason.

Early the next morning, she sat at the kitchen table with a cup of coffee, watching the deer outside the kitchen window chasing the squirrels. This was where her mother had grown up, spending her mornings sitting here with her beloved Nana watching the deer. Emily wished she'd gotten to know Nana. But she'd passed on years ago.

"Good morning, Emily." Her mother interrupted her thoughts. "It's so good to have you home. You did such a wonderful job at the

FBI office. I feel like Agent Zolinski is on our side. He believes us and knows why we did what we did."

"Thanks." Emily hugged her mother. "I think so too. Mom, I'm going to visit my father at the jail today."

"What?" Beth's eyes widened in surprise. "Whatever for?"

"I need to find out what he's thinking, if he's planning to try to get Jason, just in case. I have a lot of questions to ask him."

"Well," Beth settled into a chair across from Emily with a cup of coffee, "That probably makes sense. We need to know what we are up against so we can share this information with our lawyer."

"Where's Jason? He's not still sleeping, is he?"

"I haven't seen him yet this morning, Emily, which is rather unusual. I do worry about him, with all he's been through. He is happy to be back home with us, I know that. But the strange thing is that he misses Rob. I just don't understand the bond they seem to have created together, do you?"

"Dad must have been good to him, at least."

They halted their conversation when they heard the creaking of the old swing on the porch outside the kitchen. Beth got up, peeked out, and saw Jason swinging back and forth, a puzzled look on his face.

"Well, good morning, Jase." She sat down beside him and gave him a big hug. He was quiet, deep in thought instead of being his usual exuberant self. "Is everything okay?"

"Yeah…except I don't know why everyone is keeping secrets from me, Mom." He stared down at the floor instead of making eye contact with his mother.

"Honey, we aren't keeping secrets. There are just some things that we adults need to figure out after…well, after what happened. You know, with, ahhh…Bob. You've been through enough. We don't want you to worry. Everything will be fine. Trust me. Once we figure this out, we will all have a nice talk, okay?"

Jason nodded.

"Is anything else bothering you? Anything you want to talk about?"

"Why do you call Bob 'Rob' sometimes?"

"Sorry. The names sound a lot alike, I guess."

"He's really not a bad guy, Mom. He's my good friend, and I want to see him again. He says I made a difference in his life, did you know that? That he's a better man because of me. I feel bad that he's in jail. He didn't mean to hurt anyone, you know."

"I know," Beth sighed, holding him close. "I'm sure he will be all right, Jase." It would, however, take a lot to convince her that Rob, or Bob, had suddenly become a nice guy with no ill intent. That would be a miracle in itself.

Chapter Thirty-Seven

Walking into that jail was a humbling and humiliating experience for Emily. Was this really a good idea? She was searched, as was her handbag, and had to walk through a screening device. Then she had to show identification, her passport, and sign in before she was escorted to the visiting room. She glanced around at the bare concrete walls and sparse furnishings—just a few small tables with several chairs around them. She seated herself in one of the chairs as the guard left to retrieve her father. She was all alone.

Crossing the international border had also been a very humiliating experience. The border agent had asked what her purpose was in visiting Canada.

"To visit my father. I'll be coming back in a few hours."

He'd raised his eyebrows, his eyes scanning her vehicle. "And where is that?"

"The Fort Frances jail." She hung her head.

"His name?"

"Rob Calhoun."

After entering some information into his computer and waiting for a response, he cleared her to cross.

Now she waited anxiously for her father to arrive, not sure what to expect. Finally she heard footsteps and spun around to see her father, in a baggy orange jumpsuit, being escorted into the room by a guard. He smiled hesitantly at her, a look of humiliation upon his face. He was clean-shaven; the scraggly beard her mother had described was gone. But he looked thin, pale, with bags beneath his eyes. Who was this stranger? He bore no resemblance to her overly confident, arrogant, professional father.

"Dad?" Her eyes began to tear up as the guard escorted him to the seat across from hers and removed his handcuffs before retreating to his position by the door. He apparently planned to stand there watching them throughout the visit.

Her father slumped down in the chair across the table from her, hanging his head. A pang of pity burst through her heavy heart.

"Emily…." He shook his head sadly. "All I can say is I am sorry, so sorry for so many things. I haven't been the kind of father you deserve. I know that. But I swear to God I'm going to make it up to you once I've paid the price for what I've done."

Was that her father talking? Since when had he apologized for anything?

She leaned across the table, staring directly into his eyes. "Do you have any idea what hell you have put us all though? Kidnapping Jason? My God! How could you have done that? Were you trying to destroy my mom, after all she's done to give Jason a loving home all these years?"

He stared down at the table, hanging his head. "I admit it started out that way. I always felt she still belonged to me. You know, I really did love her. I still do in a way." He paused, trying to compose himself. "I was determined to get her back. I wasn't thinking straight. Not until…."

"Until?" She urged him to continue.

"Until Jason came into my life. I suddenly discovered that his happiness was more important than my own selfish desires. I love that kid, but I finally understand that he belongs with your mom and Seth. I harbor no more ill feelings towards either one of them."

"Really? Or are you just saying that, trying to lay the groundwork for your defense? What would you have done if the cops hadn't caught up with you? I'm not exactly stupid, you know."

"Of course I know that. Listen, I had already decided to bring Jason back home where he belonged, Emily, as much as it would hurt me to do that. We even had the old beater truck packed and ready to leave the next morning. Ask Jason. But it was too late. That's when the cops moved in and arrested me." He shook his head in frustration. "I was such an idiot, a pompous ass," he continued. "I thought I was the center of the universe. Well, I'm not. Look at me now."

"About Jason...," she began hesitantly.

"Yes, about Jason." His demeanor changed dramatically, a glowing smile now spreading across his face. "Emily, I have some shocking news. For some reason, they made me take a DNA test. I am Jason's biological father! I can hardly believe it. He is the result of my marriage to that Wanda woman. As you know she disappeared with him when he was just a baby. I never saw him again—until now. Here I thought Jason was Beth and Seth's boy, not my own son!" He watched for her reaction, but there was none. No surprise whatsoever. "What? You're not surprised?" She simply shook her head as he continued, now gripping the corners of the table tightly, his muscles tensed. "So tell me this." He lowered his voice. "How the hell did he end up with your mom? And if you knew, why didn't you tell me? All these years, and I never knew. Was that fair to me?"

"Would you have cared? Would it have made a difference, Dad? Think about it. You would have used it to harass or threaten my mom. I know what you did when Seth had to run you off the island at gunpoint."

He shook his head. What could he say? It was the truth. "You have not answered my question, Emily. How did he end up with your mom? I have a right to know. Maybe she's as guilty as I am if she took my son without my knowledge or consent. She had, still has, no legal parental rights whatsoever."

"Yes, I know," she sighed. "It's a long story, and it's one of the reasons I'm here today." She told him the whole story as he shook his head in disbelief.

Tears filled his eyes when she was done. "Thank God you rescued my son. I had no idea Wanda would neglect him like that. Drugs?"

"Yes, drugs. Big time. She died from an overdose a few years ago."

"I heard that."

"Five more minutes, Calhoun," the guide called out from the back of the room.

"Em...." He reached across the table, putting his hand over hers. "I'm sorry. I want to make things up to you also, to be a better father. I want to get to know your little Angelique. Do you have any pictures of her?" Emily quickly pulled several photos from her purse and proudly showed them to her father. "She's adorable. Looks just like you did as a baby, do you know that?"

Again, something tugged at her heartstrings as she watched her father enjoying the photos of his granddaughter.

"Anything else you want to know before I have to leave?" He nodded towards the guard who was moving closer now.

"Since we now know that Jason is your biological son, what do you intend to do about it?"

"I realize now that he belongs with your mom and Seth. I mean that. But I also want to see and spend time with him. My lawyer and I are working on a plan, an open adoption plan, to make that happen, to make it legal. It will be fair to all of us, especially to Jason."

Emily sighed with relief. This sounded almost too good to be true. It didn't sound at all like the father she'd known all her life. Still, it would take time before she would trust anything he had to say.

"One more thing before I have to go. Please tell your mom and Seth that I am very sorry, that I intend to make up for what I've done. And...," he brushed a tear from his eye, "tell Jason that I love him and look forward to seeing him again someday soon. My son!" He beamed with pride.

Emily and her father both stood as the guard approached. Bob pulled her into his arms and gave her a big hug. She hugged him back. "I love you, Em," he whispered as the guard clamped the handcuffs back on him and started leading him away. "Wait! I almost forgot. I have something for Jason." He nodded towards a large book on the table near the door.

"What is it?"

"An awesome new book about space exploration that he will love. I had my attorney pick up a copy. You know how much Jason loves space? We spent a lot of time talking about it on our camping trip."

Camping trip? Was that what you'd call the kidnapping?

He was then led from the room in handcuffs. Another guard escorted Emily back to the entrance, where she collected her belongings and walked out to her car, almost in a daze. Conflicting emotions swirled through her mind. It had gone much better than she'd dared to hope. But was it for real? Could her father have actually changed this much? And was he serious about working out some kind of a deal that would give her mom legal rights to Jason, provided he could still see him sometimes? Would her mom agree to that? Under the circumstances, she was not sure. It would take time for her mother to ever believe or trust the ex-husband who had treated her so badly, and kidnapped Jason. But maybe this was a start in the right direction.

Before starting the car, she picked up the heavy book her father had given her and opened it to the title page, where she found an inscription written in her father's handwriting. It read *To Jason, With love always from your space exploration buddy, Bob.* At least he hadn't signed it *Dad.* That could have been a problem.

With that, she put her head in her hands and began to sob. Tears of joy, love, and hope mingled with those of sadness, pity, and disbelief. Maybe a new day was dawning.

Chapter Thirty-Eight

After dinner that night, the adults decided they needed to relax with a few glasses of wine out by the fire pit overlooking Rainy Lake. They needed some time alone to talk about Emily's visit with her father. They bundled up in warm jackets, knit hats, and gloves.

As much as Jason loved their family bonfires, he decided to stay behind at the cabin. He was entranced with the book that Bob had sent home for him, and was already devouring it. Beth noticed that he kept taking breaks, flipping back to the title page. He read the inscription, over and over again, his finger tracing the words that Bob had written to him. A look of relief and hope spread across his face every time he read it.

Beth sighed as she watched her son's reaction. How could he have become so attached to someone like Rob? And in such a short period of time? It hurt to see her son hurting and wanting to maintain a relationship with his own kidnapper. Hopefully he would get over it before long. But they would have to tell him the truth soon, as much as he needed to know. Then what? Would Jason resent them and be upset that he could no longer have any contact with Rob?

Bob, she corrected herself. From now on, they would call her ex-husband by his new name of Bob as Jason had repeatedly requested. Hopefully this Bob person was a lot different from the Rob that she'd known.

Huddled around the fire together beneath a canopy of glistening stars, they listened in silence to the soothing sound of waves lapping against the rocky shoreline far below. Seth poured them each a goblet of wine. They sipped slowly, almost enjoying the peace and solitude. Nature had a way of soothing the emotions welling up within each of them. Just gazing up at the endless star-studded universe above made one realize how tiny and insignificant they and their problems actually were.

If Jason were there, he'd be chattering enthusiastically about the various constellations, planets that had recently been discovered, which ones may be habitable—and of course, his ambition to explore space someday. At least the old Jason would have done that. It was eerily quiet tonight without him. He was busy learning more fascinating facts about space from his new book, the one Bob had sent home for him. Admittedly a nice gesture, but....Emily gave them a thorough accounting of her visit with her father and her impressions. She struggled with her conflicting emotions, not sure what was real and what was not. Could her father have been transformed into a decent, caring human being? Or was that merely wishful thinking on her part?

"He actually thinks we will allow Jason to see him again?" Beth was bewildered. That was crazy after all he'd done. Terrifying.

"No way in hell." Seth stabbed the fire. "He cannot be trusted. At least he will be in prison for a while. By the time he gets out, Jason will have forgotten all about him. He loves us and is happy with us."

"Of course he is," Emily chimed in. "But he also cares about and has bonded with his biological father—who does have legal parental rights, you know."

"True, but we will work with our attorney to get those rights taken away," Seth replied.

"Yes, but...." Beth sighed. "You know we will have an ugly battle on our hands, fighting against someone like Rob...ah, Bob. If there's any way we could settle without a big battle in court, without having to drag Jason through hell, we may want to consider it. We need a legal adoption, finally."

"What is best for Jason?" Emily interjected. "What if your attorney works with my father's attorney to come up with some kind of—what did he call it? 'Open adoption' proposal? Your attorney can negotiate for you without you having to be involved directly. Just a thought."

"What does Rob *really* want?" Seth questioned. "There has to be something in it for him or he wouldn't consider allowing us to legally adopt Jason. What is he after?"

"This may sound crazy after all he's done, but I had the impression that he genuinely cares about Jason, enough to relinquish his parental rights—as long as he can still have some contact with him," Emily said softly, not wanting to upset her mom and Seth after all they'd been through.

"That remains to be seen, but I agree. We need to meet with our lawyer tomorrow to update him on this and see what he can do to explore our options," Seth conceded. "What do you think, Beth?"

Beth nodded. What else could they do? They needed to find a way to obtain legal custody of their boy as soon as possible. They wouldn't be in this mess if it had been taken care of long ago. But how could they have done so under the circumstances?

THE NEXT DAY, they all bid Emily a tearful goodbye at the International Falls airport, thanking her for all she'd done. While she hesitated to leave before the adoption process was finalized, she needed to get home to Angelique and Jacques.

The lawyers were soon hard at work, hammering out an open adoption proposal that would benefit both of their clients. Beth and Seth would have full parental rights of Jason. In return, they would allow Bob reasonable visitation, after he had completed counseling. Visitation would be more clearly defined once Bob was released from prison. The most controversial part was dropping the kidnapping charges. Of course, that was what Bob wanted. He'd probably be in prison long enough without being prosecuted for kidnapping.

Before finalizing anything, before the prosecuting attorney would consider dropping the kidnapping charges, the branch of the court handling adoption proceedings required a private meeting with Jason to determine what was in the boy's best interests and the nature of his relationship with his biological father.

It was time, finally, for Beth and Seth to have "the talk" with Jason that they'd put off for too many years.

Chapter Thirty-Nine

Jason awoke to the smell of bacon frying downstairs. His mom had promised him blueberry pancakes and bacon for breakfast, his favorite. Afterwards they were all heading to the mainland, where he was supposed to talk to somebody. He wasn't sure what that was all about.

Mom and Dad were quiet this morning for some reason, as if they had something to say but weren't quite sure how to say it. Nevertheless, Jason devoured his breakfast.

Finally, Seth cleared his throat and nodded at Beth.

"Honey," Beth smiled, touching his arm. "We have something we need to tell you. First of all, you know you are our son. You always will be, and we love you very much."

"I know, Mom. I love you too, both of you."

"You also need to know that your friend, Bob...." She paused. "Well—"

"I know, Mom," Jason interrupted her. "I already know."

"What do you know?" Seth gasped.

"Doctor Bob is also my dad. My biological father."

Beth and Seth were speechless. Finally Beth recovered her voice. "How do you know that, Jason? Who told you?"

"Nobody told me. I just figured it out when we were out there at our campsite. I never told anybody…I just got this strong feeling and I knew he was my father. You see, there was this old Indian woman who would show up sometimes, like she was watching me. Then she would just disappear like magic. You know, she looked a lot like that picture of Nokomis on the wall of your studio, Dad."

Seth nodded. So Nokomis had fulfilled her promise to watch over and guide Jason after all. He hadn't been imagining her presence there the day they rescued Jason.

"Anyway," Jason continued. "I think the idea that Doctor Bob was my father came from her somehow. It's hard to explain. Something made me feel like he was lonely and needed me to be his son—and that I really was his son. He told me I made a huge difference in his life, that he had made mistakes, but now he was a changed man. Because of me."

"Go on." Beth put her hand over his.

"Besides, you know I have the same color blue eyes as he does, right? The same color hair. I look more like him than you, Dad. I don't look like I have any Indian blood in me at all."

"Son, why haven't you told us this before?" Seth asked gently.

"Because I didn't want you to feel bad." Jason's eyes filled with tears. "You're still my real mom and dad, and I always want to be with you. But I want to see Doctor Bob too. He needs me."

Beth pulled her son into her arms and held him close. "We don't feel bad, Jason. We should have told you long ago. But you know what? We didn't want you to feel bad either."

"So what I don't get is, were you married to Doctor Bob before you married Dad?"

"I was, a long time ago."

"Wow. So then you and Doctor Bob are my biological parents."

"Not exactly. You see, after we were divorced, Bob married another woman. She would have been your biological mother."

"Wow, really?" Jason's eyes grew huge. "So who is she? Where is she? Doesn't she know where I am or anything?"

"I'm sorry, Jason, but she died some years ago. You've lived with us up here since you were a tiny baby. You've always been our son, and we are so proud of you."

"I never knew that...that is sad. But I have the two of you, and Emily...and Doctor Bob. And that makes me happy. I love you all, you know." He picked up his space book, then put it back down again. "Dad? Even if I don't have any real Indian blood in me, I still want to be an Indian like you. Is that okay?"

"Absolutely, son. You'll always be my little Indian buddy."

Chapter Forty

After breakfast they bundled up and launched the boat for their trip into Ranier. Winter would be setting in soon, and the lake would be freezing over. Then they'd be stranded on their island during the freeze-up process until the lake was frozen solid enough for them to get around by snowmobile. Later they'd be able to drive their SUV back and forth along the ice roads.

A V-formation of loud, honking Canadian geese flew overhead. They'd soon be heading south for the winter.

As they walked into the courthouse, Beth assured Jason that they'd be waiting outside while Jason talked with the nice social worker.

"I've got this," Jason announced to his parents as he walked into the office, head held high, to be greeted by a smiling older woman who immediately began to put him at ease.

"What's that big book you've got there, Jason?"

"Space exploration. It's a really cool book that Doctor Bob, my... ah, my biological father gave me. We both love space. I'm planning to be an astronaut someday."

"That's wonderful. So tell me what it's like to live on an island in Rainy Lake. Do you do fun things with your parents?"

Jason began excitedly describing the fun things they did together.

"It sounds like you have a good life there with your mom and dad, eh? You're happy, Jason?"

"Yeah. I have the best mom and dad in the world, and I love living there with them, even if they're not my biological parents. They're still my real parents, you know. I guess they need to do something to make that legal?"

She smiled at the boy. "You know an awful lot for a boy your age. So what can you tell me about Bob, your biological father?"

"I love him, too." Jason sighed, thinking back on the good times they'd had together on their camping adventure. The nights they sat by the campfire. Their talks about space. His big bear hugs. Just being together. One time he had yelled at him, but after that, he had been good to him.

The officer waited until he was ready to go on.

"The thing is, I really want to see him again and do things with him. I want to go on fishing trips with him and stuff like that. Maybe even a trip to NASA. That would be so cool. He's really a nice man and he was good to me. I feel bad that he is in jail. He needs me."

"Do you need him too?"

"Yes, I do," Jason whispered, wiping a tear from his eye. "He's my other dad, and I never knew that before. Now I want to spend some time with him. I love both my dads, and I love my mom, of course."

"Would you like to talk with Bob today?"

"Really? How?" He could hardly contain his excitement.

"Ever heard of Skype?" She pulled open her laptop and connected with Bob at the Fort Frances jail.

"Yes, I know about Skype." Jason sat down in front of the laptop as she stepped away to give him some space. She pulled out a notebook to jot down her impressions.

"Doctor Bob?" Jason exclaimed as his father came up on the screen.

"Jason! It's so good to see you, buddy. How are you?" Bob smiled warmly.

"Where's your beard? Did they make you shave it off? You look different. But, hey, I can't wait to see you again. I miss you."

"Likewise, son."

Son! That made Jason smile broadly. "I know that now. Maybe that's why I knew I loved you like a dad right away. I'm happy to be your son, Doctor Bob."

"And I am so proud that you are my son, buddy. Maybe you can start calling me something other than Doctor Bob now?"

"Sure, like what?"

"Well, Seth is already Dad, right?"

"Yeah, that's right. But now I have two dads."

"How about Pops? Would you like to call me that?"

"Yes, Pops. I like that."

"So tell me what you've been up to, Jason."

"Oh, I'm reading that great book you gave me about space. Did you know that there could be billions of planets out there in the universe, circling their own suns? And there are these supermassive black holes that are birthing new stars at a furious rate. Also, they are finding other planets that may sustain life. There's one—I think it is called Kepler62A, that is only twelve-hundred light years away from earth—and it may also support life. So Mars isn't the only one we need to start exploring. Maybe I should join the US Space Force when I grow up. What do you think about that?"

"Wow," Bob chuckled. "You never cease to amaze me. You know, I've been thinking about something. I think you'd love to visit NASA someday."

"Really? That would be so cool if you and I could do that together. We could go to the Space Center in Houston. That's where Mission Control is, you know. There are moon rocks and everything. And they train astronauts there."

"That's a great idea, son."

"Or...it would also be so cool to see a rocket launch at Kennedy Space Center in Florida!"

"I love that idea also. Maybe we could do both someday—if that's okay with your parents, of course."

Jason thought about that. Would his parents allow him to do something like that with Pops? Maybe they would once they realized that he was a nice man after all, not the way he used to be when his mom was married to him.

"But you know, I may not be going anyplace for a while. We can still talk, or Skype, or write letters until I get out. I'd like that a lot."

"So would I," Jason sighed. "I love you, Doc...I mean, Pops. And I miss you."

"Love you too, son. Goodbye for now." Bob signed off as a guard approached from behind.

Jason stood up, a big grin upon his face, as the nice lady closed her notebook. "You had a nice talk with your second dad?"

"I did. I call him Pops now. I can't wait to go to NASA with him someday!"

"You are one smart young man." She smiled at him. "Sit down while I call your parents to come in, okay?

Beth and Seth soon entered the room and sat down side by side on the sofa, a worried look upon their faces. Hopefully everything had gone well. This was all about what was best for Jason. They'd been informed that this woman was a social worker who specialized in child protective services. She worked with the court on adoption and foster care cases.

"You have one smart and amazing son, here," she began. "I will be submitting my report in favor of an open adoption as outlined in the document your attorney has provided. You will have legal parental rights over Jason. Rob will have visitation once he is released."

Beth and Seth nodded. It was the best they could hope for. Besides, they would not have to deal with visitation for some time, not until Rob was released.

"I have one additional recommendation. It is very important to Jason to maintain contact with his biological father even while he is incarcerated. That is apparent to me after witnessing the Skype conversation they just had."

"Yeah," Jason interrupted. "I just talked with him on Skype. I call him Pops now...because you are my Dad." He smiled at Seth. "I have a Dad and a Pops now. Do you know what? He said he'd like to take me to NASA someday—but only if it's okay with you, he said."

"Well, we will see about that," Seth replied quietly.

"It would be nice, maybe, if we could all do something together someday," Jason said softly, his eyes pleading with both Seth and Beth.

"Like what?" Beth tensed up.

"Well, maybe he could come to my birthday party sometime. That way you could get to know him. He's different than he used to be, Mom. You will find that out."

"We can talk about all of that later, son." Seth stood and gave him a hug. "We will work things out."

As the officer dismissed them, Beth and Seth put their arms around their son's shoulders and began to walk out when a sudden movement from behind startled them all. Spinning around, they saw the image of an old Indian woman flash through the room as warm vibrations seemed to seep through their souls.

"Nokomis?" the three of them exclaimed in unison.

Mission accomplished. Almost. Her unspoken words drifted into their subconscious minds as she disappeared once again.

Epilogue

ONE YEAR LATER

An open adoption agreement was finalized and filed with the court, granting Beth and Seth full parental rights to Jason. Rob Calhoun, who would henceforth be known under his new legal name of Bob Johnson, was granted visitation rights with specifics to be determined upon his release from prison. The old Rob Calhoun persona no longer existed.

While kidnapping charges against him were dropped as per the open adoption agreement, Bob was sentenced to only six months in prison for income tax evasion. He paid back the money he'd stolen, paid back income taxes and related fines, and cleverly negotiated a plea bargain with the court. He claimed to have been temporarily mentally incapacitated, actually believing he was entitled to the money he'd embezzled since he had made most of that money for his law firm.

The final straw in negotiating his short sentence was convincing Frank Clark, his former law partner, to drop embezzlement charges against him. Frank was well aware that the old Rob had a lot of personal dirt on him, along with information about some of his shady dealings. Frank did not want any of this revealed to the world, let alone his wife. The law firm did not need any more negative publicity.

The two former partners negotiated a buy-out agreement that was fair to them both. Rob Calhoun would not be practicing law anymore in the United States of America.

Upon his release from prison, Bob settled into his cabin in Nestor Falls and fixed it up, including a space-themed bedroom for Jason when he visited. The walls were decorated with murals of planets floating in a star-studded universe. At the center, Apollo 11 was perched upon the valleys of the moon as it was back in 1969 when the first astronauts landed there. Neil Armstrong was pictured taking his first steps upon the moon. "One small step for man, one giant leap for mankind," the caption read. Bob would never forget witnessing that spectacular moment in history upon his grainy black and white television console. He had longed so much to walk in those footsteps someday. That was not meant to be, but perhaps Jason would walk upon the moon, or Mars, someday.

Bob became a part of this little Canadian community of Nestor Falls. He volunteered his time providing free pro bono legal advice for indigent people and those living on the nearby First Nations Reserve. He enjoyed hiking up to the lodge most mornings for coffee and bull-shitting with the owner of Black Bear Camp and his guests. And he even became a real fisherman—mostly because Jason loved to fish. He always looked forward to Jason's visits. One of the highlights was fishing together on Lake Kakagi. They also enjoyed watching the Northern Lights dancing across the sky and talking about space exploration.

Beth and Seth, after many long talks and disagreements, finally allowed Bob to visit their home, but only after he'd completed intensive counseling and anger management therapy. He'd begun that process immediately after being incarcerated, knowing this was the key to maintaining any kind of a relationship with Jason.

As for Seth, Bob finally realized that he was not such a bad guy after all. No need to kill him and throw his body into the whirlpools at Kettle Falls after all! It was obvious that Seth made Beth happy. Somehow that was enough. It made him happy as well. Whoever would have thought?

Whatever had happened to him out there in the wilderness with Jason had miraculously changed his life. His obsession with Beth had even disappeared. He was moving on and had, in fact, begun dating a nice widow who lived in Nestor Falls.

Bob knew he had a lot to make up for, and was determined to do so. He set up a college fund for Jason and for Angelique, his baby granddaughter. He began to follow Emily's Facebook posts with pictures of little Angelique, and was planning a trip to Paris to meet her in person.

As for Beth and Seth, they finally realized that the old Rob had indeed morphed into his new persona of Bob Johnson, and was no longer a threat to any of them. The open adoption arrangement seemed to be the best solution for them all, especially Jason.

Jason was thrilled with the arrangement. He had two families now, both of whom loved him and taught him many things. He still cherished "being an Indian" with his dad; and he loved space exploration with his pops. In fact, he and his new pops were planning a trip to NASA to celebrate Jason's twelfth birthday next year. Not only that, Jason was now the proud owner of a naughty little German shepherd puppy who would someday grow up to be a watch dog. The puppy had been a welcome home present from his mom and dad.

Now and then Nokomis still found it necessary to whisper into their ears. She'd gently remind them that forgiving others—and forgiving yourself—were the keys to letting go of the past and embracing a future filled with endless possibilities.

Made in the USA
Columbia, SC
01 August 2022

64309296R00140